STORM SURGE

A KENZIE GILMORE CRIME THRILLER
BOOK 7

BIBA PEARCE

LIQUID MIND PUBLISHING

Liquid Mind Publishing

This is a work of fiction. All characters, names, places and events are the product of the author's imagination or used fictitiously.

ALSO BY BIBA PEARCE

The Kenzie Gilmore Crime Thriller Series

Afterburn

Dead Heat

Heatwave

Burnout

Deep Heat

Fever Pitch

Storm Surge

Night Watch (Coming Soon!)

Prefer Audiobooks? Find the Kenzie Gilmore Crime Thriller series on Audible here:

CHAPTER 1

Kenzie loved everything about the newsroom. The sounds, the smells, the vibrance. There was always something going on. A world raging around them: events occurring, memories being created, lives changing...life altering events, and she was watching it happen, her finger on the pulse.

"Kenzie, get in here!" yelled Keith, Editor-in-Chief of the Miami Herald, and her boss. She got up, eyes drawn to the window as great lashings of rain pelted against the glass, making it shudder.

Hurricane Matteo.

That's what they were calling it. It was supposed to be the worst hurricane to hit the Florida coastline in a decade. Not her usual remit, but due to the intensity and projected chaos, she was one of the reporters assigned to the story.

On one of the many flat-screen televisions positioned around the newsroom, a broadcaster was giving a dire warning of the approaching storm:

Good evening, this is a critical weather update. We're tracking Hurricane Matteo, a major storm system that's rapidly approaching the Florida coast. We urge all viewers to pay close attention to this report.

The camera cut to a satellite image of the hurricane. Dense clouds swirling around a focal point currently positioned out to sea. The anchor continued:

Hurricane Matteo has intensified to a Category 4 and is moving towards Florida with sustained winds of over 100 miles per hour. The National Hurri-

cane Center has issued a warning for the following areas: Florida Keys, Miami, Fort Lauderdale, and Palm Beach. These areas are expected to experience severe weather conditions, including heavy rainfall, destructive winds, and possibly life-threatening storm surges.

The image on the screen switched back to the reporter in the studio:

If you are in the warning area, it's crucial to act now. Secure your home, gather essential supplies, and follow evacuation orders from local authorities. Remember, the safety of your loved ones and yourself, should be your top priority.

The camera cut to footage of emergency crews preparing for the storm, including people boarding up their homes and shopping for emergency groceries and supplies.

Emergency services are on full alert and ready to respond. We advise everyone to avoid unnecessary travel, stay indoors if possible, and keep away from windows during the storm. Please keep your radios and mobile devices on for further updates. We'll be broadcasting continuously to provide the latest information and guidance. Remember, stay vigilant and prepared.

The camera panned to a flushed meteorologist standing in front of a weather map.

"What's up?" Kenzie poked her head around Keith's door.

"Take a seat." He gestured to the vacant chair opposite him. As usual, his desk was cluttered with rival newspapers and magazines as well as stained coffee cups. How he managed to function amongst all this mess, she had no idea, yet he was one of the best editors in the business. Keith had a nose for drama unlike anyone she'd ever met.

"*Matteo,*" he began, nodding backwards to the window. On cue, the wind gave a menacing howl.

"I'm on it." Kenzie sat down. "Clive's on the beach shooting the weather coming in and I've got five hundred words ready to go."

"Clive just called the office," Keith said, cutting in.

Kenzie frowned. "He did?"

"Yeah, the marina's been hit by a storm surge and some of the boats have sprung free from their moorings and are crashing up against the breakwater."

Kenzie's eyebrows shot up. "That could get messy." All those superyachts smashed to pieces on the concrete pier. Talk about an insurance nightmare.

"It is." He hesitated. "One of the yachts belongs to a friend of yours."

She stared at him, her mind whirling. Who was anchored there? "Salvatore Del Gatto?"

"You got it." His eyes gleamed.

"I'm on my way." She jumped out of the seat.

"Kenzie," Keith called after her. "Don't make me regret sending you down there."

But she'd already gone.

Del Gatto.

They didn't get more corrupt than that slimeball, except she could never prove it. Several times over the years she'd tried to investigate the Italian-American businessman, only to be warned off, reprimanded, or taken off the case. Once, he'd even sued the newspaper—she'd nearly lost her job over it.

Keith must sense a story if he was willing to send her there. Maybe he thought it was a good opportunity to nose around the billionaire's boat. Who knew what secrets it might hold?

Buzzing with excitement, Kenzie texted Clive to say she was on her way and dashed through the parking lot to her car. Zipping through the mid-morning Miami traffic, wipers wheezing back and forth in the deluge, she reached the marina just before Security locked the gates.

"We're closing," the dripping guard shouted, as she rolled down her window a crack. Even then, the spray hit her in the face. "It's too dangerous."

"Press. I won't be long." She held up her ID badge and he let her through.

Kenzie's eyes widened as she stared at the rolling swells hurling hundreds of gallons of water over the floating pontoons. The sailboats that were still attached in their slips, groaned and strained at their lines, hanging on for dear life, while those that had been ripped free from their moorings gyrated chaotically in the bay at the mercy of the raging ocean.

She got out of the car, pulling up the hood on her windbreaker. Her blonde hair was tied back in a ponytail, but even so, loose tendrils escaped and whipped around her face. She squinted through the downpour. Crew members were scattered alongside their vessels, desperately trying to secure them, but no rope would be long enough, no tether strong enough. There was a shout as a wave lurched over the floating platform and a young man was nearly swept off. No wonder they were closing the marina. Emergency services personnel in bright yellow raincoats yelled at them to return to safety, but millions of dollars were hard to let go.

Kenzie peered around for Clive but couldn't see him in the maelstrom. She hoped to goodness he hadn't been swept away. The slip where Del Gatto usually kept his superyacht was bare. So were the two on either side of it. That part of the marina was more exposed and had been hit hardest by the storm surge.

She scanned the lines of undulating platforms. Vessels that had snapped free from their mooring were being swept across the bay. Some were drifting alarmingly close to the breakwater. The sea bucked and heaved as the force of the tropical cyclone turned the usually sheltered yacht sanctuary into a washing machine.

Holy crap!

There it was, *Jewel of the Seas*, kicking and twisting amongst the waves. Even from where she was standing, Kenzie could hear the ear-splitting screeches as the hull scraped against the concrete.

She began to run.

Back through the marina, across the private beach overlooked by the Acacia Club Members' Bar, up the concrete steps and along the slippery pier. The wind lambasted her, threatening to push her into the wild seas where she'd surely be smashed against the breakwater, too. Rain stung her eyes and seeped underneath her hood, but she kept going. A sole figure stood two-thirds of the way down, leaning into the gale, camera poised on his shoulder, filming the superyacht in its final death throes.

Clive.

Kenzie didn't shout out for fear of distracting him, not that he'd have heard her in this gale anyway. Instead, she came to a halt several feet away and watched as a hundred feet of pristine, once-gleaming superyacht collided with the marina wall. *Jewel of the Seas*, a titan of luxury and human engineering, met its end in a cacophony of splintering wood and shattering glass. The impact echoed like a gunshot across the bay, sending a shockwave through Kenzie's chest. The sailboat's stern rose momentarily, defying the raging storm, before it succumbed to the waves, thrashing against the concrete.

The magnificent vessel broke apart, its pieces tossed mercilessly by the waves, a testament to the unforgiving power of the storm. Clive's camera, protected by a waterproof casing, captured every moment. His face was a mask of concentration and awe, while Kenzie stood frozen, witnessing the demise of Del Gatto's pride and joy.

Once the debris had settled, and the pieces of the yacht were washing up onto the beach, Kenzie hurried back along the pier, dragging a wide-eyed Clive with her.

"Did you see that?" Rain poured off his face and he was soaked to the bone, but he didn't notice. "Holy shit, Kenzie. Did you see that?"

"I saw."

She led him down the jagged steps and back onto the beach. The storm was intensifying as it made landfall. They had to find shelter, and quickly. Waves crashed onto the shore, tossing bits of the superyacht around like discarded Lego pieces. Parts of the hull swept up onto the sand and stayed there, gleaming amongst the foam. Wood panels from the interior, along with flotsam from the deck, joined them. Kenzie recognized several deck chairs, a twisted jet ski, and what may have once been a bed frame. In the distance, an orange lifeboat bobbed uselessly, the only part of the *Jewel* to have remained intact.

"Come on," Kenzie yelled. "Let's get to the club house." The wind picked up some of the lighter debris and hurled it down the beach. "Before we get hit by something."

They turned away, Kenzie's arm around Clive, who was shaking with cold or excitement, she couldn't tell which, his shoulders arched over his camera. She was about to lead him up the stairs to the bar when a silver gleam caught her eye. She turned, peering down the beach.

"What's that?"

Clive turned. "What?"

"Over there, in the shallows." She let go of his waist and strode over to the item, the wind buffeting her and threatening to throw her off her feet.

Looking down, she saw it was a metal case, dented and pockmarked from being chucked around. No more than a foot long and half a foot wide, it resembled a child's school case, although it was made from heavy duty metal. A wave surged up the beach and pushed it higher, then threatened to suck it back down again where it would be lost forever. Kenzie ran after it.

"Be careful!" Clive shouted.

She waded into the bubbling surf and managed to grab it before it floated too far away. Suddenly, the sand beneath her feet gave way, and she felt herself sliding back into the waves.

"Help!" she cried, reaching out to Clive.

He swung his camera over his shoulder and ran after her. "Grab my hand."

"I can't reach."

He ventured a little deeper, the water swirling around his waist, and stretched out his hand. Their fingers touched. Kenzie surged forward, grabbed it, and he hurled her out of the undertow.

She stumbled up the beach, then fell to her knees.

"What the hell, Kenz?" He stared at her like she was crazy. "You could have been killed."

"You're a good one to talk." Hadn't he been tottering on the brink of the pier only moments before? He shut his mouth.

"Come on." She scrambled to her feet. "Let's get under cover."

Holding hands, they fought their way through the gale force wind and rain, up the stairs and across the terrace to the club house. They burst through the door, startling a middle-aged man who was hurriedly checking the windows in the member's lounge. He swung around. "What the hell—? We're closed."

"We got caught in the storm." Kenzie fished in her dripping trouser pocket for her press card. "I'm Kenzie and this is Clive. We're with the Miami Herald."

"Rob Nolan. I'm the club manager." He shook his head. "You kids could've been washed away out there."

Kenzie collapsed into a chair and placed the metal case on the table. He wasn't wrong. "I know. We very nearly were. Thanks for letting us in." Clive was shivering uncontrollably. "Sit down," Kenzie told him.

"He okay?" Rob gave him a worried glance. "Does he want a brandy or something?"

Clive shook his head.

"He will be. He's just wet and cold. Do you have any towels, or a blanket?" She glanced hopefully at the man.

He surveyed the growing puddles on the floor. "Sure, I'll be right back."

"You're okay now," Kenzie rubbed Clive on the shoulders. He nodded and tried to stop his teeth from chattering.

"Oh, my gosh, Kenz. I got the whole thing."

"I know. You could have died out there on that breakwater."

"You should see the footage," he muttered, his lips almost purple. He was gripping his camera like it was his most precious possession.

"I can't wait, but we have to get you dry and warm. Then we'll take a look."

He nodded.

"In the meantime, let's take a look at this." Kenzie fumbled with the clasp. It was a combination lock, but a large vertical dent in the front of the case meant it was loose. It wouldn't take much to pry it open.

She looked around and spotted some cutlery lying on a nearby table. "Pass me that knife."

Clive did so, then watched as she leveraged it under the clasp and pushed down. It gave way, snapping easily. Shooting Clive a triumphant look, she lifted the lid off the case. Inside was a black, velvet, drawstring bag like you'd find inside a Scrabble set. Kenzie undid the cord and opened the bag.

"What's inside?" Clive asked.

Kenzie blinked. Then she blinked again.

Was this for real?

Slowly, raising her gaze to Clive, she whispered, "I think they're diamonds."

CHAPTER 2

Lieutenant Reid Garrett of Sweetwater PD faced his department. They'd been preparing for *Hurricane Matteo* for days. This was the first category 4 storm since he'd taken over as lieutenant, and he was acutely aware that the safety of his officers and community now rested on his shoulders. He was also conscious that the chaos accompanying a storm like this created ample opportunities for criminals. His team needed to maintain law and order, while providing emergency assistance to those who needed it most.

He'd spent the last few days reviewing and updating emergency response plans, including evacuation routes out of the area, shelter locations, and communication strategies should the cell towers or power lines go down.

All off-duty officers had been recalled and extra shifts had been allocated. Monroe, who was the oldest detective in the Department and confined to a desk, had done most of the administrative work.

Reid turned to him. "How are we doing on the emergency hotline?"

"Quiet, so far," Monroe replied, "but the control center is on standby. I've also acquired more emergency vehicles, generators, and supplies in case we need them."

"Great." Reid turned to Detective Vargas, his second-in-command. "Is the Public Address System up and running?"

"Good to go," Vargas confirmed. "I tested it this morning." They'd use it to issue public safety warnings or evacuation orders, should they be needed. Sweetwater was approximately fifteen miles inland, so unless the nearby canals burst their banks, they should be okay. It was the coastal zones and barrier islands that would be hit the worst. Areas like Miami Beach and Key Biscayne were particularly susceptible to storm surges and high winds. "We've also issued safety warnings via social media, local news, and community outreach."

Detective Diaz, the department's only female detective, added, "We're as prepared as we can be."

Officer Hamilton, one of the department's more recent recruits, glanced up. "Marcus Bradford called. Again. He wants to know if we've caught the guy who burgled his house."

"For goodness' sake." Reid scraped a hand through his wayward brown hair. He'd done that so many times today, he was sure it was now standing on end. Celebrities always thought the universe revolved around them. "Doesn't he know we're about to be hit by a hurricane?"

They'd taken over the case from Miami PD, who were too busy to deal with the spate of high-profile burglaries that had hit the Miami area. Three celebrities had been hit so far. Marcus Bradford, the soccer star who'd recently signed with Inter Miami; Cassandra Lee, a sultry pop singer topping the charts; and a woman called Naomi Davidson, who, if rumor was to be believed, was Congressman Leonard's little bit on the side—a fact hotly denied by both parties, of course. All three burglaries had been meticulously orchestrated, with no trace of the perpetrator found at any of the scenes. The press had annoyingly nicknamed the thief the *Bling Bandit*, on account of the high value jewels stolen. To be honest, Reid was regretting taking it on.

Wind howled around the station, rattling the windows, while rain lashed down outside. The parking lot had turned into one enormous puddle.

"Everybody got their wet weather gear?" Reid asked. "Take care out there. It's going to get crazy, and I want to see you all back here safely afterwards."

There were a series of somber nods.

"The fire departments, medical services, and other law enforcement agencies are prepped and ready to assist. We're the first-line responders, so do what you can to ensure preservation of life and call for additional help when needed."

The phone rang. Monroe answered. He listened for a moment, then said, "Send through the coordinates. We're on our way."

Reid took a deep breath. It had begun.

"We've got a tree down on SW 18th Street, near Tamiami Lakes Park," Monroe told them once he'd hung up. "It's blocking the road and there's been a non-fatal collision involving two vehicles. An ambulance has been dispatched."

"Get someone over there," Reid barked. Monroe would keep track of who was out doing what. No sooner had he dispatched an officer, the phone rang again.

After that, it didn't stop.

"Boss, there's been a report of a body at a garage off the Ronald Reagan Turnpike," Monroe said, a couple of hours later. The office was nearly deserted now, with almost everyone out on calls. Until now, they'd had no fatalities.

Reid frowned. "A body?"

"Yeah. The caller didn't give any details. She caught a glimpse of the victim by looking underneath a garage door, which she said was half rolled up."

"How does she know he's dead?"

"Said he wasn't moving."

"I'm on my way." He grabbed his high visibility waterproof jacket off the back of the chair and pulled it on. Their vehicles had been equipped with all the necessary rescue equipment and first-aid supplies, were fueled up, and ready to go. "Send me the caller's details, and the location of the body."

"Will do, boss."

The wind hit Reid as soon as he exited the building, nearly wiping him off his feet. He braced himself and pushed forward toward the squad car, squinting as the rain stung his face. Some of the gusts must be nearly eighty, ninety miles per hour already.

Reports on the radio were coming in fast and furious. Miami Beach was being torn apart by the onslaught. Palm trees had been uprooted, debris was flying around, and sailboats from the marina were smashing against the breakwater and washing up onto the beach. It sounded like mayhem.

Reid drove as fast as he dared toward Ronald Reagan Turnpike, keeping a watchful eye out for flying debris and pedestrians running for cover. He glanced out of the windshield at the windswept trees that were bent over as if cowering from the wind. Palm fronds littered the road, along with smaller branches and random items like umbrellas, a bicycle, and even a child's stroller.

The few vehicles that were on the road were moving at a snail's pace, wipers frantically sweeping across windshields, ineffective against the deluge.

Reid saw the flashing ambulance lights before he got to the garage. The emergency vehicle had mounted the sidewalk and was parked outside a steel, roll-up door. Reid surveyed the premises. Squeezed in between a warehouse and an auto parts store, it was hard to say which it belonged to. Both the warehouse and the store were closed due to the weather, their awnings tied back, and security shutters closed.

Reid ducked underneath the half-open door and announced his arrival. "Lieutenant Garrett, Sweetwater PD. I got a call about a possible forty-five."

The lead paramedic stepped forward and shook Reid's hand. "We couldn't resuscitate him—he was dead when we got here." A young man stood beside him, looking like he was about to lose his breakfast.

The garage had a low ceiling and smelled of diesel-tinged cigarette smoke. Looking around, Reid noticed several small cigarette butts scattered around. This was where the employees came to smoke. "Any idea how he died?"

"Looks like he was hit on the head. Maybe a falling tree or pot plant or something." He shrugged. "In this storm, anything's possible."

"Could it have been deliberate?" Reid studied the body of the man lying on his stomach on the warehouse floor. Caucasian, in good shape, fully dressed in wet clothes. His hair was plastered against the back of his head, though it was hard to see if that was because of the blood or rain from the storm.

"I can't say. Wouldn't have thought so, though. It looks like he crawled in here to get out of the storm, but his injuries were too severe."

"Hmm..." Reid eyed a cell phone lying a foot away from the body. He couldn't see anything resembling a weapon. "You touch anything?"

"Apart from administering CPR on the victim, no. Once we ascertained he was dead, we moved away from the body."

Reid nodded. The senior paramedic was in his late thirties, weathered and craggy-eyed. This wasn't his first rodeo. "Anybody else been here?"

"Not since we arrived."

"Good." Reid straightened up. "You did good. Any idea who he is?"

"Nah, we didn't check for ID. Left that to you guys." Once again, the veteran paramedic had done the right thing.

"Okay, thanks fellas. Don't leave, will you? I'm going to need your help transporting the body. CSI is never going to make it here in this."

Reid pulled on a pair of forensic gloves and took out his phone. He'd processed crime scenes before and knew the drill. It wasn't ideal, but if he wanted to preserve the body, he'd have to work quickly so the paramedics could take it to the morgue. The Florida humidity, especially in the middle of a hurricane, wasn't kind to corpses.

The warehouse was dirty, dust and leaves had collected on the floor. Despite this, he scanned the area around the body for muddy prints, hair, or any other kind of evidence, but found nothing. The cigarette butts were confined to one corner.

After bagging the phone, he inspected the victim's body, starting at the top and working his way down. The gash on the back of the man's head oozed blood and the wound site was swollen, but he wasn't sure it was enough to kill him.

He paused at a tattoo on the man's forearm. Initially hidden by his shirt sleeve, it was of a skull wearing a maroon beret, in front of two crossed swords. Reid pursed his lips. That looked like a military tattoo. Taking some photographs of the inkwork, he moved on.

The bulge in the man's back right pocket told Reid he was carrying a wallet. Taking it out, he inspected it. It was thin, made of black leather, and worn around the edges from overuse. He rifled through it. A few hundred-dollar bills and some credit cards. Not a mugging, then.

Taking out the driver's license, he read the name at the top.

Vince van Staden.

It was registered to an address in Miami.

The victim was thirty-six years old with a honed, muscular physique.

"What are you doing here, Vince?" Reid murmured, resting on his haunches and studying the guy. Broad forehead, square jaw, weathered complexion. This man worked outdoors. His hands were tough but not callused. He wasn't a stranger to hard work, but he didn't appear to be a manual laborer.

Had he really been injured and crawled in to escape the storm like the paramedic assumed, or was this a deliberate act? Reid bent down and peeked under the garage door surveying the sidewalk. The gutters were filled with surging rainwater, the drains at the point of overflowing, but he couldn't see any broken pot plants, logs, or other objects heavy enough to cause this kind of injury.

Of course, the man could have been hit further away, but Reid wasn't betting on it. A severe head wound would disorientate him and affect his balance. It would make him want to lie down. He'd need shelter, and quickly. An open garage would be a good place to crawl into and call 911.

Reid stared at the phone. He never got to make that call.

He was about to stand up when a thought struck him. Carefully, he raised the man's eyelids to inspect his eyeballs. Small, red veins criss-crossed the whites of his eyes. Petechial hemorrhaging. Tiny burst blood vessels that suggested this man may have died of asphyxiation. There weren't any bruises or ligature marks on his neck, although the prone position of the body and the man's deeply tanned skin made it difficult to see properly. Again, that would be something for the coroner to ascertain. Still, there was enough evidence here to suggest his death might not have simply been a result of the storm.

He called the paramedics back. "Okay, you can take him now." Until he was told any different, he would be treating this as a suspicious death.

CHAPTER 3

"Diamonds?" whispered Clive.

"I think so." Kenzie held open the neck of the bag so he could take a look. The photographer's eyes widened.

"They look like pink stones."

"They're uncut." She tightened the bag as Ron came back into the lounge. He had a blanket in one arm and two hand towels in the other.

"This is all I could find."

They accepted the towels and dried themselves off. Clive had finally stopped shivering, but Kenzie wrapped a blanket around his shoulders anyway.

"My phone's ruined." She looked at it dismally. The screen was a discouraging gray.

"Serves you right for wading into the ocean and nearly giving me a heart attack," Clive said.

She shot him a look. "I need to use yours."

He handed it over, and she dialed Reid's number. It rang for a long time, then went to voicemail. Damn. He must be busy. Frustrated, she left a message for him to call her back on—

"What's your number?" she whispered to Clive.

He rattled it off, and she repeated the numbers to Reid's voicemail.

Next, she tried the police department, but the line was busy. They must be hectic on account of the storm.

"No answer," she said, hanging up. "I'll try again later."

"You're calling the cops?"

"Yeah. They're going to want to see these."

Clive hesitated for a split second, and Kenzie knew exactly what was going on in his mind. A bagful of diamonds. Worth millions. Right here in their hands. Nobody else knew about it but them.

"No, Clive," she said, before he could say anything. "We can't. This is evidence."

"But Kenzie..."

She shook her head.

Clive's shoulders sank. "How much do you think they're worth?"

"I don't know. They might not even be real."

He arched an eyebrow. "What if they are? Isn't there a finders' keepers' rule or something?"

"I don't think so." The look in his eye was disturbing. To be fair, a cache of diamonds this big could set them both up for life.

"This is evidence," she repeated, a little less fervently. "Del Gatto is up to his neck in it now."

"How do we know these came from his boat?" Clive argued. "They could be anyone's. Maybe they swept off a pier, or one of the other yachts. Please, Kenzie, just think about it."

She shot him a warning look. "Don't, Clive. Don't say anything else."

"But—"

She held up her hand. "Of course they're from Del Gatto's yacht. I don't see any other sailboats washing up on the shore, do you?"

"Not yet." He glanced dejectedly out to sea. There were several other loose boats bucking on the frenzied ocean, but they'd drifted out into the bay, not toward the breakwater like Del Gatto's. Lucky for them.

"I've got that crooked bastard now," she hissed, hand tightening around the bag. "I always knew he was up to no good—and now I'm going to prove it. This is going to be huge."

Clive gave her a doleful look.

She snorted. "Cheer up, Clive. You've just captured the video of the year. I wouldn't be surprised if it goes viral. Any stills you can get from it will be on the cover of every newspaper in Miami before long, probably nationwide. Keith is going to love you."

He perked up at the thought.

Then, Ron gave a shout and pointed out of the window. Kenzie and Clive glanced up. It was hard to see through the driving rain and flying debris, but it looked like a body had washed up on the beach.

"Is that—?" Clive stared at the beach.

"It's a woman." Kenzie stuffed the bag of diamonds into her jacket pocket and made for the door. "Come on."

"You can't go out there," Ron called. "It's too dangerous."

"We've got to help her." Kenzie didn't stop. "She might still be alive."

"Shit, not again." Clive threw off the blanket, clambered out of his chair, and raced after her. "Call 911," he yelled to Ron as he followed Kenzie out into the storm.

The wind was so strong it nearly blew their feet out from under them. Kenzie gritted her teeth and strode forward, her hood flying back, tiny spears of rain piercing her skin. Despite her best efforts, she was barely moving. It was like fighting through an invisible wall of air.

The body on the beach lay still. It wasn't looking good.

Kenzie pushed forward, determined to reach her. Clive followed, nearly on his knees, clawing at the sand. "Kenzie, stop! We can't do this. We're going to get blown away."

"We're nearly there," she gritted, leopard-crawling through the wet sand towards the woman. Spray stung her eyes, while the wind clutched at her clothes, threatening to pull her over and toss her down the beach like a rag doll. She ducked, keeping her center of gravity low. Clive did the same. Finally, they reached the woman.

She wore nothing but a sheer evening gown. Kenzie thought it was couture, but she couldn't be certain. Not with the silk torn and covered in sand and foam. The thin straps had fallen off her shoulders, and her feet were bare. Whatever shoes she'd been wearing were now at the bottom of the ocean. Gently, Kenzie turned her over onto her back and felt for a pulse. There it was. Faint, but fluttering. "She's alive!"

But not breathing...

Worried, Kenzie tilted her head back to open the airway and began mouth-to-mouth. The woman's chest rose with each breath. Thank God Keith had made them do that first aid course last year. They'd all complained like hell, but now it was saving a life.

The woman spluttered, and water dribbled from the side of her mouth.

"Turn her on her side," Clive said. He helped Kenzie maneuver the woman into the rescue position. She gagged, sea water streaming from her mouth. After a long coughing fit, where she expelled even more water, she opened her eyes and gasped, "W—Who are you?"

"We're here to help." Kenzie patted the woman on the back. As she did so, a glittering tennis bracelet on the woman's wrist caught her eye. "You nearly drowned. Are you okay?"

The woman closed her eyes again. "I don't know."

The wind hurled sand at them, along with small twigs and leaves. It felt like sandpaper on her face. She could only imagine it was worse for the woman, who was scantily dressed, her arms bare. They had to get her back to the club.

"Can you walk?"

She looked around, dazed. Sea water lapped at her ankles while foam blew over her legs. It was obvious she'd washed up in the surf. Had she been on a boat? Washed off the pier or a pontoon somewhere? A palm frond whizzed by, followed by half a surfboard. Kenzie didn't want to think what had happened to the other half, or the owner.

"Come on. Let's get you inside."

Clive lifted the woman to her feet, and together, they helped her to the clubhouse. The wind was behind them this time, which made walking easier, but they had to be careful they didn't stumble as they were violently pushed along.

Ron was waiting at the door with the same blanket Clive had used. He wrapped it around the bedraggled woman who clutched it to her slim frame and gratefully sank into an armchair.

Kenzie crouched down in front of her. "You okay? There's an ambulance on its way."

"Actually, they're going to be a while on account of the storm," Ron said.

"There's no need. I'm fine."

Kenzie gave her a moment to catch her breath. The diamonds were still in her inside pocket, and she left them there, unwilling to bring them out in front of Ron and the woman.

Ron brought over a glass of water. The woman took a tentative sip, then gave a weak smile. "Thank you. Really. You saved my life."

"You're welcome." Kenzie smiled as she used one of the small hand towels to dry her face and arms. Once again, she was drenched. Clive, who looked like he'd had quite enough for one day, was doing the same.

"You should get checked out by a doctor," Kenzie told her.

"Honestly, I'm okay."

Kenzie wasn't going to push. With the storm making landfall, the medical services would be tied up anyway. There'd be a wait at any hospital. Besides, it looked like the woman was recovering quickly. A rosy glow had seeped back into her cheeks now that she was in the warmth of the clubhouse and, as far as Kenzie could tell, she seemed in control of her senses.

"What's your name?" she asked.

"Alexandra," the woman said, then smiled. "But my friends call me Alex."

"Alex Who?"

She coughed again, closed her eyes, and took a slow, deep breath.

"What are your names?" she asked, once she'd recovered.

"I'm Kenzie." She pointed to Clive. "This is Clive."

Alex gave them a little nod.

"Alex, do you remember what happened? How did you get to be in the ocean?"

She clutched the blanket around her. "I was at a party down the beach. We thought it would be fun to take a look at the wild seas. This surge of water came out of nowhere and knocked me off the rocks. The next thing I knew, I was floundering in the waves. I heard people screaming, but then I must have lost consciousness. When I woke up, you were kneeling over me, and I was vomiting sea water."

Kenzie shot her a worried look. "Is there anyone you want me to call?"

"I live alone," she said.

"Won't your friends be worried?"

"Yeah, but I'll call them when I get home."

"Okay, if you're sure." She glanced at Clive. "Can I use your phone again to call the police?"

Alex looked up. "There's no need to call the police."

"It's not about you. We found something on the beach, that's all."

"Oh, yeah?" She burrowed into the blanket like she wanted it to absorb her.

"Yeah, but it's a police matter."

Alex gave a tired nod. "Do you think I could call a taxi? I'd really like to go home now."

"You won't find one in this weather," Ron told her.

"That's okay. I can give you a lift home," Kenzie offered.

"You're too kind."

Reid's phone rang and rang. Kenzie was about to hang up when he answered. "Kenzie? You okay?"

Relief flooded her when she heard his deep, gravelly voice. "Yes, I'm fine. You?"

"Fine. What's up?" He was always curt when he was busy. In the background, a siren sounded, accompanied by the muted howl of the wind.

"Sorry to bother you." She moved away from the group to the other side of the club house. "It's just, I'm at the Acacia Yacht Club and we've found something on the beach that I think you should see."

"The beach in front of the club?"

"Yeah, next to the marina. Del Gatto's yacht just got smashed to pieces on the breakwater."

"I heard a couple of boats had washed up. What did you find?"

"You have to see it to believe it," she said. "I don't want to discuss it over the phone."

"Kenz, I'm at a crime scene. Can't you just tell me?"

"I really think you need to come down here. I can't trust anyone with this." Clive was still giving her furtive looks. Not that she thought he'd do anything, but millions in uncut diamonds was one hell of a motive.

A sigh. "Okay, fine. I'll swing by the yacht club on my way back to the station."

"Thanks, Reid."

"See you soon."

REID STARED at the contents of the bag, then up at her, then back at the bag. "Is this what I think it is?"

"I think so."

They were in the manager's office, where she'd asked to talk to Reid in private. Ron still didn't know what they'd discovered. Alex was still covered with the blanket and Clive was sulking, no doubt thinking of the untold riches he would never have.

Reid shook his head. "There's a fortune in uncut diamonds here."

"I know," she hissed. "That's why I wanted to give it to you as soon as possible. Clive is giving me funny looks and I can't tell anyone else what's in the bag for fear of being mugged—or worse."

He gave a tight nod. "You did the right thing. Having these on you makes you a hot target."

She shivered and handed them over. "Here, take them. I don't want them anywhere near me."

"I'll lock them in the safe box in my car." He hesitated. "The fewer people who know about this the better, just until I get them to evidence lockup."

"Del Gatto's a controversial figure," Kenzie said. "If he's involved in diamond smuggling, or whatever this is, it's going to be a major story."

"You don't know for sure these are his."

"How could they not be?" She gestured in the direction of the beach. The point was, there was no proof. Not yet.

"Who's the woman in the blanket?" Reid asked, stuffing the diamonds into his jacket pocket.

"Her name's Alex. She washed up on the beach just after we found the diamonds. I don't know who she is, but Clive and I helped her. She'd swallowed half the ocean and was unresponsive when we found her."

"You managed to resuscitate her?"

She nodded. "Thanks to the CPR course I did last year."

"Well done." The pride in his voice gave her a warm, fuzzy feeling.

"What about you?" she asked. "You okay?"

"I've been downtown. Someone reported a dead body."

Her eyes widened. "I'll let you go."

"What did these wash up in?" he asked. "You said there was a container?"

"Yeah. They were in a metal case. It's on the table in the club house."

"I'll need that for analysis."

"Sure. I'll get it for you."

"Let me lock these away first, then I'll feel a whole lot better. I'll meet you back inside."

"Okay."

Kenzie went back into the lounge to check on Alex while Reid shot out a side door into the driving rain. Five minutes later, he was back, wiping his face on his sleeve. She heard him jingle the car keys in his pocket and breathe a heavy sigh of relief. No one was getting their hands on the diamonds now.

"Are you okay, Miss?" Reid asked Alex, who was clutching the blanket around her like her life depended on it.

She gave a watery smile. "I am now, thanks to my two saviors."

"Do you need a lift? I can take you home or to the hospital if you'd prefer?"

"That's okay. Kenzie already offered."

Reid turned to Kenzie. "Not sure you should drive in this. It's manic out there."

"I'll be fine. I can drop Alex on the way home. I know you have to get back to the station."

She could tell he was torn between seeing her safely home and going back to work, where he was needed. "Okay, but please drive carefully."

"I will."

"Good. I'll call you later."

KENZIE CRAWLED along the almost deserted causeway to Alex's condo in Brickell, a trendy part of the city. Beneath them, the water of the usually placid Biscayne Bay churned and heaved and spat foam in the air. Kenzie gripped the steering wheel as the wind howled like a banshee and buffeted her small car, threatening to push it into the ferocious waters below.

Alex gulped. "Maybe we should have waited it out at the club house."

She was probably right. Kenzie hadn't realized it had gotten so bad. Turning around now, however, would be even more dangerous. "We're nearly there," she gritted out, her eyes burning with concentration.

"Thank goodness," Alex whispered, once they were off the causeway and out of the full-frontal attack of the wind.

The urban environment created a natural barrier, protecting them from the worst of it, but debris still shot through intersections, which had turned into natural wind tunnels. Kenzie swerved as a mangled bicycle nearly hit them.

Big puddles had formed along the side of the road, as the storm drains were overwhelmed by the deluge. The city, usually vibrant and full of life, was now a ghost town, its inhabitants hunkered down and braced against the storm.

Finally, after what felt like an eternity, Alex gestured to a sleek skyscraper and Kenzie pulled up in front of the building.

"I never caught your last name?" Kenzie said, turning to face Alex.

"Delacroix," Alex said, still clinging onto the dashboard. "Alex Delacroix."

CHAPTER 4

Reid, hair damp from the dash through the outdoor parking lot, handed the black velvet bag containing the uncut diamonds to Captain Pérez. The captain's office still smelled the same—coffee and printer ink. Standing here now... It felt like the last four years hadn't happened. That he was still a Miami PD detective reporting to his boss. He cringed at the unwanted memories.

"You found these on the beach?" Pérez asked incredulously, feeling the weight of the bag in his hand. The windows shook as the rain pummeled them.

"Kenzie did. They washed up shortly after Del Gatto's yacht, *Jewel of the Seas*, broke apart.

"You're kidding me? That's the name of his boat?"

"Yeah. It escaped its berth and smashed against the breakwater. There are pieces of it all over Miami Beach."

A soft snort. "You think the diamonds were onboard?"

Reid shrugged. "Possibly. No way to know for sure."

"We should bring him in for questioning."

"You think he's going to admit to having a fortune in diamonds onboard his sailboat?"

"They might be legit."

Reid shot him a look.

"Okay, fine. Still, I think it's worth questioning him about it. At the very least, we can gauge his reaction."

"He'll lawyer up, and we've got no proof they came from the yacht."

"It's our only play here." Since the diamonds had been discovered on Miami Beach, they fell under Miami PD's jurisdiction. "As soon as this hurricane dies down, we'll ask him to come in."

"Be my guest." Reid had enough on his plate with the hurricane, the jewel thefts, and this morning's homicide.

"How is Kenzie Gilmore?" Pérez asked, a hint of a smile on his lips.

"She's good." Reid didn't meet his gaze. Pérez didn't know about their relationship. It was still pretty new, and they were still getting used to being a couple.

"Her career has taken off. I read her articles on Maria Lopez. Gripping stuff."

Pérez had overseen the Morales Cartel investigation during which Kenzie had been kidnapped by the notorious female cartel boss. Kenzie had then gone on to coerce information out of Maria for the DEA by agreeing to write her memoirs from prison.

"She's done very well." Reid agreed, not without a touch of pride.

"What about you two?"

Reid tried, but failed, to look innocent. "What do you mean?"

"Come on, Garrett. The sparks were flying between you two."

"Were they?"

Pérez threw up his hands, just as a palm frond hit the window. "Okay, I get it. None of my business."

Reid glanced outside. "I'd better get going."

Pérez reached into the bag and took out a small handful of diamonds. He studied them, as if he hadn't heard Reid, tilting his head to the side. "How much do you think they're worth?"

"Not sure. Assuming they're real, between five and ten mill. I've counted them and got the weight written down in my report, so there's no doubt how many are in there."

He didn't take his eyes off the haul. "Any idea where they came from?"

"If Del Gatto's involved, it could be anywhere."

Pérez gazed at the uncut gemstones for a while longer, then put them back in the bag. "Makes me nervous having these at the station."

"I know what you mean."

"Not least because of the temptation they provide. Just one of those stones is probably worth more than I earn in a month."

Reid watched as Pérez stood up and locked them away in the safe.

"I'll take them to the lab myself. The chain of custody must be preserved at all costs."

"You're a good man, Captain. An honest man."

He chuckled. "I don't have a choice. You've weighed them."

Reid laughed, but he knew the captain wouldn't have taken them anyway, despite the temptation. Reid had felt it too. No one was immune to the lure of millions of dollars at their fingertips. "How long do you think it'll take?"

Pérez gestured to the window. "In this? Hell, we'll be lucky if we get a result in the next forty-eight hours, but you never know. There might be someone close by who can take a look. They'll have to bring in an external appraiser."

Reid nodded. He turned to go.

"Any leads on those burglaries?" Pérez asked.

Reid paused, turned, and said, "It's on hold until this storm is over. We're swamped at the moment with callouts. I should be getting back."

"Understood. We're in the same boat." Pérez motioned to the squad room where officers darted around like balls in a pinball machine, answering phones, running out and coming back soaked and bedraggled, before heading back out again. "Let me know if you find anything."

"Will do."

The wind whistled around the building, screaming like a banshee. Reid was not looking forward to going back out in that.

"Good luck." Pérez called, as his desk phone rang.

Reid raised a hand in reply and left the captain's office. He was just stepping out of the elevator when he got a call from the coroner.

"Garrett," he answered, hanging back in the lobby. It was too loud, windy, and chaotic outside to take a phone call.

"We prioritized your victim before we got hit with a backlog from the storm," the coroner said grimly.

"Great, thanks." He'd wondered why the coroner was calling him so soon after the body had been delivered to the morgue. "Find anything?"

"Actually, yeah, but I think you might want to come down here and take a look."

"What is it?" Reid glanced at his watch. He wanted to get back to the station to help the others. It was getting late, and the storm was getting worse. He'd heard there were now electricity outages on the west side of Sweetwater, and some of the communities in the Glades, including his own place, were in darkness.

"We found something in the victim's stomach."

"You did? What was it?" Probably drugs. The cartels used civilians as drug mules, but when something burst, or they didn't deliver, it could turn deadly.

"At first we thought it was a stone, but on further analysis, we discovered it was a diamond."

"The hurricane victim swallowed a diamond?" Diaz repeated, frowning. Reid was back at Sweetwater PD briefing his team on the dead guy he'd found in the garage on Ronald Reagan Turnpike.

"An uncut diamond," Reid added. "But that's not all."

"It's not?" Diaz asked.

"Earlier today, Kenzie Gilmore found a cache of uncut diamonds on Miami Beach. They appeared to have been onboard a yacht that sprung loose from the dock in the storm surge and broke apart against the breakwater."

Detective Vargas's eyes widened. "Diamond smuggling?"

"Maybe. It's impossible to know for sure."

"Whose yacht was it?" Diaz asked.

"Salvatore Del Gatto's yacht."

Vargas let out a low whistle.

"Kenzie must be thrilled," Diaz said quietly. "She's been gunning for Del Gatto for years."

"She is pretty excited by the prospect," Reid murmured.

Diaz grinned. "It won't be easy proving his involvement."

"That's Miami PD's job, not ours. It's their case." Reid rubbed his chin where the stubble was growing.

"But it was our victim who had the diamond in his stomach," Vargas said. "The two cases have to be related."

"We don't know they are yet," Reid said, but he'd been thinking the same thing. Too much of a coincidence otherwise, and he didn't believe in those. "I'm still waiting on forensics. I've sent the diamond found in our vic to the same lab as the cache found on the beach." He'd also let Pérez know. "We'll find out tomorrow if they are from the same source."

"Two uncut diamonds showing up on the same day." Diaz pulled a face. "Come on."

Reid held up his hands. "Tomorrow. Right now, let's see what you can dig up on our victim, Vince van Staden."

He had to check-in with the national weather service on the hurricane status. Now that it had made landfall, he was hoping it would start petering out, but so far, it only seemed to get angrier.

Diaz and Vargas concentrated on van Staden, while Monroe fielded calls from dispatch regarding the hurricane.

"There's flooding at the Tamiami Trailer Park," Monroe called, his hand over the phone receiver. "We need more officers to assist with the rescue operation. Emergency services are stretched thin."

"We're on it," Reid said, and left with Officer Hamilton, who'd just walked in sopping wet and shivering. All he'd had time for was a cup of coffee before Reid had marched him back out again. "Need your help with an evacuation," he said.

To his credit, the rookie officer hadn't complained. He'd simply grimaced, downed his beverage, and turned to walk straight out again.

On the way to the trailer park, Reid filled him in. "Flooding. The canal burst its banks and many residents are stranded, including old folks and young mothers with babies. They need our help."

The reality was even worse. Flood waters had risen so high the park had turned into a vast lake. Most of the homes were underwater, and residents had climbed onto their vehicles, mobile homes, and trailers to get away. The constant downpour and vicious wind made their plight even more perilous.

Reid and Hamilton split up and for the rest of the day, waded through chest-high water, or when it got too bad, used flotation devices to carry frightened residents to safety. By sundown, however, everyone was safe and, apart from a last frenzied search for a missing pooch, they'd had no loss of life or major disasters.

It was after nine o'clock when Reid and Hamilton finally stumbled back into the police department, wet and exhausted. They collapsed at their desks, unable to even think straight. "I need a minute," he told Monroe, who'd come over.

"Pérez has been calling for you," the desk sergeant said.

"What does he want?"

"Don't know, but he said it was urgent. Oh, and there's pizza if you're hungry."

He was starving.

"You're a lifesaver," Reid told Beatrice, as he got up to grab a slice. While civilians weren't usually allowed in the ballpen, they did make allowances for spouses and partners, particularly when they brought food, and Griffith's wife looked after them well.

Officer Dwayne Griffiths, a former Miami beat cop, stood with an arm around his wife grinning from ear to ear.

"Told you that you wouldn't regret hiring me," he said to Reid, who, despite his fatigue, chuckled.

"You were right about that."

Pizza slice in hand, Reid went back to his desk and called Pérez on his cell.

"I got news on your diamonds," the captain said. Reid could hear the underlying excitement in his voice.

"That was quick."

"Yeah, turns out there was a trade show nearby that had been cancelled on account of the storm. The conference hotel was filled with diamond experts." He snorted. "We got lucky."

"What did they say?"

"They're a match." Pérez gave a soft laugh. "Your victim's diamond matched those Kenzie found on the beach."

"Can't say I'm surprised. Van Staden must have been in contact with the cache of diamonds. You talk to Del Gatto yet?"

"No, I was saving that pleasure for tomorrow. We've had one emergency after the other down here. I'm still at the station."

"Same," Reid said, and the day was only going to get longer. The night shift couldn't cope with the barrage of hurricane calls. They needed all hands-on deck. It was going to be a long night for everyone.

Pérez sighed. "You know what, Reid? You take it."

"You want me to question Del Gatto?"

"Yeah, your vic is obviously involved somehow, and I'm not going to take another homicide on. We've got enough on our plate. It was your Kenzie who found the diamonds, so why don't you take it from here. Just keep me posted."

"You sure?" Reid ignored the 'your Kenzie'. One of the reasons he didn't want anyone to know about their relationship was because it could so easily be misconstrued. A police lieutenant with a reporter girlfriend. People would naturally assume Kenzie had a hotline to the police department—which she did—and that anything he was working on would get back to her—which it didn't.

He treated Kenzie like any other journalist.

Okay, that wasn't strictly true. But he was careful about what he

shared and, while she often got an exclusive, he only divulged information on a case once it was solved. The problem was, she frequently
helped solve it, so the lines got blurred. He rubbed his forehead. With
Kenzie, the lines were always blurred.

"I'm sure," Pérez said. "Have fun questioning Del Gatto."

Reid grunted and hung up.

He turned to Vargas, who'd been speaking to the fire chief on the
phone. "The diamonds match."

Vargas put down the phone and said, "They're connected. Now
what?"

"Now we try to link our victim, Vince van Staden, to Del Gatto."

Vargas consulted his notebook. "The victim's name wasn't in the
system. However, I did check out his tattoo. It's a special forces symbol,
commonly used in regiments operating in Africa."

"Africa?" Reid frowned. The vic was a white guy in his forties. He
didn't look African.

"Where in Africa?"

"South Africa. According to my research, the tattoo is the insignia of
a now defunct reconnaissance unit based in the north of the country."

Reid frowned. There were diamonds in South Africa. But what was
an ex-South African soldier doing in the United States? Then it struck
him. "Van Staden was a mercenary."

Vargas gave a grim nod. "It looks that way."

Reid scratched his head. It sounded like a riddle. What do a corrupt
billionaire, a cache of uncut diamonds, and a dead mercenary have in
common?

He didn't have a freakin' clue.

CHAPTER 5

Kenzie gaped at Alex. "Your last name is Delacroix?"

"Yeah."

"As in Calvin Delacroix, the late Hollywood film star?"

"He was my father." She frowned. "Did you know him?"

"Oh, my gosh." Kenzie blinked several times. "Y—Yes. I was there when he got shot. At the party, I mean." She'd helped a very grumpy detective solve the murder.

"You were there?" Now it was Alex's turn to look astounded. Kenzie couldn't blame her. What were the chances?

"I was one of the reporters covering the event. I work for the *Herald*." Before she'd been promoted to the crime beat. Before she'd met Reid.

"Really?" Alex's face fell. "I wanted to be there, but I was writing my finals and couldn't make it."

"You were in California?"

"Yeah, UCLA. I was finishing up my college degree."

A party up the beach. The designer dress. The tennis bracelet. It all made sense now.

"Did he...did he suffer?" Alex asked, her eyes hovering just this side of tears. "I always wondered what had happened, but the police didn't tell me much, only that he'd been shot."

"It was very sudden." Kenzie thought back to that summer evening at the sprawling mansion. Palm trees, cocktails, the well-heeled guests... then, a loud bang and a collective gasp.

Kenzie had run to the study door, only to find it locked. When another guest had kicked it open and they'd found their host's body, chaos ensued. She'd been an entertainment reporter then, covering the party for the society column. Solving that murder had caught the attention of the *Herald*'s esteemed editor, Keith, and catapulted her to the crime beat, where she'd been ever since.

"I doubt he suffered." Delacroix had been dead when they'd broken the door down.

Alex let out a shaky sigh. "Thank goodness. Thank you, Kenzie. You've put my mind at rest."

"It must have been a terrible shock," Kenzie said. Alex still had the blanket wrapped around her and cut a slim, fragile figure with her damp hair and pale skin.

"It was. I thought about dropping out, but my tutors wouldn't let me. I was at the very end of my course, so I got a deferment for the last couple of exams and took them the following year when I'd recovered. It was a traumatic time."

"Is that when you moved to Florida?" Kenzie asked. Delacroix had retired in the Sunshine State to get away from the constant buzz of Hollywood. She hadn't known he had a daughter back in California.

"Yes," she said in a whisper. "I wanted to see where it had happened. It made me feel closer to him, you know?"

Kenzie nodded. She understood—better than most. Her mother had died violently too, and on the anniversary of her death, Kenzie often visited the place she'd grown up. There was a certain comfort in it.

"Is your mother still alive?" she asked Alex.

"No, she died when I was a child. I don't remember her."

"I'm sorry." Kenzie didn't mention her own mother or the circumstances surrounding her murder. She didn't know Alex nearly well enough to relate that story, no matter how much they had in common.

"Well, thanks for the ride." Alex reached for the door handle. "And for saving my life."

"You're welcome. You sure you'll be okay?" Kenzie asked.

"I'm sure. Thanks again, Kenzie."

Kenzie fished in her purse and pulled out a business card and a pen. Turning it over, she scribbled down a phone number. It was for her burner phone, the one she used to contact her sources, but she'd have to use it until she could get another device. "This is my cell. Give me a call and let me know how you're getting on, okay?"

"Will do." Alex smiled and pocketed the card.

"Good luck."

Alex opened the door and the wind grabbed it. It flew wide open and nearly came off at the hinges. Alex ducked out and, after pushing the door closed behind her, ran toward the entrance of the block, the blanket still clutched tightly around her.

Kenzie watched as the security guard opened the door and let her in, then she called Keith.

"Kenzie, where the hell are you? I've been worried sick. Clive came back looking like a drowned rat with some insane footage of the storm. Are you okay?"

"I'm heading back now. Had to give someone a ride home. I won't be long, the roads are deserted." She wanted to get back to the office as soon as possible and stay there until the storm had died down. There'd been more than enough drama for one day.

"Is it true? Did you find a case of diamonds on the beach?"

Clive had been blabbing.

"Yeah, I've handed them to the police." She lowered her voice. "Keith, they were from Del Gatto's yacht, I'm sure of it. He's dirty. The bastard's been smuggling diamonds into the United States, and I'm going to prove it. You were right to send me down there."

Keith gave a soft snort. "We have to tread carefully here, Kenzie. Not a word until we have proof."

A shiver went down her neck that had nothing to do with the rain. "I'm going to expose him for the criminal he is, Keith."

"I know you will, Kenzie. Just try not to get us sued in the process."

CHAPTER 6

Detective Vargas stood outside Vince van Staden's Miami Beach apartment and gazed up at the sleek high-rise with its architectural lines, dripping glass frontage, and sweeping panoramic views over the bay.

Seriously? *This* was where the victim lived?

He checked the address again, just in case, but it was correct.

Vargas blinked against the insistent drizzle, surveying the discreet, high-end security cameras positioned at strategic points around the building's exterior. Maybe there was some footage of van Staden leaving the building on the morning of his death.

The wind tugged at his hair, sweeping it away from his face. The storm had persisted, but the wind had shed its brutal edge.

Vargas walked up to the front entrance. A realtor's sign outside advertised available spaces, amenities such as a rooftop pool and a state-of-the-art fitness center. He whistled softly under his breath.

After showing the concierge his badge, he was given a master key to Vince's apartment. Because the victim had died under suspicious circumstances and there was possible involvement in criminal activity, he didn't need a warrant.

"He's on the ninth floor," the concierge said.

"Was," Vargas corrected. Vince wouldn't be coming back here.

He took the elevator up, a smooth ride which ended in a soft sigh as the doors breathed open. The landing was plush, with inset lighting and upmarket artworks on the walls. Four apartments shared this landing, so Vince's was easy to find.

Vargas let himself in and stood in the entrance, getting a feel for the apartment. It was deathly quiet, almost as if it knew the person who'd lived there was never coming back. He shivered, then pulled himself together. He had a search to conduct.

Vargas got to work, moving methodically through the apartment. Reid had been specific in his instructions. Look for any sign that would prove Vince worked on the yacht, knew Del Gatto, or had something to do with the diamond smuggling operation.

He started in the living room, with its plush furnishings and state-of-the-art entertainment system. Vince wasn't short of cash, that was for sure. He sifted through stacks of magazines, mostly on yachting or weapons, which wasn't surprising. Vince hadn't had a gun on him or any other kind of weapon when he'd been found.

He opened drawers and even flipped through the pages of books resting on the coffee table, hoping to find hidden compartments or concealed messages, but there was nothing.

The kitchen was next, its stainless-steel appliances gleaming under the bright LED lights. Vargas opened cabinets and inspected boxes of cereal and cans of food, hoping to find a gun or incriminating paperwork stuffed next to mundane groceries. Yet, all he found were used condiment bottles, cooking utensils, and an unopened bottle of bourbon. Vince had expensive taste.

The bedroom's closet and dresser, cluttered with casual beachwear, offered no clues relevant to the investigation.

Vargas didn't discover anything out of the ordinary in the bathroom either. Frustrated, he was about to give up when he noticed a small, nondescript cabinet in the hallway. Flat and streamlined, it blended into the wall and was easy to overlook.

Pulling open a drawer, he found a clutter of miscellaneous items: keys, loose change, a flashlight, and—buried beneath it all—a crew card on a lanyard.

Vargas took it out and studied it. It was for *Jewel of the Seas*. The name "Vince van Staden" was clearly printed on the badge, alongside the yacht's insignia.

Bingo.

Vince did work on the yacht. He must have worn it to gain access to the marinas and the yacht club. Smiling, Vargas dropped it into an evidence bag.

He was about to close the drawer when something rolling around the back caught his eye. He reached down and pulled out a bullet casing. It was from a .45 caliber. He squinted at it, studying the unusual markings on the casing. Now that was interesting. What was a crew member doing with a bullet casing?

Vargas put the casing in another evidence bag and left the apartment. As soon as he was back in his squad car, he called the station.

Hamilton picked up. "What's up?"

"Hey, it's Vargas. Can you look into the victim, Vince van Staden, and find out if he ever owned a gun?"

"What kind of gun?"

"One that takes .45 casings."

"Sure." There was a pause as Hamilton jotted down the request. "You heading back to the station?" he asked, a moment later.

"Yeah, why?"

"Salvatore Del Gatto has just walked in with his head of security. The boss is about to question him about the diamonds."

"I'm on my way." Vargas hit the gas. He didn't want to miss this.

CHAPTER 7

Reid watched as Salvatore Del Gatto arrived at the Sweetwater Police Department in a sleek black limousine accompanied by his bodyguard, Samson Quinn, who he introduced as his Head of Security.

Most of the department had pulled an all-nighter, and now that things were calming down, they were either packing up or about to head home for some much-needed rest.

Quinn was a straight-backed, broad-shouldered hunk of a man with a military bearing. His blonde hair was cut short, and there was a fine scar above his right eye that glistened silver when it caught the light. He stood at the entrance to the interrogation room with his feet slightly apart, his arms hanging loosely by his side, and his eyes focused on his boss, who was being led inside by a weary Hamilton. The stance wouldn't look out of place in a western. All he needed was two matching pistols in his holster and a Stetson.

"Wait here." Reid stepped past him into the room. Quinn glanced at Del Gatto, who gave a tiny nod. No question who called the shots there.

Del Gatto was short for a man at roughly five, seven, but what he lacked in stature, he made up for in presence. Confidence radiated off him, along with an expensive aftershave that made Reid's nostrils twitch.

Del Gatto sat down, his back straight, and gazed at Reid like he was conducting a business meeting. He tried to move the metal chair inwards, but when it refused to budge on account of being bolted to the floor, he settled for leaning back instead.

Reid took the seat opposite, placing a folder on the table in front of him. "Do you know why you're here, Mr. Del Gatto?"

Hamilton had already cautioned the billionaire businessman, who'd rejected the presence of a lawyer, saying he had nothing to hide. "Something about my boat, I imagine."

"Kind of. Do you recognize this?" He opened the folder and took out a photograph of the metal case. Calmly, he passed it to Del Gatto.

The billionaire couldn't keep the impatient tone out of his voice. "No, what is it?"

"It's a case, Mr. Del Gatto."

"I can see that much." He fixed his dark, piercing eyes on Reid. "I mean what's it got to do with me?"

"We think it came from your boat."

Del Gatto folded his arms across his chest. "Do you?"

So that's the way this was going to go. Del Gatto would make a great poker player. If he knew about the diamonds, it wasn't evident in his expression.

Reid pushed on. "Yesterday morning, pieces of your yacht, *Jewel of the Seas*, washed ashore on Miami Beach. This case was part of the flotsam from the wreckage."

Del Gatto's gaze darted back to the photograph. "I've never seen that before. It certainly isn't mine."

"Are you sure? It's highly likely it came from your boat."

A shrug. Nonchalant. Like it didn't matter that the case had millions of dollars' worth of diamonds inside.

"We managed to open the case," Reid said. Del Gatto continued to stare at him, his face impassive. "You'll never guess what was inside."

"Surprise me," Del Gatto replied in a deadpan tone.

"Diamonds."

The stare intensified. "Diamonds?"

"Uncut diamonds, a lot of them. Are you sure they don't belong to you, Mr. Del Gatto?"

"I wish I could say they did." He scoffed. "But sadly, no. They don't belong to me."

"I would have thought the owner would want them back," Reid said. "Unless, of course there was a reason not to."

Del Gatto didn't move.

"Like they were brought into the country illegally."

"You're implying that they were smuggled into the United States?"

"Yes, on board a yacht, maybe."

There was a pause. The two men sized each other up. Eventually, Del Gatto broke the silence. "Well, I don't know anything about that."

"When was the last time you used your yacht, Mr. Del Gatto?" asked Reid.

"Not for months. I keep a crew on board, however, and I rent it out when I'm not using it. It's a profitable little sideline. Yachts are expensive to run, you know."

"So I've heard." Reid tapped his pen on the folder. "Could I have the names of the crew?"

"Sure, I don't know them all off the top of my head, but the captain is a man called Hector Esparza. He's skippered the *Jewel* for nearly a decade."

"You got a photo?" Reid asked. He wanted to see what the guy looked like.

"Yeah." Del Gatto pulled out his phone and scrolled through a seemingly endless number of photographs. "Here," he said finally, thrusting his phone in front of Reid.

Standing proudly on the deck of a sleek sixty-footer was a dark-haired, well-built man in his early thirties. He wore sunglasses, and his deep tan and windswept hair spoke of someone who was right at home on the boat.

"That the *Jewel*?" Reid asked.

"Was." Del Gatto's shoulders sagged. "Thank God I was insured."

"Do you mind sending that to me?" Reid jotted down his number and handed it to the billionaire.

"Sure." He did as instructed, then put the phone back in his pocket.

"Do you trust Hector?" Reid asked.

Del Gatto scowled. "What kind of question is that? Of course I trust him, that's why he's in charge of running my million-dollar yacht. If you're insinuating he was smuggling diamonds—"

"I'm just asking if you trust him." Reid glanced back at his notes. "What about the other crew members? Could any of them have been involved in smuggling diamonds?"

"I have no idea."

Reid gave a stiff nod. "What about the customers who hired the yacht?"

"I don't deal with them either. My assistant—"

"We'll need a list of their names, too."

"I'll get her to send everything over." He might not be happy about it, but at least he was being cooperative.

"Do you know this man?" Reid slid another photograph across the table. It was a photograph of the dead man found in the garage. Taken at the crime scene, the man lay on his stomach on the dirty ground, his head twisted to the side.

Del Gatto stared at it for a long time.

"Sir?" Reid prompted.

"That's Vince," Del Gatto croaked. "He was part of the crew. Is he—Is he dead?"

"I'm afraid so. We found his body yesterday near Ronald Reagan Turnpike."

Del Gatto shook his head. "How did he die?"

"He was murdered."

"Murdered? Jesu—"

"Do you know anyone who would want to harm him?" Reid cut in. "Did he have a beef with anyone?"

"Of course not. Vince is a good guy. Honest, loyal, hard working." Reid noted Del Gatto was still speaking about his former employee in the present tense. Either the man's death hadn't hit him yet or he was a practiced liar.

"Van Staden isn't a very American name." Reid prompted.

"I believe he's originally from South Africa."

Reid nodded. It was as he thought. "Did you do a background check on him before you hired him?"

"Yeah. I vet all my employees, or rather Quinn does. One can't be too careful these days."

"Military background?"

Del Gatto nodded, looking impressed that Reid had done his home-work. "That's right. Some covert ops unit out of South Africa."

"Was that a prerequisite for the job?" Reid studied the billionaire from across the table, looking for tells, but there were none.

"Not necessarily, although it doesn't hurt. There are many threats out there on the high seas, lieutenant. It helps having someone onboard who knows how to handle themselves."

Especially when your cargo is worth several million dollars, Reid thought wryly.

"Vince was an asset to the team," Del Gatto continued. "He'll be sorely missed."

"How long was he with you?"

Del Gatto scratched his head. "Seven, maybe eight years. I hired him a couple of years after I bought the *Jewel*. He's been with me ever since. This is a tragic loss."

"I'm sorry," Reid said. There was a slight pause. "When did you last see Vince?"

Del Gatto pursed his lips, then sighed. "I don't remember. Not for a while. Like I said, I don't use the yacht all that often."

"Take a guess," Reid urged.

Del Gatto frowned. "A couple of weeks back, I think. We spoke at the yacht club. The *Jewel* had just got back from the Caribbean and Hector and Vince were giving me an update. There were a couple of things that needed repairing."

"This would be the Acacia Yacht Club."

A nod. Del Gatto shifted in his seat. "Is that it, Detective?"

"Just about Mr. Del Gatto. I've only got one more question for you."

"Yeah?"

"Where were you yesterday morning?"

Del Gatto's eyelids flickered. "You think I had something to do with Vince's death?"

"If you could just answer the question please, sir."

He huffed. "I was at my club."

"Bit stormy for a round of golf, wasn't it?"

"I have a weekly squash match on Thursday mornings." He kept his voice steady. "The Palmetto Pointe Country Club. You can check it out."

"Oh, we will."

Del Gatto got to his feet. "Can I go now? I have appointments."

"Sure." Reid got up and opened the door. "Just don't leave town, okay?"

Del Gatto flashed him a dirty look, then strode past Reid into the corridor. His head of security cocked an eyebrow. "Ready?"

Del Gatto nodded. "Let's get out of here."

Reid hung back and watched them leave. Moments later, the sleek, black limousine eased away from the police station entrance and was lost in the rain.

CHAPTER 8

Keith gazed at Kenzie over the computer print-out he'd been reading. "It's a good story, Kenz. I like that you've focused on the damage caused by the hurricane and not Del Gatto per se. Clive's pictures will illustrate the carnage, especially since this'll go out with our online edition, where I believe his video is already going viral."

"The follow-up will be about the diamonds," Kenzie said. "We'll leave the readers to leap to the obvious conclusion. That way we should avoid a call from his lawyers."

Keith snorted. "You're learning."

"Once we have proof the two are connected, we can merge them and do a major story on how corrupt he is."

Keith rolled his eyes. "I knew it was too good to be true."

"You know that's why you sent me to the marina." Kenzie fixed her clear blue gaze on him.

"I know. There's a story there, we just need to tread lightly."

"Which I'm doing," she rationalized.

He gave an uncomfortable nod. "We're not getting into hot water over this."

"I'll do my best," she said, with a parting grin.

Poor Keith. He knew as well as she did the billionaire was as crooked as they came, but he also had to look out for the interests of the newspaper. Budgets were tight, production was down, and they were under scrutiny from the media company who wouldn't need much of an excuse to cut print production.

At least their online division was thriving. Thank goodness for podcasts. Kenzie had been on a couple and was impressed by how efficiently they were run, as well as the traffic figures they were pulling in. It seemed these days people wanted news snippets at their fingertips and in-depth reports on the topics they cared about, in a form they could readily listen to. The glory days of the broadsheet were over.

Keith knew it, and she knew it. It was only her constant scoops that were keeping the paper afloat. The Maria Lopez story, followed by the legacy of her daughter, Emmanuelle, had intrigued readers for the last few years, but that was wearing thin now. They needed something fresh and juicy to replace it.

Kenzie had just sat down when Carla, the Style Editor, hurried over to her desk. Kenzie could tell by her pink-cheeked breathlessness that something was up. "Kenzie, Salvatore Del Gatto is hosting a charity masked ball tonight at his mansion."

"He's what?" Kenzie nearly fell out of her chair. How had she missed that one? "What charity?"

"The Breathe Hope Foundation. His wife is a patron." She'd read that Bethany Del Gatto was an enthusiastic donor..

"I couldn't get a ticket for love nor money." She huffed. "He's not inviting the press. It's only the black-tie event of the season. Everyone who's anyone in Miami is going to be there."

Damn.

Kenzie's mind whirred. How could she get an invite? Who did she know who could get her in? A masked ball was the perfect cover. Nobody would even know she was there. Then it struck her.

Alex.

Her new friend and Calvin Delacroix's daughter.

Alex would be connected enough to get her a ticket. In fact, she was probably already going. Besides, the socialite owed her. Kenzie had saved her life.

"Leave it with me," Kenzie said. "I'll see what I can do."

"Thanks, Kenz." Carla shuffled off.

It was easier than Kenzie had imagined. A quick phone call and— "Sure, no problem. I wasn't going to go, but if you're going, it'll be fun. We can go together."

Unfortunately, there wasn't a ticket for Carla. Kenzie decided not to tell her she was going, which meant she couldn't raid the newspaper's stock of ball gowns that the Style Editor kept under lock and key. She'd just have to make do with what she had at home.

THE CHAUFFEUR-DRIVEN Mercedes dropped Kenzie and Alex outside the arched entrance of Del Gatto's mansion. Kenzie had done her homework and looked up the specs earlier that day. The sprawling Mediterranean style residence, nestled on the exclusive Palm Island, exuded a sense of secretive luxury. It loomed over two acres of meticulously manicured grounds, bordered by 300 feet of pristine waterfront. As she stared, the setting sun glinted off the expansive windows, mirroring the deep, blue waters of the bay and the orange glow over the distant skyline of Downtown Miami.

"Wow," Kenzie breathed, as they walked up the marble steps to the house. A liveried guard checked their tickets before letting them in. Security was tight, with two more guards at the entrance, both with suspicious bulges under their jackets.

Kenzie stared up at the soaring ceiling and gawked at the spiraling staircase that seemed to defy gravity. "Is that a Jackson Pollock?" she murmured as they walked past an expansive living room expertly decorated and into an exotic courtyard where the guests were accumulating. The air was thick with the scent of designer perfume and luxury, a heady mix that made her senses tingle.

Kenzie followed Alex as she weaved around the expensive ballgowns and elaborate masks, finally stopping to accept a glass of champagne from a hovering waiter. The courtyard, which was more of a covered lounge, consisted of elegant sculptures, a fully staffed bar area, and lush, indoor plants. Kenzie could just imagine the high society soirees and lavish parties the Del Gatto's must have held here. Yet, amidst this splendor, a hint of mystery lingered, as if the glitzy facade hid an underbelly of secrets, lies and corruption.

Because it was a masked ball, conversations were both riotous and awkward. Guests mingled, trying to guess who each other was, laughing in embarrassment when they were wrong, cackling with delight when they were right.

Men, bolstered by the disguise, flirted with beautifully dressed women, but Kenzie hid behind her mask, observing. She spotted Del Gatto's elegant wife, Bethany, resplendent in a cobalt blue ball gown, a glittering shawl, and a mask with blue peacock feathers. Surrounded by what Kenzie assumed were VIPs, Bethany held court rather majestically, smiling and engaging them all in conversation.

Del Gatto himself was talking to a group of men, all dressed in tuxedos with bandit-style masks over their eyes. She recognized Congressman Leonard, whose campaigns Del Gatto so generously supported, as well as a Supreme Court judge. Beside him, as always, was his Head of Security, the eagle-eyed Samson Quinn.

Chatter filled the courtyard, and the women split up, Alex mingling with the guests while Kenzie sipped her champagne, blending in. A nod here, a laugh there. I *love* your dress, is it Alexander McQueen? After all these years, she was something of an expert at it.

Kenzie watched Alex work her way over to Del Gatto's wife. Slow, practiced movements, her classic features visible beneath her mask effortlessly drawing the gaze of the men and women in her vicinity. The men lustful, the women envious. It seemed Alex was also something of an expert.

Alex greeted Bethany Del Gatto, said something about the general ambiance or how spectacular the decor was, making the older woman smile. She replied, then touched Alex's hand in a gesture of friendship. Kenzie was surprised, she hadn't realized they were so close.

Then Alex was back, her lips glossy red beneath her mask. "There are tons of eligible men here tonight," she whispered conspiratorially. "Who do you want me to introduce you to?"

"Who's here?" Kenzie asked.

"You can choose between a recently divorced dog food billionaire, a shipping magnate's son, or the divisional head of the biggest asset management group in Miami."

Kenzie laughed. Alex was good company. When a vaguely familiar film director came up and engaged her in conversation, Kenzie murmured something about the powder room and seized her chance to slip away. Slowly, without attracting attention to herself, she edged toward the grand staircase.

Damn.

One of Del Gatto's security guards, a huge, bulky guy in an ill-fitting suit, stood sentry at the bottom of the staircase. How was she going to get past him?

A diversion. That's what she needed.

Edging back into the crowd, Kenzie searched for an opportunity. One of the waiters holding a tray of flutes filled with champagne walked by. She stuck out her foot and tripped him up. The poor guy went flying.

Everybody turned as the glasses shattered onto the marble tiles, and a few of the women gasped or yelped in surprise. The guard quickly zeroed in to see what had happened. When he saw the mess, he ushered the guests away until it could be cleared up.

Kenzie seized her moment and darted up the stairs. She'd purposely worn a dark teal dress that clung to her body and flared gently at the knees so she could blend into the shadows and any sudden flash of movement wouldn't draw the eye. Glancing over her shoulder, she was pretty certain no one had seen her. If anyone stopped her, she would just say she was looking for the powder room.

Kenzie crept along the upper landing towards the east side of the mansion. The corridor was dimly lit, the soft glow of recessed lighting casting long, flickering shadows against the walls. Her footsteps were silent on the plush carpets as she poked her head into room after room, looking for Del Gatto's study. If there was anything to be found, it would most likely be there.

At the end of a long corridor, she found what she was looking for. Surprisingly, the study door was ajar, a warm glow coming from inside. Someone had left the desk lamp on. Kenzie paused, listening for any sign of movement. Hearing none, she slipped inside, closing the door softly behind her.

The study was a stark contrast to the rest of the mansion's flamboyant extravagance. It was a room of power, lined with dark wood panels and filled with heavy furniture. It even smelled faintly of Del Gatto's aftershave.

The large desk, positioned to oversee the room, was cluttered with papers and artifacts. Bookshelves lined the walls, another surprise. She hadn't thought of Del Gatto as a reader. Yet it was filled with volumes that spoke of a man who valued knowledge as well as wealth.

Kenzie surveyed the room, searching for evidence of the diamond smuggling. The most obvious choice was the desk. She deftly sifted through the papers scattered on top, careful not to disturb their order. Opening the drawers, she examined the contents, scanning documents and letters, looking for anything out of place, any document or note that hinted at Del Gatto's illicit activities.

She found nothing.

With a sigh, she glanced up. An incandescent painting of two ships on a stormy sea at night caught her eye. It seemed oddly out of place, its frame slightly askew. Sensing something amiss, she approached it and saw that it was by Winslow Homer, the famous American artist. Was it an original? It looked real, but then it might just be a clever forgery. You never knew with rich people.

Kenzie gently lifted it off the wall and peered behind it. Expecting to see a safe, she was surprised to find a hidden alcove in the wall. Like a safe without a door. How strange. She'd have thought Del Gatto would be more careful than that, especially with the study door left ajar. Then again, the confidence of these wealthy men always astounded her. They thought they were untouchable, that no one could get past their security, that no one would dare. Or maybe he just hadn't had the front of his safe fitted yet.

Either way, he'd left himself wide open. Nestled among various personal items, was a small, leather-bound ledger. Kenzie's heart raced as she extracted it. It looked important, and well used. Could this hold the key to unraveling Del Gatto's diamond smuggling empire?

Flipping through the pages under the dim light, she scanned the various entries, but couldn't make any sense of them. The ledger was filled with coded transactions, but she'd need her research assistant, Raoul's help in deciphering them.

Kenzie hesitated, unsure what to do. If she took the ledger, Del Gatto would know his security had been breached, the party would be shut down, and the guests searched. Either she had to get the ledger out of the house undetected—she could throw it over a wall or something and pick it up later—or she had to photograph the pages and put it back.

Given she was in a revealing ball gown with only a tiny purse slung over her shoulder, and it was pouring rain outside, she opted for photographing the ledger, or as much of it as she could in the time she had.

Hurrying, she got out her new cell phone and turned to the page containing the most recent entries. She'd taken one shot when she heard a voice outside in the corridor. A chill flew down her spine as she recognized it as Del Gatto's Head of Security.

"Yeah, Salvo. I'm almost there now. I'll lock up."

Shit.

Del Gatto must have remembered he'd left the study door open and asked his sidekick to come up here and lock it up. Heart racing, she replaced the ledger, ensuring everything was as she had found it. With a final, sweeping glance to confirm she hadn't left anything behind, she made for the door. There might just be time to nip out or admit she was lost and looking for the restroom.

"I'm here. You did leave it open, yeah." The voice was right outside the door. There was no time to do anything. She was trapped.

Kenzie went cold. Now what?

She looked around the room, her heart thumping.

Hide. She had to hide.

Her gaze darted to the window covered by rich drapes that pooled at the floor. During the day, they were pulled back and fastened to the wall with elaborate ties, but right now, they were drawn, blocking out the incessant wind and rain.

Pulling back the drapes, she slipped behind them. To her surprise, she discovered it wasn't a window, but a balcony. The glass doors were firmly shut, while the tailwind of the hurricane moaned dolefully behind her.

The door creaked open. Kenzie held her breath.

She heard rustling and pictured the man stepping behind the desk and turning off the lamp. The room was plunged into darkness. Kenzie had the benefit of the security lights out in the rain-drenched garden, but the heavy curtains prevented them from filtering into the room.

Please don't let him check the balcony door, she prayed.

Sensing the guard was still in the room, Kenzie stood stock still, holding her breath. The drapes fluttered.

Crap.

Her heart pounded painfully in her chest. She was seconds away from being discovered and then it would be game over. She'd be frog marched out of the house by Quinn, maybe even Del Gatto himself. It wouldn't matter that she had an invite. The billionaire businessman would be furious she'd snuck into his study. He'd probably press charges and she might even lose her job at the newspaper.

Bracing herself, Kenzie waited for the inevitable.

"Excuse me, could you show me where the restroom is?" came a clipped feminine voice with a Californian twang.

Alex.

What the hell was she doing here?

"What? Miss, you can't be up here." Quinn moved away from the balcony.

Thank God.

Kenzie exhaled, going weak, and leaned back against the cold glass for support. Her legs were shaking. Boy, that was close.

"Oh, I'm sorry, I didn't realize." Alex was putting on a good show. "Should I go back downstairs or is there somewhere up here I can duck into?" The voices trailed away.

How had Alex known Kenzie was in the study? Had she seen her sneak up the staircase? Once Alex and the guard were out of the room, Kenzie emerged from behind the drapes. It was so dark, she couldn't see anything, so she switched on the flashlight on her phone. The study was illuminated by the murky glow. Sneaking toward the door, Kenzie was about to turn the handle when she heard the key turn in the lock.

Her heart skipped a beat.

She'd been locked in.

She thought hard. There was the balcony, but it was a long way up, and she was wearing a floor-length ball gown and strappy heels. Plus, it was still raining, although not as violently as before. The storm was starting to ease up now, but it was still coming down hard enough to get soaked through. There was no way she could return to the party in that state.

Was Alex still around? If she'd seen Kenzie come into the study, maybe she'd be back to unlock the door.

Two minutes passed. Then five.

Maybe Alex really had been looking for the restroom. Kenzie disregarded that thought the moment she had it. The timing had been too perfect. Alex's lucky appearance could not have been a coincidence.

Kenzie bit her lip, then sent Alex a text message.

Locked in the study. Help!

Waiting, she stared at her phone.

Please respond.

Then she saw three dots and sighed in relief. Alex was typing.

Coming.

Kenzie paced up and down. While she did, she read the titles on some of the books in the bookcase. Del Gatto had everything from popular crime fiction to what looked like a first edition of Moby Dick.

Her phone buzzed.

No key.

Darn. Kenzie went over to the door. "Alex?"

"I'm here. He's taken it with him." Alex hissed through the door.

Shit.

Kenzie heard scratching on the other side of the door.

"What are you doing?" she whispered.

"Trying to pick the lock. Hang on."

Really? Kenzie pursed her lips in surprise. She wouldn't have thought a wealthy socialite like Alex would know how to do that. Even Kenzie didn't have those kinds of skills, although it was probably about time she learned. She was pretty sick of being locked into places.

There was a low click and the thick door creaked open. Kenzie looked into Alex's smiling face. "How on earth did you do that?"

Alex held up a bobby pin. "Easy. It's a basic pin tumbler lock. Come on, we have to get out of here."

Any more questions she had could wait until later. They made their way back to the landing only to find a guard positioned at the top of the staircase.

"That's a no-go," Alex whispered.

"We could distract him with a diversion?" Kenzie suggested.

"Or we could look for another way out."

Kenzie nodded, and they moved back the way they'd come.

"This is Del Gatto's section of the house," Alex whispered, creeping past the closed doors. "I've heard his wife sleeps in the other wing of the mansion."

"I hope there's a separate entrance." Kenzie murmured, turning a corner.

"Knowing Del Gatto, there probably is." They darted to the end of the corridor where there was a heavy wooden door with an old-fashioned lock. Alex twisted the handle. Kenzie wasn't hopeful, but to her surprise, it opened with a muted creak. Her heart surged.

"It's so his mistress can come and go unseen," Alex whispered.

"Seriously?" Kenzie rolled her eyes. Poor Mrs. Del Gatto. All that elegance and charm and her husband was cheating on her.

Alex said, "There's a staircase."

"Let's go." Kenzie looked over her shoulder, but no one was coming. With a quick nod, Alex tiptoed down the stairs. Even in heels, she didn't make a sound. Kenzie followed, slightly less stealthily, making sure to close the door behind her.

When they reached the bottom, there was a short, tiled corridor and, at the end, another door. This one was sturdier than the one at the top of the stairs and had a hefty latch mechanism as well as a thick bolt across the top. A cold draft crept in underneath it.

"This is definitely the way out," Alex reached for the bolt.

"They'll know we left this way," Kenzie warned. "We can't lock it behind us."

"It can't be helped." Alex drew back the bolt, then turned the latch. "Ready?"

Kenzie nodded, and they slipped out into the rain.

CHAPTER 9

"He did have a squash match," Vargas said the following morning, when Reid asked if he'd checked Del Gatto's alibi. "I spoke with his opponent. They played three games and Del Gatto won 1, lost 2."

"Then we can rule him out." Reid went to his desk and sat down.

"Do you believe him about the diamonds?" asked Vargas.

"I'm not sure." He knew what Kenzie would say. She was convinced Del Gatto was dirty. "The skipper, Hector Esparza, could have been bringing them in behind his back. I mean, if the yacht is rented out, the crew could easily have picked up and brought in illegal diamonds."

"Where would they get them?" Vargas asked.

"I don't know. Someone down the coast, a cargo ship, some sort of dealer or middleman." He shrugged. Diamonds weren't his specialty.

Vargas nodded.

"Any luck in tracing the skipper?" Reid asked.

"Not yet. I ran his name through the system, but nothing popped up. He doesn't have a criminal record."

"Got an address?"

"He's not registered with the DMV, but I'm looking at some other sources. I'll let you know if I find something."

"What about Vince van Staden?" Reid asked. "Found anything on him?"

"I'm waiting for a call from Immigration. They said they'd have something on him. I've also asked his apartment's management company to send us a copy of the security footage from the day he died.

It might tell us what frame of mind he was in when he left his apartment."

"Okay, great."

Reid gave a tired nod and went back to work. Hurricane Matteo had left widespread devastation in its wake. Parts of the Glades were still without power, while the residents of the trailer park were slowly returning to find their trailers and motorhomes destroyed. The hostels and motels were overflowing, and a makeshift shelter had been set up in the community center next to St. Mattias's church.

Local residents and charities were supplying food, clothing, toiletries, and other essentials. In other areas, looting was taking place and store owners were reporting broken frontages and deliberate vandalism. Funny how it took a natural disaster to bring out the best and the worst in people.

Dias approached his desk. "Marcus Bradford wants to know if you've found his fiancé's engagement ring yet. What shall I tell him?"

"The truth. That we've had our hands full with the storm and will get back to the jewelry thefts when things settle down."

"Hey, boss. I've got an address for Hector Esparza." Vargas held up a piece of paper. "Managed to trace him through the social security database, although they made me jump through a few hoops to get it."

The SSA were sticklers for protocol. They required a formal request from law enforcement personnel, which included proof of an active investigation or a threat to national security, before they'd hand over sensitive information. It protected the privacy rights of individuals but was a pain for cops.

"Great."

"There was something weird, though."

"Oh yeah?"

"It seems Hector's forty-seven years old and was born in San Diego."

Reid frowned. He didn't think Esparza was that old. "Sure you've got the right guy?"

"There are no photographs on the SSA database, but it does list his current address as Miami."

Reid got up and put his cell phone in his back pocket. "Okay, then. Let's go check it out."

. . .

HECTOR ESPARZA LIVED in a modest apartment complex situated in the heart of Little Haiti. Unlike the impersonal skyscrapers dotting Miami's skyline, this neighborhood thrived on its close connections, colorful street art, and the lively rhythms of Caribbean music that filled the air. The residents were a blend of families, artists, and immigrants. Many of the buildings were adorned with murals depicting scenes from Haitian folklore and landscapes.

"If this is him, he's not paid as well as van Staden," Vargas observed as they approached the building, its facade painted in bright, welcoming colors. Instead of an elevator, a staircase led them to Hector's apartment on the second floor.

"Apartment two-oh-four is this way." Vargas said, noting the hand-painted numbers beside the stairs. Reaching the second floor, they found themselves in a hallway bathed in natural light from windows at the end. The air was filled with the scent of exotic spices, and they could hear voices behind the colorful doors of the apartments they passed.

Hector's, however, was silent.

Reid pressed the buzzer and waited. They couldn't hear any signs of occupancy, no music, no chatter of a television.

"Are we going in?" Vargas inquired.

"Can't," Reid said, scrutinizing the closed door. "No reason to." They were about to turn away when a smash from within made them freeze.

"Did you hear that?" Reid questioned.

Vargas's expression hardened. "Sounded like glass breaking. You think someone's in trouble?"

"It sounded that way." Cases of potential danger didn't require a warrant.

Reid knocked firmly on the door. "Sweetwater Police. Open the door."

After a tense pause, Reid nodded. "Let's do it."

Together, they retreated a step, then, on the count of three, unleashed their collective strength against the door. The hinges gave way with a groan, the door flying inwards.

Reid surveyed the basic yet cozy living area—a quick but thorough sweep—before calling out "clear." The window was open, but he ignored it for now and moved on to the kitchen. It was small but functional, the countertops holding a mix of cooking spices and utensils, but there was nobody there. "Clear!" he called out again.

Vargas then advanced into the bedroom and Reid heard him give the all clear.

"He went this way." Reid went back to the open window that led to the fire escape. The curtain fluttered in the soft breeze.

"Damnit," muttered Vargas, moving to the window to take a look. "We must have just missed him."

"See anything?"

"Nah, he's in the wind."

Reid sighed and turned back to survey the apartment. "It's definitely the right guy." He motioned to a fading photograph on a cabinet sideboard of Hector, standing between a man and a woman of similar age. "And he's not forty-seven."

"Must have lied on his social security application," Vargas mused.

"Unless Hector's not his real name."

There was a sail in the background and, beyond that, a tousled, blue-green sea. Reid cocked his head. "Could be Del Gatto's boat, although it's hard to tell."

"You think those two are part of the crew?" Vargas asked.

"Maybe." Reid turned the frame over, but there was nothing on the back. "If they are, this'll help us find them." He slipped it into his pocket.

The apartment was simple, but lived in. There were a couple of colorful paintings on the wall, including a block-mounted black-and-white picture of a small boy standing in what looked like a small harbor beside a smiling, older man. The man had one hand on the boy's shoulder and they were both holding fishing rods.

"Doesn't look like San Diego." Reid said.

"Could be Mexico," Vargas replied, taking a look. "Or somewhere in the Caribbean."

Reid gave a grunt and put the photograph back on the wall. They continued their search but didn't find anything incriminating. No weapon. No documents from the yacht. Only a well-used guitar standing in the corner and some fishing gear.

Reid was about to suggest they leave, when Vargas broke the silence. "Hey, boss. Over here."

Reid went into the bedroom and joined his colleague in front of a large, built-in dresser. On the floor were a pair of work boots. They were dirty, the soles covered in mud, like he'd been out in the storm.

"What's this?" Reid inquired, peering closer in the dim light.

Vargas pointed to the toe on the right boot. Reid had to tilt his head to see it, but there, on the dried mud was a red smudge. It looked like blood.

.   .   .

REID GOT BACK to the station to find Del Gatto waiting for him. He raised an eyebrow at Hamilton, who shrugged. "He came in twenty minutes ago, insisting he talk to you."

"Thanks." He lowered his voice. "Put a BOLO out on Hector Esparza. He took off out the window as we got to his apartment."

Hamilton nodded. Reid approached the disgruntled businessman who was sitting in a metal chair against the wall near to the entrance. They didn't have a waiting room. "Mr. Del Gatto, what can I do for you?" Reid shook his hand. Vargas disappeared to log the boots into evidence.

"Lieutenant, I want to report a burglary."

Reid stared at him. His mind was still on what they'd found in Hector's apartment. "A burglary?"

"Yeah, it happened last night. My wife and I hosted a charity ball at my house and it was during this event that I was robbed."

"Okay, follow me." Trying to clear his head, he took Del Gatto into the interview room and gestured for him to sit down. A charity event? In the back of his mind, he recalled Kenzie saying she was going to a fundraiser last night. Could it be the same one? Nah, that was impossible. Del Gatto would never invite her. He distrusted all reporters, particularly her.

Reid sat down opposite him. "Why are you reporting it to us? Isn't Miami PD closer?"

"It might be closer, but I don't know anyone there. I know you, Lieutenant, on account of our little chat yesterday evening."

Reid sighed. Just his luck. "What was stolen?"

Del Gatto, who was perspiring, swiped a hand across his forehead. "Five hundred thousand dollars' worth of jewelry."

Reid's eyebrows shot up. Five hundred thousand dollars. That was a lot of jewelry. No wonder he was sweating. "Where was it stolen from?"

"My wife's bedroom."

Reid noticed he'd said his *wife's* bedroom, not *their* bedroom. Interesting. Then again, the billionaire probably had twenty rooms to choose from. Why wouldn't they have their own bedrooms?

"What was the item or items stolen?"

"An emerald necklace. The stones were very rare. Egyptian, I believe. I got them from a Sultan in Cairo many years ago. They're irreplaceable."

"I take it they were insured?"

"Of course."

Not a total loss then.

Reid thought for a moment. "Did you notice a particular time that they went missing, or was it just during the course of the evening?"

"My wife said it was in the safe before she went down to the party, but when she got back to her room afterwards, it was missing.

"At first I thought it was the *Bling Bandit*, but it couldn't be—not unless he was one of the guests."

Reid cringed. "What makes you say that?"

"Because I had topnotch security at my event. There is no way anyone could have broken in. Only the guests had access to the house."

It made sense. Attending the party as a guest was a smart way to get into the normally secure Miami mansion. "I see. In that case, I'll need a guest list."

Del Gatto looked uncertain. "You're going to question all my guests?"

"What else would you have me do? You've just said yourself that one of them must be the thief."

He sighed. "It was a fundraiser for my wife's charity. There were a lot of important people there. I don't want them harassed."

"I understand that, but if you want us to investigate, we have to question the guests. One of them could have seen something."

Del Gatto gave a reluctant nod. "Okay, but please be discreet. I don't want them to think they're being accused of anything."

"We will do our best, sir. What is the name of your wife's charity?"

"It's called the Breathe Hope Foundation, and she's their patron and a founding member."

Reid nodded, tapping his finger on the desk. "Did you notice anything unusual at the fundraiser that evening? Anything out of the ordinary?"

"It was a masked ball—everything was unusual." He hesitated. "Although—" He shook his head.

"What?"

"There was a door left open in my study. A balcony door. I thought I'd locked it, but when I checked before bed, it was unlocked. It can't have anything to do with the burglary though."

"Why not?"

"Because it's on the opposite side of the house to my wife's bedroom."

"Could the thief have gotten in that way?"

"I told you, the thief was at the party."

Reid tended to agree, but there was always a chance the thief had used the party as a distraction to break in. "How can you be so sure?"

"Because my guys would have noticed someone scaling up to the balcony, Lieutenant." He shot Reid a pained look. "Besides, it was raining. If they'd come in that way, they'd be wet and there was no water in the study."

He had a point there. "Okay, do you mind if we send an officer around to take a look at the layout of the house?"

"Not at all. I'll be in this afternoon."

"Do you have any CCTV or surveillance cameras on the property?"

Del Gatto hesitated. "Only at the gates, not in or around the house. I like my privacy," he added, when he saw Reid's surprised look.

"Will you send them over so we can take a look?"

"Sure, I'll get my Head of Security to send you a copy."

"Thank you. Now, if you give my officer a description of the necklace, we'll circulate it to the other law enforcement agencies. It won't be an easy item to offload."

Del Gatto grunted. "It will to the right people."

Unscrupulous people. Collectors who didn't care whether it had been stolen. That was the problem with jewelry theft, it was all so murky. Give him a good drug deal any day. Drug dealers were relatively easy to identify and tended to have long rap sheets and be on police databases. Conversely, buyers of stolen gems were successful, wealthy individuals, outwardly respectable, with no criminal history. Much harder to pinpoint.

He watched as Del Gatto strode over to Hamilton, who would take down a description and provide him with a case number for his insurance claim.

The Bling Bandit strikes again. Reid ground his jaw. Until he had a sighting on Hector, maybe he could get to the bottom of these thefts once and for all. Pushing his notes on the recent homicide aside, he shouted across to Vargas, "Give me everything we've got on the cat burglar."

CHAPTER 10

Kenzie stared at her ruined ballgown discarded at the foot of the bed. Sun streamed in through her windows, making last night's adventure seem like a crazy, distant dream.

Hiding behind the bougainvillea bushes in the rain...racing across the sodden lawn to the water's edge...scampering over the pier into the neighbor's property. Then, Alex's chauffeur picking them up on a Palm Island side-street, drenched and shivering in their thin dresses.

To be fair, he hadn't asked any questions, simply driven them back to Alex's where Kenzie had picked up her car and gone home. They hadn't said much on the way back, not wanting to make the driver any more suspicious. Hopefully, he'd think they were drunk and silly, cavorting in the rain.

Except it was very real. The muddy hem and the rip in her dress proved it. So did the pictures of the ledger she'd found in the alcove.

The ledger.

Kenzie had been trying to decipher it all morning. At first glance, she hadn't been able to make any sense of the coded entries, but now she thought she might be making some headway. It was a shame she hadn't been able to take any more photographs before she'd been disturbed. She might have been able to make more sense of it if she had. One page wasn't enough to work with.

Kenzie stared at the letters and numbers she'd transposed into her notebook.

. . .

KM-52
   JS-8/15-640.5
   RT2->M1
   CUST-Y7
   FM-100K
   EJ-MF
   A1-SI2

THE FIRST THOUGHT she'd had was that 8/15 could be a date. August fifteenth. It was late August now, so whatever had happened had occurred two weeks ago. She tapped her pencil on the desk. There was no proof this had anything to do with the diamond smuggling operation either. It could just be business transactions, meetings, or some other illicit enterprise. Del Gatto probably had his greedy fingers in a lot of illegal pies.

Except the JS. Could that be his yacht? *Jewel of the Seas*?

Tenuous, she knew. Kenzie sighed as she scratched her head. What about the numbers? 640.5? She pondered them for a while, but they meant nothing to her.

She scanned down the list. MF could mean Miami, Florida, but it could also be someone's name, along with EJ, FM, and KM. Lots of initials. Were those the people involved in whatever this was?

Supposition wouldn't get her anywhere. She needed proof. To get that, she needed Raoul.

Raoul was her research assistant at the *Herald*, a brilliant, computer brain. This was just the sort of puzzle he enjoyed.

Her phone rang, and, seeing it was Reid, she closed her laptop. She'd talk to Raoul about the coded entry on Monday, when she got to the office.

"Hey," she said, softly. They hadn't seen each other since she gave him the diamonds and she missed him. Unfortunately, that was the nature of their relationship. His job was demanding and often kept him at the station for long hours, while hers was the same. Unless they made a concerted effort, they were lucky if they saw each other once a week. That had always been their problem.

Still, they'd grown so close in New York and she was determined that things wouldn't go back to normal. She smiled at the memories. Since being back, she'd made a huge effort to embrace their newfound romance, and she hadn't regretted it.

"Hey. How are you doing, Kenz?" Reid's voice warmed as he said her name.

"I'm good. What about you?" He must be exhausted after the last few days. "You at work?"

"Yeah, the clean-up effort is ongoing, but things are slowly getting back to normal."

"That's good." She paused. "How are you holding up?"

"We're all a bit ragged around the edges, but we're hanging in there. It's nearly over. We'll take off early today." Just like him not to make it about himself.

"If you need to go home and sleep, I totally understand," she began, even though she had to hold back her disappointment. It was the weekend, after all.

"I want to see you," he said quickly. "I've got a few things to finish up at the station, then I'll come over. Is that okay?"

"That would be great. I'll cook us something nice for supper." She smiled as a warm sensation spread over her.

"Sounds perfect."

A thought struck her. "Oh, Reid. Did you find out anything about those diamonds?"

He hesitated, then his voice dropped. "Let's talk about it when I see you."

"Okay, sure." That meant he had but didn't want anyone to know he was talking to her about it. To be fair, theirs was a complicated situation, her being a reporter and him a cop. Their interests didn't always align. How could they? She wanted to right the injustices of the world by exposing the truth, he wanted to apprehend the guilty party, but to do that, he had to follow police protocol.

It took a certain amount of trust, their relationship. Luckily, they'd built that up over the last few years. Whenever they investigated the same case, she shared what she discovered, which sometimes even contributed to the case being solved, then he gave her an exclusive once they'd caught the bad guys. She trusted him not to work with any other media outlet and he trusted her not to publish anything until he gave the say so. It worked.

Trust. Not an easy thing to accomplish, but they had.

There was another pause.

"Did you hear Del Gatto was burgled last night?" Reid asked.

Kenzie gasped. "No."

"Yeah, he reported it this afternoon."

Her pulse ticked up a notch. Had Del Gatto found out about the ledger? But how could he have? She didn't take it, only a photo. That wasn't a crime, was it? He couldn't have known she'd broken into his study, could he? "What was stolen?"

"An emerald necklace."

Kenzie sank down on the couch, her head whirling. A necklace? She had not been expecting that.

"I don't understand. There was a party at the mansion last night. Are you saying he was burgled during the party?"

A sharp intake of breath. "You were there?"

She cringed. "Yes. I went with Alex."

"Alex?" He grunted. "The woman you rescued on the beach?"

"Yes, she's really nice. Do you know she's Calvin Delacroix's daughter? That movie star that I—Oh, never mind. Anyway, I asked her to get me a ticket."

"To Del Gatto's? I'm surprised he let you in the door."

She gave a wry chuckle. It was a fair question based on their previous history. Ever since she'd claimed Congressman Leonard had been doing drugs on Del Gatto's superyacht, she'd been in their crosshairs. The subsequent lawsuit shook up the newspaper, and nearly ruined her fledgling career.

"It was a masked ball. Nobody knew I was there. I was Alex's plus one."

"The anonymous plus one."

"That's right." She bit her lip. "What did Del Gatto say?"

"Just that when his wife unlocked the safe later that night, it was gone. Did you see anything? Anyone acting suspiciously?"

Only me.

And Alex.

She went cold.

Alex.

Alex had been snooping around upstairs, too. She'd come to Kenzie's rescue, but how had she known Kenzie was up there to start with? Then there was the lock picking. Alex had been pretty damn good at that. Too good, really, for a socialite. Could Alex have stolen the necklace?

She avoided the question. "You think someone at the party stole the emeralds?"

"It's possible. Del Gatto sent through his surveillance tapes. We're going through them now."

Crap!

Surveillance tapes.

"I didn't think he had any?" she gulped. That'll teach her for believing Alex. She should have done her own research. What billionaire doesn't have surveillance tapes somewhere on his property?

"Not at the house, but at the gate, yes. We think they might have picked up the thief leaving with the necklace."

There were voices in the background and Reid said, "Kenz, I've got to go. See you tonight."

"Okay, see you later."

He hung up, and Kenzie closed her eyes. Damn surveillance tapes. She tried to think back to the gate. Where were the cameras positioned? Would they have a view of the driveway, or the lawn? Maybe a partial, at best.

She bit her lip, anxiety forming a hard lump in her stomach. If she and Alex were on those tapes, they'd have a lot of explaining to do.

CHAPTER 11

Kenzie opened the door. Her heart beat a little faster when she saw Reid standing there. "Hi."

"Hi."

"Come on in." He looked a little bleary-eyed and disheveled, but that only made him seem more attractive. She thought so, anyway. He walked in, hesitated, then bent down and kissed her. They were still getting used to this new status quo.

She reciprocated, then threw her arms around his neck and hugged him. "It's good to see you."

"You too." He was smiling when she released him.

"Come on in. Supper's nearly ready. Want a beer?"

"That would be great." He followed her into the kitchen where she had two filet mignons cooking in the oven. Before he'd arrived, she'd seared them in the pan in butter and olive oil, and the smell was glorious.

"Smells great," he confirmed, taking a seat at the island.

She grinned and handed him a beer. "Filet steaks with red wine reduction, mashed potatoes, and grilled asparagus."

"Sounds amazing." He fixed his eyes on her. "Tell me what happened at the party."

"Nothing happened." Her smile faded. Her default position was to lie, but it wouldn't work with Reid. He could see right through her.

"Kenzie—I saw the surveillance tapes."

Shit.

She squeezed her eyes shut, and he shook his head. "I knew it. I knew that was you."

"I had a close call." She tried to explain. "I was snooping and got locked in Del Gatto's study. That creepy sidekick of his found the door open and locked it while I was inside."

He gawked at her. "Del Gatto's Head of Security?"

"Yeah. You know him?"

"Samson Quinn. We looked into him. He was dishonorably discharged from the military when an operation he was leading in Iraq went south. Since then, he's worked mostly in the private sector. My contact at the DOD said he was court martialed over his actions in Iraq. Apparently, several civilians were killed."

Kenzie grimaced. "I was wary of him."

"Did he know you were in there?" asked Reid.

"I don't think so. I hid behind the drapes. Luckily, Alex came looking for me and let me out."

Reid gave her a worried look. "That was dangerous, Kenz. Quinn means business. If he'd caught you—"

She took his hand. "He didn't. I got away safe and sound. Del Gatto doesn't even know I was at the party."

Reid shook his head. "Let's hope he doesn't recognize you and your new best friend on the surveillance footage."

Kenzie cringed. "How obvious is it that it's us?"

"Not very. It's dark and the weather's bad. There's a glimpse of you two running across part of the lawn, but that could easily be explained by the party. Drunk guests fooling around outside in the rain." He shot her a hard look. "It happens."

She exhaled. "It does."

"Nobody would be able to say for sure that it was you two."

"How did you guess?"

He cocked his head to one side. "Because I know you, Kenzie. I knew you were at that party and I recognized you in the footage. Not you so much as your physique and how you moved."

"Thank you," she whispered. "For not turning us in."

He shrugged, but she could see he was uncomfortable with it. He'd had to cover for her and Alex, and that wasn't fair. "I know you didn't steal the emeralds."

Kenzie felt a sinking in her stomach. *She* hadn't stolen the emeralds, but she couldn't be certain about Alex. She studied Reid, who was so stoic and loyal, and felt a twinge of guilt. By not mentioning her suspicions, she was in effect lying. Still, she wasn't sure Alex was the thief. More investigation was necessary before she could take her findings to Reid. Then she would. She absolutely would.

"Tell me about the necklace," changing the focus of the conversation. "When did it go missing?"

"Apparently, Del Gatto's wife noticed it was gone when she returned her jewels to the safe before bed."

Kenzie frowned. "It was in a safe?"

"Yeah, whoever stole it managed to crack the combination."

"The safe wasn't left open?"

"Del Gatto insists not. It also had a complex security system. It would have taken a pro to get in there."

Kenzie exhaled silently. Alex couldn't have stolen the necklace from Bethany Del Gatto's bedroom. Cracking a high-security safe like that required not just skill but also specialized equipment. Kenzie had done extensive research into safe cracking for an article she'd once written. The thief would have needed tools such as a safe-cracking auto dialer, which could tirelessly work through thousands of combinations, or a stethoscope for the more 'old school' method of listening to the lock's tumblers fall into place. The equipment was bulky and conspicuous.

Alex had arrived at the party with nothing but a small clutch purse, barely large enough for her phone and a lipstick. The notion that she could have concealed even the most basic lock-picking tools in there, let alone something as substantial as a drill or an auto dialer, was laughable. Kenzie was pretty sure that her friend wasn't a seasoned criminal.

Her skills, as far as Kenzie could see, didn't extend beyond picking a simple door lock, a far cry from the complexities involved in bypassing a state-of-the-art safe.

That left one other theory. "You think this is the work of the *Bling Bandit*?"

"It fits the MO," Reid reasoned. "Bethany Del Gatto is a wealthy woman. There's no sign of forced entry. No DNA or other trace evidence left at the scene."

"Definitely a pro," she murmured.

Reid nodded.

A hiss from the oven brought Kenzie back to the present. "Enough about Del Gatto. Supper's ready. Let's eat and you can tell me about the diamonds I found on the beach."

SUPPER WAS DELICIOUS. Kenzie had really gone out of her way to make it a special meal, something Reid appreciated because it showed how much she cared. While he ate, he felt the tension of the last few days start to dissipate.

"The diamonds have been sent to the lab." He figured she had a right to know that much. After all, she'd been the one to find them and hand them over to the authorities. She could have kept them for herself or split them with that photographer friend of hers. No one would have known. But that wasn't Kenzie.

Her strong moral code was one of the things he loved about her. Sure, she had a habit of getting into trouble, particularly when she was going after a story, but it was always for the greater good. Always in search of the truth. She would never hurt anybody, and she'd never commit a felony. That was something he was sure of.

"Do you know where they originated from?" she asked as he put his knife and fork together.

"Not yet. The lab has brought in an appraiser to work on it. It's difficult because the diamonds have to be guarded at all times. That amount of money—" He didn't have to finish. She knew the dangers.

"What about Del Gatto? Did you question him about the diamonds?"

"We did, but he claims no knowledge of them."

She snorted. "He would."

"We have another suspect, Kenz."

"Oh?" She put her cutlery down.

"I can't say much, but it's not Del Gatto."

Kenzie pushed her plate away from her. "Come on. You don't honestly believe Del Gatto had nothing to do with this."

Reid shrugged. "I have to go where the evidence leads."

"What makes you think this other suspect was involved?"

He sighed. "I shouldn't be discussing this with you."

She gave him a look. "This is me, Reid. I'm not just any civilian. You know I'm going to keep digging into Del Gatto, so you may as well tell me if you have someone else in mind."

Unfortunately, he did know her. She wouldn't quit until she'd uncovered the truth. Maybe what he had to say would discourage her.

"We found a body, the morning of the storm," he began. "The coroner discovered an uncut diamond in the victim's stomach."

She gasped. "His stomach? As in, he swallowed it?"

He gave a tight nod.

"Was he on the yacht?" she blurted out. Reid both loved and hated the way Kenzie's mind worked. It made keeping anything from her extremely difficult.

"Yeah, he was part of the crew."

Kenzie stared at him, deep in thought. "You think he was involved in the smuggling operation?"

"We don't know."

"He must have been in contact with the diamonds. Maybe he was stealing from the shipment."

"It's a theory."

"You said he died."

Reid nodded.

"Was he murdered?"

Reid didn't reply. He couldn't answer that. Turned out he didn't have to.

Her eyes grew even bigger. "He was! Oh, my gosh. Do you think it was Del Gatto?"

Reid shook his head. "Del Gatto has an iron-clad alibi. It wasn't him."

"What about his henchman, Quinn?"

"I don't know, but Kenzie, you can't tell anyone what I've told you. You can't print it. You can't insinuate it. You get that, right?"

"I know, and I won't." She gazed distractedly at her empty plate. "But if you don't suspect Quinn, who do you suspect?"

"I can't discuss that." He hated saying that to her, but there were lines he just couldn't cross.

Her face fell. He'd disappointed her. "I'm sorry, Kenz, but you know how this goes. It's not the first time we've been in this situation."

She gave a frustrated nod. "Yeah, I know."

Reid thought about the party. How she'd snuck into Del Gatto's study and hadn't mentioned it until he'd told her he'd seen her on the security footage. Knowing Kenzie, there was probably more she wasn't telling him too.

He reached for his beer. They both had secrets they had to keep.

CHAPTER 12

"I've got a puzzle for you," Kenzie told Raoul, when she got to the *Herald's* offices. Situated on the fifth floor of a downtown high-rise, the newsroom offered exquisite views over the city, the Port of Miami, and the barrier islands.

The bay was deceptively calm, the waterfront glistening in the early morning sun. How different from the violent maelstrom of the other day. You'd never believe a Category 4 hurricane had blasted through, creating a storm surge that had ripped yachts from their moorings and tossed them around the marina like they were toys.

"Oh, yeah?" Raoul looked up. Despite sitting next to the window, Kenzie couldn't remember her researcher ever looking out of it. He had eyes only for the jumble of code flitting across his screen.

Kenzie dug her hand in her pocket. He watched her expectantly. "For your eyes only." She handed him a piece of paper.

He gazed at it for some time, then said, "What's this?"

"It's a ledger entry. I need your help to decipher it since it appears to be in some sort of code and I can't make head or tail of it."

He adjusted his glasses and took a long, hard look at the handwritten entry. "I'm going to need context. *A lot* of context."

"I'll email you what I have."

"No," he barked, shaking his head. "No emails. Tell me."

Raoul was right. Emails could be hacked. Computers could be seized and used in lawsuits.

She pulled up a chair. "I've got a story to tell you."

He listened intently while she told him about the diamonds that had washed up on the beach, the charity ball, and finding the ledger in Del Gatto's study. She purposely left out Alex's involvement, as well as how she'd gotten locked in and their frantic race to freedom across the soaked lawns of the mansion.

"Whoa! Back up."

"Shh..." Kenzie hissed. "Keep your voice down."

"Sorry, I'm struggling to get around the fact that you found millions of dollars' worth of diamonds on a beach and *gave them to the cops*." He gaped at her incredulously.

She gave an embarrassed nod.

"Are you crazy? You could've been set for life?"

"I'd rather catch Del Gatto," she murmured.

Raoul shook his head. "Sometimes, I don't understand you, Kenzie."

"I'm an investigative journalist, Raoul. This is what I do. I investigate, and the diamonds are a perfect opportunity to bring down Del Gatto and that corrupt cohort of his, Congressman Leonard."

He gave a snort. "You like making enemies, don't you?"

She shrugged. "Comes with the territory. Now, are you going to help me or reprimand me for not stealing the diamonds and keeping them for myself?"

His gaze turned back to the paper she'd given him. "Do you suspect this coded entry has something to do with the diamonds?"

"Maybe. That's what I'm trying to find out."

"And this is the only entry you have?"

"There were others, but this is the only page I managed to photograph."

"It would have been better if we had others to compare them to," he grumbled.

"I know." She'd had the same thought. "But we'll have to work with what we've got."

"Okay, it'll involve some research. Give me a few hours and I'll see what I can dig up."

"Thanks, you're a star. Remember, not a word to anyone or I could get into serious trouble."

"Why? Do they know it's missing?"

"No, I left the ledger there, but there was a theft that night during the party. If anyone finds out I was sneaking around the mansion, I might inadvertently become a suspect." She thought of the surveillance footage of Alex and herself.

"A theft?" He cocked his head.

"Yeah. Someone stole Del Gatto's wife's emerald necklace. He reported it missing the next day."

Raoul whistled under his breath. "You like playing with fire, don't you?"

"It's not my fault he was burgled."

"Quite the coincidence, though, isn't it?"

It was.

"Kenzie!" boomed a loud voice.

She glanced up. Keith was beckoning to her from across the newsroom. "I'd better go."

He grimaced. "The boss is on edge today. Head office rang him first thing—circulation numbers have plummeted along with print ad revenue. He's been given an ultimatum to boost figures or start cutting staff."

Her heart skipped. "Seriously?" She didn't ask how Raoul came by this information, the urgency in his tone said enough.

"Dead serious," he replied, his features tightening. "Everyone is online these days. People would rather listen to the latest influencer than read mainstream newspapers. We're in hot water."

Kenzie felt a chill run down her spine. Could her job be at stake? Was the situation worse than she'd originally imagined?

As she walked across the newsroom to Keith's office, a heaviness began to descend on her. The newspaper was more than just a workplace, it was her life, her reason for being. Without it, she didn't know what she would do.

"Keith, what's up?"

He slumped in his chair, his shoulders sagging. Up close, Kenzie noticed that his skin was sallow, he had dark rings under his eyes and he looked terrible. Her heart sank. This was not good. "Is something wrong?"

"They're shutting us down, Kenz."

"What?" She bent over like someone had sucker punched her in the gut. "You're kidding?"

"Wish I was."

"But why?"

"The shifting dynamics of media consumption," he replied bitterly.

"They're ditching the paper edition and going a hundred percent digital. Starting next month, we're going to be an online subscription service only."

Kenzie sank into the chair opposite him. "What does that mean for us? Do we still have a job?"

"You do," he said. "I managed to negotiate deals for most of my reporters, but obviously there are online editors already, so you'll have to work with them."

Kenzie stared at him, horrified. "What about you?"

He snorted. "Nobody wants an old hack like me around. Not anymore."

Kenzie couldn't believe what she was hearing. The *Herald* wouldn't be the same without Keith. Keith wouldn't be the same without the *Herald*. "Y—You can't leave."

"I have no choice, Kenzie. I've been given a redundancy package. A golden handshake, if you like." He gave a humorless laugh. "I've got the month to clear out."

"But...but...we haven't heard anything," she stammered.

"Not yet. They're going to announce it this afternoon. If you check your email, you'll see a department meeting has been scheduled for four o'clock."

"Who's giving the meeting?" Surely Keith would be the one to tell his staff they were closing down the division.

"Someone from HQ. I don't know who." He sighed. "We've had a good run, eh? Better than we should have done, given the current climate."

"It wasn't enough," Kenzie whimpered, dropping her head into her hands. She felt like crying. How could it all be coming to an end?

"No," he murmured. "It wasn't enough."

They sat in silence for a moment, then Kenzie looked up. "What are you going to do, Keith?"

"I don't know. I haven't thought that far ahead yet. Play golf. Fish. Spend more time with my grandkids." He shrugged. "Maybe I'll write a novel. I haven't written anything in a very long time. I used to be good, you know." He gave a sad smile.

"I know," Kenzie managed a weak smile. Keith had won awards in his day. Like her, he'd been a tireless seeker of the truth. "What about if I get a scoop? Would that help? Del Gatto? He's a big fish."

"You can't beat the system, Kenz. Taking down Del Gatto would be a major win, but it won't make any real difference."

She fought back tears.

"It's happening everywhere." Keith gave an empty smile. "The world is changing. The way we consume information is changing. Digital platforms offer so much more in the way of distribution, and their costs are lower. The broadsheets can't compete."

"That doesn't mean we should lose them completely."

"You don't have to worry, Kenzie. HQ recognizes the value of high-quality journalism. They know it attracts and retains subscribers, and you're one of the best. Your future is secure." He leaned forward onto the mounds of paper scattered all over his desk. "If you play your cards right, you can still have a great career in investigative reporting. Maybe you can even start a podcast." He gave a dry laugh.

They discussed the reasons for the decision in more detail, arguing the finer points like they always did. Kenzie couldn't believe this was probably one of the last times she'd do this with Keith. When she finally returned to her desk, she'd forgotten about the ledger, about Alex, and even the diamonds. All she could think about was how her life, her career was about to change — and she didn't know if she was ready for it.

CHAPTER 13

Reid walked across the parking lot to the police station, relishing the heat of the sun on his back. Hurricane Matteo was fast becoming a distant memory. Communities were rebuilding, streets were being cleaned of debris, and windows were being fixed. Soon, his district would be back to normal.

He said hello to Monroe, Hamilton, and Diaz before going to sit at his desk. Vargas came over a short time later carrying a bulging folder. "You wanted to see the stuff we've got on the burglaries?"

Reid gestured to the empty chair opposite. "Yeah, take a seat."

"I don't get it," Vargas mused, as he sat down.

"Don't get what?"

"In every case, the victim doesn't know they've been burgled until after the event. The thief seems to know exactly where the jewels are hidden. They get in and out without so much as a sound, they never raise the alarm. They leave no DNA, no evidence of their crime, and they're gone before the theft is discovered."

"They're a pro." Reid arched an eyebrow.

"I can't help thinking they must have inside information." Vargas pursed his lips. "Or be working with an accomplice who does."

It was a good theory, one Reid had considered, but hadn't had time to develop yet. "You think someone is giving them the information? Telling them where the valuables are kept, how to access them, that sort of thing?"

"Makes sense, doesn't it? Maybe a maid or member of the staff. The victims are always wealthy celebs or high net worth individuals."

Reid gave a thoughtful nod. "I know we haven't really looked at this in any great detail, but that's a good place to start. Why don't you speak to each of the victims and compile a list of staff, caterers, gardening services, et cetera. We'll cross reference them and maybe something will jump out at us."

Vargas nodded. "I'm on it."

"Also, let's check with other police departments in Florida. Could be our jewel thief is moving from one metropolitan hub to another when it gets too hot."

"Yeah, okay."

They were finishing up their discussion when Detective Diaz rushed over. "Boss, I can't trace any of the guys in Del Gatto's crew. They've vanished."

He scowled. "What do you mean vanished?"

"Gone. Disappeared." She put her hands on her hips. "The crew list I got from Del Gatto's assistant was no help whatsoever. Apart from Vince and Hector, who we already know, everyone else on it was either a non-registered immigrant or used a false name."

"How convenient." He grimaced. "What does Del Gatto say about that?"

"He claims he had no idea. He didn't deal with the hiring and firing of staff. That was the skipper's responsibility. He chose his own crew."

"The same skipper who's our prime suspect," murmured Reid.

Diaz nodded.

Reid tapped his pencil on the table.

"I might have an idea," Diaz said, cautiously. "But it's a long shot."

"Oh yeah?"

"I thought I'd pay a visit to this beach bar where the yachting crowd usually hangs out and see if anyone knows anything. Del Gatto's yacht is, or was, pretty conspicuous. Somebody must know her crew."

"Good idea. I'll come with you." Reid stretched and got to his feet. He needed a change of scenery and the sun streaming in the window was making him long to be outdoors. Too much desk work was not good for anyone.

"We can't go in looking like cops." Diaz tilted her head as she studied him.

He grinned. "Don't worry. I've got a change of clothes in the car."

· · ·

THE CREST WAS a rustic beach bar situated half a mile down the beach from the Acacia Yacht Club.

"Cute place," muttered Diaz, as they walked in. Made mostly of sunbleached wood and reclaimed sails, it had a chill, laid-back vibe to it. Reggae music played softly in the background.

Reid looked around. "I'd have thought there'd have been more hurricane damage." Both he and Diaz wore dark sunglasses and casual beach attire, blending in with the sun-bleached surfers and weathered deck hands.

"Looks like they got off easy."

They walked over to the bar and took a seat. Reid ordered a couple of beers from the bartender, a tanned, young man rocking a Hawaiian shirt. "Hey, you don't know anyone who worked on *Jewel of the Seas*, do you?" he asked, casually.

The bartender narrowed his eyes. "Why?"

"I'm looking for a crew, and since the *Jewel* washed up in pieces after the storm, I thought those guys might be looking for work."

The bartender surveyed him, taking in the surf shirt, the khaki cargo pants, and leather strap he'd tied around his wrist. A nice touch, he'd felt. Kenzie had suggested it a while back on an undercover operation, and he'd taken it to heart.

"Nobody here from the *Jewel*," the barman said, apparently satisfied with Reid's story. "I'll give you a shout if they come in." He moved away to take another order.

A short time later, a lone man entered the bar dressed in casual beachwear, with a nervous energy about him that clashed with the relaxed atmosphere. He scanned the room, his eyes briefly meeting Reid's before darting away.

He and Diaz watched surreptitiously as the man made his way to the other side of the bar, where another man, rugged and lean with wavy dark hair and a prominent anchor tattoo on his left forearm, greeted him.

"That's Hector Esparza," Reid said, putting his hands on the bar. "I recognize him from the photos."

The two men exchanged terse words, barely audible over the mellow reggae beats, grabbed a couple of beers, and retreated to a secluded corner table.

"The conversation seems tense," Diaz whispered to Reid. The nervous man was constantly checking over his shoulder as if he were looking out for someone. Someone he didn't want to see. After a brief exchange, the jittery man stood up and quickly left the bar.

"I'll go after him," Reid said, standing up.

"Okay, I'll wait here and keep an eye on Hector." The skipper seemed to be in no rush to finish his drink.

Reid nodded, then followed the man outside.

"Hey, wait up," Reid called out, his tone friendly but firm. As the man turned, Reid saw the flash of fear in his eyes. "You're from *Jewel of the Seas*, aren't you?"

The guy broke into a run.

Great.

Reid took off after him. The sand was soft and hampered the fleeing man's progress. He aimed for the water, where the sand was firmer, but Reid had tennis shoes on and easily caught up. He tackled the guy in the shallows and the two went rolling into the waves.

"Don't kill me," the nervous guy said, spluttering.

"Relax, I'm not going to hurt you."

"You're not?"

"No. My name's Lieutenant Reid Garrett from Sweetwater PD. I just want to ask you some questions."

The fear was replaced by denial. "What about?"

"Who did you think I was?"

He was rewarded with a sulky silence.

"Okay, let's try this. Who wants you dead?"

The man didn't say anything but stared at his feet.

Reid sighed. The guy was clearly more afraid of the person or persons after him than the cops.

"You're coming down to the station with me." Reid cuffed the guy's hands behind his back.

"But I haven't done anything!"

"Then you won't mind answering some questions." Reid led the guy back to the squad car. Diaz was there waiting for him, her hands on her hips.

"Where's Hector?" he asked, then he noticed her cheek and winced. "What happened to you?"

"Bastard ducked out the back. I tried to catch him, but he took a swing at me and ran off."

"You okay?

"Yeah, he just clipped me. Nothing serious." Diaz was underplaying it. It was already turning a deep shade of purple.

"Nice friends you've got," Reid said to the jittery guy and pushed him into the back of the cruiser.

"He isn't my friend."

"Really? Isn't he your crew mate?"

The man hung his head sulkily. "Doesn't mean he's my friend."

Reid shot Diaz a triumphant look. "Okay, let's go."

"Am I under arrest?" the man asked.

"Not yet." Reid started the engine.

"Then why am I in cuffs?"

"You're being detained for questioning," Diaz said, twisting around in her seat. "But we can arrest you if you'd prefer?"

He shut up after that and they drove the rest of the way to the station in silence.

REID AND DIAZ got back to find two unmarked black SUVs in the station parking lot. Reid studied the plates.

"Feds," he muttered.

Diaz gave him a startled look. "What are they doing here?"

"Guess we're about to find out."

They walked in with their detainee, who was still sulking, when Hamilton intercepted them.

"The FBI is here," he whispered, nodding to two men wearing identical government black suits.

"Thank you, Hamilton." Reid nodded to the men. They were the same height, same build, and if it wasn't for their differing hairstyles, could have been clones of each other. One had curly dark hair, while the other had a severe brush cut, military style. They were standing at Vargas's desk.

"Boss, these men are from the FBI. They're here about the diamonds," his second-in-command told him.

"Right. Hamilton, take this guy to the holding cell. He's not under arrest, but he is a flight risk." The young officer nodded and took custody of the suspect.

"Is there somewhere we can talk in private?" Brush Cut said.

"No." Reid made no apology for the fact that his desk was in the bullpen. They weren't a big department, and the three spare rooms were used for printing, interrogating suspects, and storing evidence. Besides,

Reid preferred sitting with his team. He was a hands-on boss. He wanted to be in the thick of it.

"Okay. I guess we'll have to talk here," the other one said.

"Guess so." Reid walked around them to his desk and sat down. He gestured for them to take a seat.

They looked around, grabbed a couple of vacant chairs, and pulled them up to Reid's desk.

"We're taking possession of the diamonds," Brush Cut told him, getting straight to the point. Reid had been expecting that. The Feds had a habit of sweeping in and taking over cases, and this was a juicy one.

"I'm afraid I can't allow that," Reid said, more because he didn't like the man's tone than for any other reason. "This is our case."

"Not anymore," Brush Cut replied. He must be slightly superior to his partner. "This is a federal matter. We're taking over the investigation. You need to hand over the diamonds."

"I can't." Reid repeated.

"You can't or you won't?" Brush Cut leaned forward.

Reid held his gaze. "I can't because they're at the lab under armed guard, getting tested."

Brush Cut exhaled noisily.

"When will you get them back?" Curly Locks asked.

"Soon." Reid saw no reason to lie. "I believe they're working with an appraiser to trace the origin of the gems."

"They're most likely from west Africa," Brush Cut said, frustrated.

Vargas shot him a curious glance. "How do you know that?"

The two agents looked at each other.

"Care to fill us in?" Reid asked softly.

"After you tell us everything you know about the diamonds," Brush Cut said.

Reid fixed his gaze on him. "You first."

Brush Cut hesitated, then gave an arrogant shrug. "I guess we can fill you in on the basics."

Reid waited.

The FBI agent rested his clasped hands on the desk. "The bureau is investigating a professional diamond smuggling outfit. It's a large, complex organization with key players in politics, industry, and local businesses. We've known there was a Miami connection for some time, but we haven't known how the diamonds are being smuggled into the country."

"Until they washed up on our beach," Reid said.

"Yeah, that's right. Salvatore Del Gatto is now a person of interest in this investigation."

"I've interviewed him," Reid said. "He denies any knowledge of the diamonds or the smuggling operation."

"We'd like to ask him that ourselves," Brush Cut said.

"Be my guest." Reid almost smiled as he pictured the billionaire's reaction to the FBI bringing him in for questioning. His lawyers would have a field day with them.

"What about his crew?" Brush Cut asked. "Have you interviewed them?"

"Not yet," Reid said honestly. He didn't mention that one was dead, and the other in the wind. "But we've got a list of names."

"We'd like a copy of everything you've got," Brush Cut said.

"Sure." Reid met Vargas's gaze. "Detective, won't you give the agent a copy of the file?"

Vargas nodded and walked over to his desk.

"You made any headway?" Brush Cut asked.

"We haven't had much time to work on it with the hurricane and all." Reid didn't mention that he had one of the crew in the holding cell.

Brush Cut nodded. "We'll take it from here."

"You said the diamonds were from west Africa?" Reid said, before they could leave. He figured he may as well get as much information out of the two agents as possible.

Brush Cut studied him for a moment, then muttered, "What the hell. They come from a country called Sierra Leone. There are several diamond mines over there. One in particular, Kimbala, is most likely where your diamonds are from. Previous shipments have ended up in high end jewelers all down the east coast."

"They can trace the diamonds back to the exact place they were mined?" Vargas asked, coming back with the file. He dropped it on Reid's desk in front of the agent.

Brush Cut acknowledged it with a quick nod. "Pretty much, yeah. Something about the chemical makeup and the soil elements in that region. Kimbala is where the majority of the smuggled gems originate from."

"What about South Africa?" Vargas asked.

Brush Cut shot him a suspicious glance. "Why'd you ask about South Africa?"

"I thought that's where the diamond mines were," Vargas said hastily, realizing his mistake.

Reid didn't say anything. It was better if the FBI didn't know about Vince, the dead crew member. That was his homicide investigation, and he wanted to find the killer, regardless of whether it had anything to do with the diamond smuggling operation or not. He didn't want the Feds taking that case away from him, too.

"I don't know about that," Brush Cut said. "All I can tell you is the diamonds we've seized so far have been from west Africa."

"Thanks for filling us in." Reid tied up the conversation. He wanted to talk to his suspect in the holding cell and find out what had happened on their last voyage, and why his fellow crew member was dead. It was time the guy told them the truth.

CHAPTER 14

The Palmetto Pointe Country Club was situated in an exclusive coastal enclave overlooking a picturesque bay. As Kenzie drove up the elegantly curving driveway toward the club entrance, she passed a sprawling golf course and a signpost that read: *Private Beach Access*. The marina was sprinkled with yachts, and both grass and clay tennis courts.

Palmetto Pointe was one of Miami Dade's most exclusive clubs. It was talked about in hushed whispers amongst the *nouveau riche*, all who were desperate to be invited to be members. The membership roster was secret and, unless you owned one of the revamped multi-million-dollar mansions in the area or were an A-list celebrity, you were not getting in.

"Is Del Gatto a member?" Kenzie asked, as Alex led her out onto the terrace.

"Yeah, I've seen him here. I think he likes to play squash. That's his mistress over there, Christina Gomez." She nodded toward an attractive blonde in her mid-thirties wearing a tiny tennis skirt and a top that showed off her expensive boob job. "She's actually not a bad tennis player."

Alex had automatic membership thanks to her father, the late Calvin Delacroix, a Hollywood legend and a descendant of Vivien Swanson, a Golden Globe winning actress and model and a darling of the Golden Era of Hollywood.

"I used to play in the league," she confided to Kenzie as they sat down in the restaurant overlooking the ninth hole. Beyond the golf course, the azure water of the private beach glittered enticingly. "But it's too pretentious for my liking. Still, I thought it might be a good place to have lunch. The fresh salmon salad is to die for."

Kenzie took in the luxurious decor, impeccably trained waiters, and expensively dressed members. The men reeked of power and influence and the women were dazzlingly attractive, with their salon-chic hairstyles and sculptured bodies draped in designer sportswear.

"I can understand that," she murmured. Truth be told, she'd always wanted to visit the prestigious club, if for no other reason than to peek at its secretive members. So far, she'd seen two heiresses, a famous talk show host, and a state senator.

Dragging her gaze away from the members to the menu, she nearly balked at the prices. The main courses were eye-wateringly expensive. "Have whatever you want," Alex told her with a wave of her hand. "Lunch is on me."

"Are you sure? I invited you out."

"Yes, but I suggested the country club. Please, Kenzie, it's the least I can do after you saved my life."

Kenzie glanced at her over the menu. "I think you paid your dues the other night when you got me out of Del Gatto's study."

"That was nothing," she said dismissively. "I'm just glad I was there when you needed me."

"About that," Kenzie said.

The waiter came over to take their order. Kenzie bit her lip. She deferred to Alex and went with the salmon salad.

"You won't regret it," Alex told Kenzie gaily.

"Alex, why were you upstairs at the party?" Kenzie asked, impatient to get back to the topic of discussion.

Alex hesitated. "This is going to sound silly, but I was curious to see where you were going."

"You saw me go upstairs?" Kenzie studied her. Alex sat comfortably, her hands in her lap. Her dark hair framed her face in a jagged bob and the smattering of mascara she'd applied made her eyes appear even more green than usual, or maybe that was the reflection from the golf course in front of them.

"Yes, there was that commotion with the champagne glasses, and I spotted you slip away and go upstairs. I was intrigued, so I followed."

"You were intrigued?" Kenzie frowned. "Why?"

"Okay, now you're going to think I'm really silly, but I've always wanted to be a reporter, right from when I was a little girl and, when you disappeared, I thought you might be up to something, so I followed." She grimaced. "I hope you don't mind."

"*You* wanted to be a reporter?" Kenzie repeated.

"Yeah. I studied journalism at college. Graduated with a 4.0. Loved my course, but my parents didn't want me to work. Not at a newspaper." She turned up her nose like it was a bad thing.

"Why not?"

Alex sighed. "This is going to sound ridiculous to you, but people like me don't work, Kenzie. We volunteer, we do charity work, and we sit on the board of nonprofits."

"I'm sure you could—"

"Oh, I tried. Mother and I were always arguing over it. After she died, I became manager of my grandmother's estate. Then after my father was murdered—" She looked down at her hands. "It seemed a bit late to start a career."

"I'm sorry," Kenzie murmured. No amount of money in the world would make her give up her job, even if she was forced to work on the digital edition of the newspaper. She loved it too much. In that respect, she sympathized with Alex.

"What were you doing in Salvatore's study?" Alex asked, her gaze flickering back to Kenzie.

When Kenzie didn't immediately reply, she leaned forward and whispered conspiratorially, "You're investigating him, aren't you?"

"I, er, well...yes, I am."

"How exciting!" Her eyes flashed. "What's he done?"

"I can't really talk about it."

Alex would not be deterred. Kenzie had come here hoping to pump her for information, but instead, she found herself in the firing line. "Has it got something to do with that case that washed up on the beach?"

Kenzie studied her across the table. "What makes you say that?"

Alex flicked her hair off her face. She had her actress grandmother's bone structure. The same effervescent features that had won the hearts of adoring fans the world over. "Let's see. First, Salvatore's million-dollar yacht smashes to pieces and a mysterious case washes ashore. Then, after you rescue me, that good looking detective friend of yours arrives, and takes the case away with him. It doesn't take a genius to figure out that the two must be related."

It seemed she'd underestimated Alex Delacroix.

Kenzie gave a faint nod. "You're right. About all of it. There was contraband in the case. Once I realized it, I called Lieutenant Garrett." She settled for a paired down version of the truth.

Alex clapped her hands. "I knew it! That's why you wanted an invitation to the party and that's why you were snooping in Salvatore's study. You were looking for clues that linked him to whatever was in that case."

Kenzie spread her hands. "You got me."

Alex grinned. "You should have told me. I'd have helped you."

"Then we'd both be locked in the study," Kenzie said, pragmatically.

Alex gave a tinkling laugh. "True. So, did you find anything?"

Kenzie shook her head. "Unfortunately not. I didn't have much time before Samson Quinn locked the door."

"That's a shame." Alex thought for a moment. "You're convinced the contraband came from *Jewel of the Seas*?"

"You know his yacht?" Kenzie asked.

Another laugh. "Of course. I've been on it enough times."

"Oh, I didn't realize you were such good friends." Kenzie bit her lip. Maybe it was time she shut up about Del Gatto. If Alex told him about this discussion, there's no telling what he'd do.

"We're not, but I adore his wife, Bethany."

"I wasn't aware," Kenzie said.

"She's a wonderful woman. Gives so much to that charity of hers."

"Cystic fibrosis, isn't it?"

"That's it. Her sister suffers with it. She's been in and out of hospitals all her life."

"I'm sorry to hear that," Kenzie said. It explained the masked ball fundraiser, and why Bethany had been the Belle of the Ball.

Their salads came. As the waiter put them on the table, a handsome man in golf clothes walked past.

"Alex, hi. Haven't seen you around in a while."

"Hi Harry. Yeah, I know. I've been busy." The man's gold Rolex glinted in the midday sun.

"This is my friend, Kenzie Gilmore."

Harry nodded politely, although his eyes barely touched on Kenzie before flitting back to Alex. "Hope to see you at the prizegiving."

Alex's smile was fake. "Wouldn't miss it."

"That's Thomas Henry Rutherford III," Alex whispered, once he'd moved on. "Quite the catch of the season."

"He seems to like you," Kenzie remarked dryly.

Alex laughed, her green eyes glittering. "Not interested."

Kenzie stared after the golfer. His name rang a bell. "Didn't his wife commit suicide?" she asked suddenly, as it came to her.

"Oh God, that was a terrible tragedy," Alex whispered. "He found her body in the garage. She'd gassed herself."

Kenzie shook her head. "How awful." She remembered reading about it in the papers.

"My heart goes out to him," Alex continued. "A girl in my dorm killed herself at college, and I'll never forget it."

"Oh, my gosh," Kenzie turned to her, horrified. "Did you—? Were you the one who—"

"No, I didn't find her. It was during the day and I was out. One of the students in her tutor group found her. Apparently, she was deeply unhappy."

"She must have been," Kenzie mused.

"Anyway, I've tried to put it behind me," Alex said. "It helped, moving to Miami."

"Fresh start," Kenzie said.

Alex nodded.

After lunch, Alex gave Kenzie the grand tour. It really was a beautiful club. Before she left, Kenzie excused herself to go to the restroom. While she was there, she heard a woman on the phone in the next cubicle.

"He promised he'd leave his wife," the woman whined. "It's been four years, and he's still with the bitch." Kenzie's eyebrows shot up.

There was a pause as the person on the other end of the line replied, to which the woman in the cubicle said, "I can't give him an ultimatum. He's not the kind of guy you can push around."

Another pause as the person spoke.

"I don't want to leave him," the woman wailed. "I love him, but I've had enough. I don't want to sneak around like I'm his dirty little secret."

Kenzie cringed. It sounded messy.

She washed her hands and was about to leave the restroom when the cubicle door swung open. Out stumbled Del Gatto's mistress. She glared at Kenzie through smudged eyes, mascara streaming down both cheeks.

Kenzie shot her a sympathetic grimace, then hurried out.

Now that was interesting.

. . .

WHEN SHE GOT HOME, Kenzie made a strong coffee and took her laptop over to the sofa. Collapsing on it, she googled Alexandra Delacroix.

Surprisingly, there wasn't much online about her. She didn't have a social media footprint, which Kenzie thought strange for a journalism major, and there were no mentions of any charity work or appearances in Los Angeles.

The Miami Herald had an article on Calvin Delacroix's death that Kenzie had written herself, and the Miami New Times had an obituary, which said he was survived by his only daughter, Alexandra, but other than that, there was zilch.

Intrigued, Kenzie picked up her phone and called Raoul. "No, I haven't deciphered the code yet," he said, as soon as he picked up.

She laughed. "That's not what I'm calling about."

"Oh? That's a relief. What is it?"

"I need you to do a deep dive on someone for me."

"Is it urgent?"

"No, not really. It's just someone I met. I want to know whether I can trust them."

"A man? I thought you were seeing that detective, what's his name again?"

She ignored the question. Raoul knew very well what Reid's name was. "It's not a man."

"Okay, text me the details and I'll take a look first thing tomorrow."

"Thanks Raoul."

"No worries. Have a good evening, Kenz."

"You too."

Kenzie shut down her laptop and turned on the TV. She was just in time to catch the six o'clock news. The *Bling Bandit* got a mention, as did the latest victim, Bethany Del Gatto who was filmed outside a designer store wearing a broad-brimmed hat and dark glasses, cradling her pet chihuahua. Somehow, the theft of the five hundred-thousand-dollar necklace had been leaked to the press. For once, it wasn't her.

Then, the news anchor went on to mention that Del Gatto was offering a twenty-thousand-dollar reward for information pertaining to the burglary.

Kenzie sat bolt upright. Whoa! Reid would not be happy about that. She thought about calling him but decided against it. They didn't need to speak to each other every night, even though secretly, she longed to hear his voice.

It would be great to talk through what she'd discovered with him, but of course, she couldn't. He didn't know that Alex had picked the lock to get her out of the study, and he didn't know about the ledger.

She squeezed her eyes shut. Maybe it was time to come clean.

CHAPTER 15

Reid studied the man perched across from him in the interview room. With a lithe and sinewy frame, he struck Reid as a greyhound poised at the starting line, quivering with the pent-up energy of an imminent sprint. His arms were tanned to a dark mahogany, no doubt from all the deck work, and crows' feet clawed at the corners of his eyes from endless hours squinting into the sun.

The man stared stoically at Reid, but there was fear behind his eyes, Reid could see it. He'd interviewed a lot of people in his career, both at Miami PD and here at Sweetwater, he knew when a suspect was scared and trying to hide it.

The man still hadn't said who he was, but it wasn't tough to figure out. Out of the six crew members that Del Gatto's assistant had given them, the first mate, Vince, was dead and Hector, who they knew to be the yacht's skipper, had eluded them. The navigator, Carl Ramos, didn't have a recent address on record, and the cook and stewardess, Alejandro and Lucia Martinez, lacked legal work status in the States. Vargas was on the hunt for them, piecing together clues from the photograph they'd found at Hector's place. That narrowed it down to Pedro Gonzales, a deckhand who did whatever odd jobs were needed aboard.

"How are you doing, Pedro?"

The man glanced up, surprised.

"That is your name, isn't it? Pedro Gonzalez."

"How did you—?"

"Your boss, Salvatore Del Gatto, told us."

Pedro seemed to sink into himself.

"Does that bother you?" Reid asked.

"No. Why should it?"

"I don't know. You looked scared, that's all." He paused. "Are you scared, Pedro?"

"Why would I be?" he countered. "You've got nothing on me."

He was right. They didn't.

Yet.

"Do you know this man?" Reid slid the photograph of Vince van Staden across the table. Pedro glanced down, his eyelids flickered, then he looked away.

"No."

Pedro was lying. Clear as day. Reid had seen something in that look. It was fleeting, but it looked like sadness.

"He was found murdered," Reid said, emphasis on *murdered*. "We found him with his head caved in."

Pedro stared at the table as if he wished it would swallow him up.

"Who do you think could have done that to him?"

"I don't know," he muttered.

"Do you think Hector could have killed him?"

Pedro seemed startled. His eyes darted to the door like he wished he could slink through it.

"Ah, hell," Reid said nonchalantly. "Maybe Vince deserved it. Maybe the guy was a thieving scumbag who deserved to have the shit beaten out of him. Maybe he deserved to die."

Pedro's face twisted into a scowl.

"Was he a bad guy, Pedro?" Reid asked quietly. "Did he deserve to die?"

Pedro shook his head.

Reid exhaled silently under his breath. Finally, they were getting somewhere.

"He was your buddy, wasn't he? You worked together on *Jewel of the Seas*."

Pedro stared at the photograph on the table. "Vince was a good guy, a good friend. He didn't deserve...that."

Reid nodded sympathetically. "When last did you see Vince?"

"About a week ago, when we docked. I didn't know...I didn't know he'd been killed until yesterday."

"Is that why you were at the beach bar? You were meeting Hector there to talk about Vince?"

Another nod.

Reid leaned in. "Pedro, do you have any idea why Vince was killed?"

"No." Fear filled his eyes, making him squirm.

"Do you think Hector could have killed Vince?"

Pedro lowered his head. "I don't know."

"Was it to do with the diamonds?" Reid asked, softly. "Did Vince try to steal some of the diamonds and Hector found out?"

Pedro paled beneath his tan. "W—What diamonds?"

"We know about the smuggling operation." Reid hoped he sounded more confident than he felt. "We know you were bringing them in from West Africa."

Pedro shook his head. "W—We crew the yacht for paying customers, that's all. We sail around the Caribbean, the Keys, the Florida coast. I don't know about any diamonds." The words flowed from his mouth like a river of rehearsed dialogue. He'd been told to say this if they were ever questioned.

"Right." Reid sat back and studied him. "Then why were the diamonds found on Del Gatto's yacht?" Close enough. Pedro wouldn't know they'd washed up on the beach.

Pedro's gaze hardened. He was becoming more entrenched in his story now, surer of his lines. "I told you, I don't know about any diamonds. I'm just a deckhand."

"What were you meeting Hector about?" Reid said, trying to unsettle the suspect by jumping around. "Did he call you?"

"Yeah, he told me about Vince. Said he wanted to discuss my future now that the yacht was gone."

It was probably partially true, although Reid strongly suspected Hector had invited Pedro to the beach bar to get him out in the open, so he could kill him too.

"Who hired you?" Reid asked. "To work on the yacht."

"Hector."

"Who's Hector's boss?"

"You know who."

"Del Gatto?"

Pedro nodded. "All we do is crew, man. That's not illegal."

He was right. Nothing the deckhand had said so far gave Reid an excuse to hold him. He was about to try a different angle, when there was a commotion in the hallway.

"Wait here." He got up and opened the door to the interview room.

"I demand to see my client," a loud voice demanded.

"Who are you?" Reid asked, even though he knew. Not the man's name, but he knew what he was.

"I'm this man's legal representative. How dare you interrogate my client without his attorney present?"

Del Gatto. There was no way Pedro could afford a lawyer.

Reid beckoned for him to come in. "There's no need. I'm done with your client."

"You are?" Pedro glanced up hopefully.

"Yeah, you're free to go, Mr. Gonzales. Thank you for your cooperation in this matter. If you think of anything else, you know where to find us." Fat chance of that happening, but he enjoyed the look of consternation on the lawyer's face.

Pedro hurried out of the interrogation room as if he was petrified Reid would change his mind. The lawyer lingered. "This was unlawful, Lieutenant, and you know it."

Reid shrugged. "I was just asking him some questions, that's all."

"You detained him."

"He ran when we approached him. It looked suspicious."

The lawyer shot him a scornful look before straightening his suit jacket and striding out of the police department. Pedro had already left and was waiting outside where he felt safer. Reid wasn't sure he was. Kenzie's words rang in his ears.

You don't honestly believe Del Gatto had nothing to do with this.

Reid got the uncomfortable feeling that young Pedro had just jumped out of the fireplace and into the proverbial fire.

Hamilton came over as Reid was standing at the window watching them leave. "I've got that list of names you asked for," he said. In the background, the phones started ringing.

"The yacht customers?" Reid asked, distracted. What the hell was going on?

He turned to Monroe who threw up his hands.

"No, the close friends and staff members of the victims of the *Bling Bandit*," Hamilton said. "Was I supposed to get a list of the yacht customers too?"

"No, sorry. Don't worry about that. Someone's already sending that through." Reid shook his head. Too many cases. Too many lists.

"I'll put it on your desk." Hamilton moved away.

"Hamilton?" Reid said. "Can you do me a favor?"

The young officer spun around. "Yeah?"

Reid pointed to the car outside, that had yet to move. "Tail them. I want to see where they go."

"WHAT'S WITH THE PHONES?" Reid asked, going back to his desk.

"I don't know, but we're being inundated with calls from people saying they know where Del Gatto's necklace is."

"What?"

"They're asking about the reward."

"Goddamnit!" Reid took out his cell phone and called Del Gatto but got his voicemail. He left a message demanding the businessman call him as soon as possible, then went back to his desk. The phones didn't stop.

Half a painful hour later, Reid was trying to finish up some paperwork when his cell phone buzzed. It was Hamilton. "Boss, you'll never guess where they went."

"Del Gatto's place?"

"Exactly. What do you want me to do?"

"Wait there. Make sure Pedro gets home safely."

"What if he doesn't?" Reid could hear the concern in Hamilton's voice. He had taken stock of the situation and knew the young deckhand could be in danger.

"If he's not out of there by midnight, call dispatch, and we'll send a couple of patrol officers around to check on him."

"Okay." Hamilton didn't sound convinced.

"That's all we can do, Hamilton. We can't go in without a reason."

A sigh. "I know."

IT WAS a balmy seven o'clock when Reid finally left the station. The sun was low in the sky, which was already beginning to change from powder blue to vibrant orange, like it had been dipped in paint. He hoped it wasn't too late to call Kenzie. After the day he'd had, he really felt like seeing her.

To his relief, she answered straight away. "Reid?"

"Yeah, how are you doing?"

Her voice lightened. "I'm good. How are you?"

"Fine. I'm leaving work now. You want to come over? We can order a pizza and sit out on the deck. It's a great evening for it." It had become something of a ritual. The two of them out on the deck, sipping a beer and listening to the sounds of the swamp at night. It was kind of romantic.

"I'd love to."

Reid found he was smiling. "Great."

He was about to end the call when she said, "Reid?"

"Yeah?"

"Er, there's something I need to talk to you about."

"Okay. Is it serious?"

She laughed. "No, not at all. Just something I've been meaning to tell you."

"Okay, sure. I'll see you when you get here."

"See you soon."

CHAPTER 16

Kenzie watched in awe as the sun melted into the swamp. The surface of the water was strewn with orange and crimson hues, mirroring the sky. It was a sight to behold. The air was warm and heavy, filled with the scent of damp earth and lush vegetation.

"It's so quiet," she whispered, absorbing the stillness. It felt like the swamp was holding its breath, maybe in awe of the spectacle in front of them. The gentle rustle of the sawgrass and the distant calls of the marsh birds were the only sounds that broke the silence.

Reid nodded and put his arm around her. They sat side by side on the new wooden swing bench, gazing out at the tangle of mangroves and open water. It was their happy place.

"It's always different," he said pensively. "That's one of the things I love about it."

Before he'd moved to the Glades, Reid had lived in the city and worked at Miami PD. When his undercover colleague had been killed, he'd quit his job and moved out here for solitude, or to punish himself, Kenzie still wasn't sure which, and had led a lonely existence until she'd come along and they'd solved their first case together.

After that, Reid had been asked to come back to Miami PD, but he'd refused, instead taking over the practically defunct Sweetwater Police station, a tiny, threadbare department with a bad reputation and an even worse closure rate. It was known as the place where old cops went to die.

Reid had gotten rid of the corrupt elements and restored the department's reputation. It continued to go from strength to strength. Now, it had become known as the place rookie cops applied to when they graduated from the academy. It was small enough not to be intimidating, and they could learn from the best—Lieutenant Reid Garrett. Kenzie smiled as she thought of what he'd accomplished.

"We found one of the other crew members today," Reid told her. She turned to him, surprised. It wasn't often he offered up information.

She tried to keep her voice even. "Did he say anything about the diamond smuggling?"

"No, sorry." Reid stroked the outside of her arm. "I was going to push him, but his lawyer turned up. Or rather, Del Gatto's lawyer turned up."

Kenzie's eyes widened. "Del Gatto's lawyer? What was he doing there? Del Gatto must be worried about something."

"I didn't think he was involved," Reid admitted, "but now I'm not so sure."

"Did they leave together?" Kenzie asked.

"Yeah. Hamilton followed them to make sure the suspect got home okay."

"And did he?"

"Not yet. The lawyer took him to Del Gatto's place."

"Are you worried?"

He shrugged. "Even if I was, there's nothing we can do about it. The Feds have taken over our investigation."

"What?" Kenzie turned to face him. "You're kidding."

"I wish I was. They took all our files on Del Gatto and the diamonds."

Kenzie couldn't believe it. "And you just handed them over?"

"I had to. It's an international smuggling ring and, therefore, their area."

Kenzie frowned. "That sucks."

"Yeah, but they won't find much in the files. The list of crew members Del Gatto's assistant gave us was useless. Out of the six crew members, one is dead, one's on the run, and one is at Del Gatto's. Of the remaining three, one gave what we think is a fake name and address, and two are unregistered. The Feds will have a hard time tracking them down."

Kenzie couldn't resist a grin. "Did you tell them about the man you had in custody?"

"Hell no. He hadn't identified himself at that point. We had no idea who he was." His eyes sparkled. "He could've been anybody."

She laughed. Typical Reid.

"Besides," he added. "I wanted to find out if he knew the dead guy."

"Did he?" Kenzie probed.

"Yeah. They crewed together on Del Gatto's yacht."

"Do you think he was caught stealing?" Kenzie asked.

Reid shrugged. "It's the only thing that makes sense at this point. Unless he was going to blow the whistle on the whole operation. Maybe he saw something he didn't like and wanted out. We'll probably never know."

Kenzie leaned against him. "I'm sorry, Reid." Damn the Feds for taking over like that. To be fair, an international smuggling operation was bigger than Sweetwater PD. It was bigger than all the police forces in Miami put together.

He sighed. "It is what it is. I'm not going to let them compromise my murder investigation, though."

Kenzie grinned. "And here I thought you were just going to sit back and let them take over." He chuckled.

"I presumed you know Del Gatto offered a reward for his emeralds," Kenzie said.

Reid's expression turned sour. "I gathered. We were inundated with calls this afternoon. We don't have the manpower for that."

"You don't think it'll work?" Kenzie raised an eyebrow.

"I think we'll get thousands of opportunists making up stories to get their hands on that twenty grand." He pulled a face. "Damn stupid idea."

A few moments went by where they listened to the gentle lapping of the water under the deck. Now that the sun had gone down, the night creatures were starting to come out. Kenzie heard the deep baritone of a frog, accompanied by the high-pitched chirp of an insect.

"It comes to life as soon as the sun sets." She cocked her head to listen.

Reid nodded. "It's when the predators go hunting." On cue, the distant hoot of an owl resonated through the trees, making Kenzie shiver.

"I went to the Palmetto Pointe Country Club for lunch today," she said, to lighten the mood.

"That's fancy."

"Alex invited me. I saw Del Gatto's mistress there."

Reid's eyes narrowed. "He has a mistress. I thought he was happily married."

"Apparently not."

Reid shook his head. "It's like a bad soap opera."

"Get this. He has a side entrance to his suite, so she can come and go without being seen," Kenzie elaborated. "His wife lives on the opposite side of the house."

"You have been busy." He glanced across at her. "How did you find out about this?"

"At the party. After Alex got me out of the study, we left via the side entrance. It was after that you saw us running across the lawn." It was on the tip of her tongue to tell him about the ledger, but she didn't want to ruin the mood. Anyway, his mind was back on the investigation.

"Could someone have gotten in that way?" he asked.

"No way. There is no handle on the outside, and the door is bolted firmly from the inside. They'd have to be let in."

He ground his jaw thoughtfully. "But the thief could have left that way, like you two did?"

"I suppose so." For reasons she couldn't explain, she didn't want to draw attention to Alex. Not until she'd done some more digging. A splash beneath the deck sent shivers down her spine.

"Gator," Reid muttered.

Kenzie snuggled closer to him. Suddenly, the tranquil setting had lost some of its sheen. "Shall we go inside?"

She could tell Reid was feeling it, too. "Yeah, good idea."

They ordered a pizza and, when it arrived, sat together on the couch to eat. It was much cozier inside, with his old radio tuned into a blues station and a soft breeze wafting through the window.

"Did you know they can trace diamonds to their place of origin?" Reid told her between bites. "I didn't know that." She could tell his mind was still on the investigation. She got like that too when she was involved in a case, so she understood. Sometimes it helped to talk about it. She didn't mind being his sounding board.

"Where were the diamonds that I found on the beach from?"

"Sierra Leone." There was a distant look in his eyes. "A mine in west Africa with a strange name. Kimbala, I think."

"Wow, that is far away. I wouldn't have thought the yacht could have made it across the Atlantic."

"It didn't," Reid said. "The Feds told me that diamonds are usually smuggled out on cargo ships, using corrupt port officials and forged customs documents. These cargo ships meet up with private yachts in international waters, and the diamonds are transferred."

"Then Del Gatto's crew brings them into the United States," Kenzie finished.

"Exactly. Nothing declared, nothing reported to customs. No checks of any kind."

"It sounds so easy," Kenzie mused.

"If you've got a million-dollar superyacht," Reid said. "Going out into the shipping lanes is no joke."

Kenzie snorted. "Do you think the crew were in on it?"

"Definitely," Reid said. "The skipper is still missing and is our prime suspect in a homicide."

"You still think he's behind it?"

"If he isn't, why is he running?"

"Maybe he's scared of Del Gatto. Now the game is up, he wants to silence those who know about the operation."

Reid was silent for a moment.

"Kenzie, we've issued a warrant for the skipper's arrest. There's evidence that suggests he killed Vince van Staden, another crew member."

Kenzie blinked at him. "What evidence?"

"Blood on his shoes. We found them when we searched his apartment. I got the results back before I left the office. It's a match."

She shook her head. "Just because he has the victim's blood on his shoes, doesn't mean he killed him."

"Well, he was with him when he died," Reid reasoned. "And if we can find him, he'll get a chance to explain. At the moment, he's in the wind. It's looking like he's our guy."

"You think because he killed the man with the diamond in his stomach, he must be running the operation," she surmised.

"You have to admit, it makes sense."

It did.

But where did that leave Del Gatto? Was he really as innocent as he claimed to be?

They finished their pizza and were about to turn in when Reid's cell phone rang. Kenzie saw Hamilton's name flash on the screen.

"Garrett," Reid answered.

Kenzie watched as his expression changed. His eyes grew hard, and his jaw tensed. It was obviously bad news. "What?" she mouthed.

He shook his head. "Okay, I'll be right there."

"What's happened?" Kenzie asked, the moment he hung up the phone.

"That was Hamilton," Reid said. "Pedro Gonzales, the suspect I had in custody this morning, has just been shot and killed."

CHAPTER 17

"Where's Pedro?" Reid asked, as soon as he arrived at the crime scene.

Damn it!

How had this happened?

Hamilton's last report had said the young deckhand had been dropped off at his apartment safe and sound.

"He's inside." Hamilton motioned to the whitewashed four-story apartment block. "Second floor."

Reid pulled on a pair of disposable forensic gloves as he strode toward the building. "What happened? I thought he was home safe."

Hamilton, already wearing his gloves and carrying his crime scene backpack, fell into step beside him. "He was. The taxi dropped him off shortly after eleven. I watched him walk inside."

"So?"

Hamilton let out a shaky breath. "I was about to leave when I heard the gunshot. The perp must have been waiting for him in the apartment." He hung his head.

"It's not your fault," Reid said. "You couldn't have known there'd be someone there."

Hamilton didn't reply.

"You see the shooter come out?" Reid asked, as they took the stairs two at a time to the apartment.

"No. I'm guessing he used the fire escape. I ran in right after I heard the shot. There wasn't time for him to come down this way. I would have seen him."

The stairwell was damp and drafty, and smelled faintly of urine. They reached the second-floor landing and turned into the corridor.

"Number nine," Hamilton said.

Reid stopped outside Pedro's apartment and looked down. The deckhand's body filled the doorway, his boots sticking out over the threshold. Poor bastard hadn't even made it inside. He bent down and felt for a pulse, even though he knew there wouldn't be one. Standard protocol.

Reid inspected the body. The victim lay on his back, eyes open as if he was staring upwards at the ceiling. A naked bulb flickered above them, casting erratic shadows on the peeling walls. Hamilton hung back, out of the way.

"Center mass." Reid nodded to the leaking wound in the middle of the man's torso. "Whoever did this knew what they were doing."

"You think it was a deliberate hit?" Hamilton asked.

"Could be." Reid studied the bullet hole, then looked up. "Any evidence of a break in?"

"The door's intact. Pedro's key is still in it." His voice faltered a little. "I haven't been into the apartment."

"Okay, you take a look. I don't want both of us in there." They'd already compromised the crime scene just by checking the body. The CSI team wouldn't be happy about that.

Reid stepped aside so Hamilton could enter. "Look out for the blood."

Hamilton stepped around the crimson puddle that had formed beneath the body and entered the apartment. "Not much here," he called, as he went into the living area. "Needs a lot of work done to it, but it doesn't look like it's been burgled."

"He's probably renting," Reid said. "Deckhands don't get paid much."

Hamilton did a quick lap of the flat, then came back and stood on the other side of the body. "He was living in squalor. It's disgusting in here. Considering the cargo they were bringing into the country, you'd think they could have paid him better."

"Looks like the shooter was about ten to fifteen feet away," Reid said, standing up. A ballistics expert would confirm, but it didn't appear to be close range, and there wasn't enough space in the hallway for it to be any farther.

"What's that over there?" Hamilton tilted his head to the side.

Reid reached over to pick up a small package that had fallen under a side cabinet a few feet away. He hadn't seen it from where he'd been standing. "It's a brown paper bag."

Hamilton crouched forward. "What's in it?"

Reid took a look. "Cash. Lots of it."

"Really? Do you think Del Gatto paid him to keep quiet?"

"Maybe. Could be severance pay. I mean, the guy just lost his job." Reid thumbed through the bills. "There's a thousand bucks in here."

Hamilton held open an evidence bag. "You'd think it would be more if it was hush money."

"Did he have this on him when he got out of the cab?" Reid dropped the brown paper bag inside.

Hamilton frowned. "I'm not sure. I only caught the back of him as he walked towards the stairwell."

Reid straightened up. "Let's assume he did, because I doubt the shooter put it there. It looks like he dropped it when he fell."

Hamilton nodded. "Pedro opened the door, surprising the intruder, who discharged his weapon and killed him."

"Not sure about that." Reid narrowed his gaze. He surveyed the dirty apartment and then the victim. "Look how he fell? He's lying on his back inside the flat."

"Yeah?" Then Hamilton's eyes widened. "If he'd been shot after he opened the door, he'd have fallen backwards, not forwards."

"That's right. The force of the bullet would have sent him flying backwards into the corridor." Reid put his hands on his hips. "Ballistics will confirm, but I think the shooter was out here in the corridor."

"Lying in wait?"

Reid gave a grim nod. "What if Pedro got home, opened the front door, then noticed the killer standing in the corridor? He turned, was shot in the chest, and fell backwards into the apartment."

Hamilton's expression hardened. "So, he was facing his killer when he was shot."

Reid nodded. "Looks like it."

REID PEELED off his shirt and pants and climbed into bed beside Kenzie. "You okay?" she whispered, snuggling up to him. She was warm and soft, and he closed his eyes in an attempt to block out the last few hours— even just for a minute. He'd seen a few dead bodies in his time, but they always unnerved him. Maybe because it highlighted the frailty of life.

One bullet and you're history.

Poor Pedro wouldn't have known what had hit him. There he was, thinking he'd scored. He was holding a month's wages in his hand when...bam! It was all over in a piercing, lead-filled heartbeat.

"Yeah." What more could he say?

"Do you think Del Gatto's men shot him?" Kenzie asked.

"I don't think so. He still had the cash on him that Del Gatto had given him."

"They paid him off?" She glanced up.

"Nah, it's not enough. My guess is they paid him a month's wages in lieu of crewing. I mean, the yacht's lying at the bottom of the bay. Also, if Del Gatto wanted to get rid of Pedro, he could have done it before now. Why wait until he was back at his apartment to shoot him?"

Kenzie frowned. "Then who?"

"My money's on the missing *Jewel of the Seas* captain. We suspect he killed his first mate and now his deckhand has been shot. It looks like he's tying up loose ends."

Kenzie shivered, and he put his arm around her. "What about the other crew members?" she whispered. "Do you think he's going to go after them, too?"

"I expect so."

Kenzie was quiet for a moment, then she said, "Reid, you have to find them before he does."

Reid closed his eyes, even though he knew sleep would not come. "I know," he whispered into the dark. "I know."

CHAPTER 18

The atmosphere in the newsroom was thick with gloom. Everyone was still grappling with the fallout from Monday's meeting, coming to terms with the harsh reality that the print edition was being discontinued. Despite the whispers that had been circulating, the finality of the decision hit hard—they were transitioning to an all-digital format.

A handful of the die-hard reporters had already handed in their resignations. No way were they going to work for the online edition. There were still broadsheets out there who'd have them and, if not, they'd freelance.

"You can't fight change," Keith had told her, when he'd strolled in around ten. His tardiness said it all. Keith was never late. It pained her to see he'd lost his va-va-voom. The stalwart editor had always been the driving force behind the *Herald* ever since she'd been there.

Kenzie gritted her teeth as she read a piece by the *Herald's* Economics Editor praising Congressman Leonard's latest project, the modernization and upgrading of the downtown tram system. Granted, it would benefit thousands of commuters, but what annoyed her was that Del Gatto was one of Leonard's biggest supporters and donated millions to his campaigns, so the project was probably funded by dirty money.

Maybe even the proceeds from the conflict diamonds.

Reid was under the impression the billionaire businessman wasn't involved, but she couldn't shake the feeling that he had something to do with it.

"Hey Kenzie, you have a moment?" Raoul stood beside her desk holding the piece of paper with the ledger entries on it.

Her spirits lifted. "Have you found something?"

"Maybe." He pulled up a chair and sat down. They both leaned over the piece of paper, sheltering it with their shoulders. Kenzie looked at the coded letters and numbers again.

KM-52
    JS-8/15-640.5
    RT2->M1
    CUST-Y7
    FM-100K
    EJ-MF
    A1-SI2

"TELL ME WHAT YOU'VE GOT." She shifted her gaze to his.

"Using what we know about Del Gatto and the research I've done on the diamond industry, I've come up with a few educated guesses."

"Guesses?" Kenzie couldn't hide her disappointment.

"That's all they are, Kenz. I can't know for sure until we can prove the theory. We still don't know Del Gatto is actually involved and, until we have dates and events to match to the code, we won't know if we're on the right track."

She sighed. "Okay, let's hear what you have got."

He nodded and pointed to the second line of code. "These letters stand out. JS for example could be *Jewel of the Seas*, and 8/15 could be August fifteenth, but you already knew that."

She gave a soft grunt. She'd managed to get that far on her own.

"It would help if there was a way to check that date to see if the yacht was at sea."

Kenzie gripped his wrist, making him jump. "We can check with the marine master. They'll have a record."

"Okay, good." He glanced back down at the entries. "CUST could relate to customs or a customs official, someone they used to sign off on the cargo in Sierra Leone, or wherever the ship sailed from."

Kenzie released his arm. "That makes sense."

"Except I'm not sure what Y7 is. Could be his name, his number, the dock number. No idea."

Kenzie was getting excited now. "We can try to look up how the port authority works in Sierra Leone. That might give us an idea."

"I'm looking into that. So far, I haven't been able to come up with much. They don't have a reliable computer system and the power outages in the area mean the servers are usually down."

Kenzie gave him a skewed look. "You can't hack into them, you mean?"

He ignored her and continued with his assessment. "100K could be a hundred thousand dollars, and FM could be the initials of the person or organization who facilitated the deal."

"Like a middleman?"

"Yeah, but it could be here, it could be that side, who knows." He scowled and adjusted his glasses. Kenzie knew he hated not knowing. Raoul was a data geek and anything that didn't make sense, irked him. It was one of the reasons he was so good at his job. "If you got the names of the people involved, maybe we could figure it out, but without a crib, we can't know for sure."

"A crib?"

"A clue. Something that will validate our assumption. If we can prove there is a man called FM who is involved in the smuggling operation, we can confirm that line of code, and apply it to the rest. Same with the dates and the 100K."

"I see." Kenzie frowned. "Is that it?"

"Well, MF could be Miami, Florida. Going on the same pattern as before, BB could be the name of their contact here in Miami."

"But to be sure, we need to find someone with those initials in Miami."

"Correct. My guess is you'd be looking for a fence or a diamond appraiser. Someone who has the skills to grade diamonds and forge false authenticity certificates."

Kenzie jumped up. "Thank you. That helps tremendously. I've got my work cut out for me, but at least we have a plan."

"I'm not done," Raoul said.

"Oh?" She sat back down.

"There's one thing I'm pretty certain of."

"Yes?" She stared at him. "What is it?"

"I looked into how diamonds are graded, and I'm pretty sure that the last line of code is a grading system."

Kenzie glanced at the entry. "How can you be so sure?"

"Because A1 is a grade A diamond, and SI2 means with small inclusions."

"How on earth do you know that?"

"Look at this." He pulled up a website on his phone and showed it to her. It was a diamond grading system, and the text read:

SI1/SI2 - Slight Inclusion
   Slight Inclusion (SI1/SI2) diamonds have noticeable inclusions under 10x magnification.

"Wow, that's pretty definitive," she whispered, her heart racing. It was the one line of code that made sense. One line that gave her confidence she was on the right track. One line that confirmed Del Gatto was involved in this.

"What I didn't find was any mention of carats, and that's a big one with diamonds, which makes me think that the 640.5 may be the total carats of the consignment."

Her eyes widened. "That's a lot of carats."

"It's a lot of money. If these are A-grade diamonds with minimal flaws, you're looking at a street value of about $3,000 to $18,000 per carat."

"Holy crap!" Kenzie felt the color drain from her face as she did the math. An average value of ten grand per carat would mean she'd been holding potentially six and a half million dollars in her hands.

"Exactly. Do you know how many washed up on the beach?"

"The bag was quite heavy. I'd say at least two or three handfuls." Her voice was hoarse.

"About six hundred and forty?"

She cleared her throat. "Could be."

Raoul peered at her over his glasses. "Maybe your detective boyfriend can tell us that?"

"The diamonds are at a lab for analysis, under lock and key, and after that, the FBI are taking custody of them."

"They would have weighed them. Lieutenant Garrett could find out exactly how many were in the shipment. It could be the crib we need. If these figures are from the most recent page in the ledger, it might be this shipment that's recorded."

It was.

Pity she'd only had time to photograph the last page of the ledger. But if Del Gatto was involved, then she wanted to know.

"I'll see what I can find out."

CHAPTER 19

Reid held the phone away from his ear as he listened to Captain Pérez rant about the obscene number of calls the Miami PD had received about Salvatore Del Gatto's missing emerald necklace. "My team is spending all day answering phones. We're not a goddamn hotline. What the hell does he think he's playing at?"

"Same here," Reid replied, but didn't say anything else. When Pérez was in this kind of mood, it was better not to provoke him. He'd fizzle out after a few minutes. His old boss needed to let it out before he calmed down.

"Did you know about this?" Pérez growled.

"No, sir. First I heard about it was when our phone lines went nuts."

Pérez made a clicking sound with his tongue. "Twenty grand? Doesn't he know he's going to get every wacko in Miami calling with anything they can think of to get a piece of that?" He didn't need to tell Reid that. Sweetwater PD was trying to filter the information as best they could, but most were crank calls. There'd been nothing useful so far.

"I'll talk to him," Reid said. "Get him to rescind the reward. That should stop the calls." When people realized there was no reward, the information would dry up.

Pérez grunted. "Do it soon, Garrett. We're drowning here."

"Will do, boss."

"What's with the boss shit?" he said irritably. "You know I'm not your boss anymore."

Reid grinned. "You still outrank me, though."

A grunt.

"Sorry to lay this on you, Reid, but we're getting the brunt of it." Miami PD was one of the largest police departments in Miami-Dade County. It would be the department of choice for most callers in the bay area. Del Gatto hadn't specified who to call with news, so all the departments were being inundated. Pérez wasn't the first irate caller he'd had today.

"I understand. Don't worry about it. I'll call Del Gatto now."

"Thanks. Oh, and let's meet for a beer sometime. I think we both need it after this debacle."

"Sounds good, Captain."

He heard a wry chuckle before his old boss hung up the phone.

"WHERE ARE we on the staff list of the Bling Bandit victims?" he asked Vargas on his way to grab a coffee. He needed caffeine before he called Del Gatto.

"Getting there." Vargas rifled through some papers on his desk. His second-in-command was usually pathologically neat, but everyone was feeling the strain of the incoming calls, the two homicides, the missing suspect, and the jewel thefts.

"I've spoken to Cassandra Lee and Marcus Bradford," Vargas said, mentioning the two celebs that had also been burgled, "but so far, nobody jumps out. Neither hired the same staff members, caterers, landscapers, decorators, or any other service personnel that I can see."

"Well, keep digging. Get on to Del Gatto's assistant for their list, and if we don't get any hits, we'll extend the search to include friends and family."

Vargas nodded and got back to work.

"Hey boss?" Diaz looked up from her desk. "I checked with most of the other police departments in the state. Nobody else has reported any high value thefts with the same MO as our bandit. It looks like it's isolated to the Miami area."

"Really?" He frowned. "What does that mean? That our perp is local?"

"Could be. I'll call the rest, but I think you're right." She reached for the phone.

· · ·

IT TOOK ALL of Reid's patience and skill, but Del Gatto finally agreed to publicly rescind the reward offer. His office had also been inundated with calls and, even though he wouldn't admit it, Reid could tell he realized it was a bad idea.

"Doesn't anyone have any integrity anymore?" Del Gatto barked into the phone at Reid, who nearly choked on his coffee.

IT WAS late afternoon when Vargas approached his desk. "Hey, boss. The forensic report came back with the findings on the shooting at Pedro's flat."

"Yeah? Anything significant?"

He gave an excited nod. "A shell casing from a .45 caliber was found outside his apartment."

Reid frowned. He didn't remember seeing any, but then they hadn't stayed long, not wanting to contaminate the scene more than necessary.

"According to ballistics, the casing bore a distinct marking, indicating it was fired from a Colt M1911." He raised his eyebrows.

Reid knew what a Colt M1911 was. A lot of old timers used them, particularly mobsters and retired military personnel. He also knew that it was an extraction mark on the head stamp, a factory problem. Not all M1911's had the issue.

"There's something else," Vargas shot him a knowing look. "The extraction mark on the casing is similar to the casing I found at Vince's apartment"

Reid frowned. "I still don't understand why Vince had that casing. It doesn't make sense."

"Evidence," Vargas suggested. "Against someone using the Colt."

"Maybe." Reid shook his head.

Vargas continued, "The bullet was a hollow point round, designed to expand upon impact, causing maximum internal damage."

Reid cringed. "That's not the standard choice for a casual shooter."

"No, and the gunpowder residue pattern indicated that the shooter was at a distance of approximately fifteen feet from the victim, just like you said."

Reid stared at Vargas. "This was a calculated hit rather than a close-range confrontation. The shooter knew what he was doing."

Vargas lowered the report. "Does this mean Hector's a pro?"

Reid raked a hand through his hair. "What do we know about Hector? Vince van Staden was a mercenary, maybe Hector was, too."

"There's not much on him," Vargas said. "I'll dig a little deeper and see what I can find out. If he has a military background, it must be on record somewhere."

"Ask Del Gatto," Reid suggested. "He seemed to know the guy better than anyone else."

"Will do."

It was a shame Pedro was dead. Reid had a feeling the young deckhand would have had a lot to say about the *Jewel's* skipper.

"I haven't managed to find anything on the remaining three crew members," Diaz said, coming over. "Carl Ramos was most probably a fake name, and we can't find anything on the cook and steward."

"If we can't locate them, let's hope Hector can't either."

"What if Hector is doing Del Gatto's bidding?" Vargas asked suddenly, as the thought occurred to him.

Reid frowned. "It's a possibility."

"If he is, Del Gatto isn't going to just hand him over." Vargas held the phone in the air.

He had a point.

"Okay, Vargas, why don't you go over to Del Gatto's place and talk to him there. You'll be able to gauge whether he's covering for Hector or not."

"Got it." Vargas got up. "Oh, the security footage from van Staden's apartment block just came in. I haven't had time to look at it yet."

"I'll check it out," Reid said. He went back to his desk and opened the file that the management company had sent through.

The first thing he noticed was the tempest of relentless, driving rain. Along with the howling gale force wind, it decreased visibility and made everything he was looking at seem blurry. Vince van Staden had died on the day the hurricane had hit the Florida coast.

The footage began at 6am and extended throughout the day. Reid forwarded the footage, slowing it down whenever he saw someone coming or going in the frame. The camera was positioned at the front entrance and covered the rain-drenched marble steps leading to the front of the building, a portion of the pavement, and a sliver of street. Not a lot to go on.

At nine thirty, a solitary man came out of the building. His height and build caused Reid to think it might be Vince, but he was facing away from the camera. Reid froze the footage, leaning in as if to penetrate the screen's barrier, squinting against the grainy, washed-out effect of the rain. It was so damn hard to tell for sure. The man paused on the pavement and checked his watch. Strange, it was pelting down and yet here he was standing in the rain. Why?

Then another man entered the frame. Shorter, this time, but well-built with a thick head of hair. "Well, I'll be damned," Reid murmured, pausing the video again. The man was facing the camera and Reid recognized the tanned arms and the pear-shaped smudge on the man's forearm.

It was Hector.

REID DROVE straight to Kenzie's house after work. He wasn't staying over, just stopping by for dinner. That was his excuse, anyway. Truth be told, he just wanted to see her. After the revelation that Hector had been with Vince the morning of his death, Reid was more certain than ever that the skipper had killed the South African, along with Pedro.

To his surprise, Kenzie opened the door and pulled him into a tight hug. Suddenly, the world seemed a slightly better place than it had moments before.

"You feel good," he murmured, into her hair.

She held him for longer than usual. "So do you."

Reluctantly, he released her. "You okay?"

"Not really."

He walked inside and she closed the door behind them. "What's up?"

To his surprise, her eyes filled with tears. "The newspaper's restructuring."

"You're kidding." He stared at her dejected expression and knew that she wasn't. "Shit, Kenz. I'm sorry. Is it official?"

"Yeah, they told us on Monday, but I think it only really hit home today. We've got one month left and then we're being incorporated into the digital team." He heard the bitterness in her voice.

"Why didn't you tell me before?"

"I didn't want to think about it," she admitted. "I think I hoped it wasn't true." She shook her head. "Silly, huh?"

He knew that feeling well.

"It's not silly. You were processing. It takes time."

She nodded and wiped her eyes on the back of her sleeve. "Well, I've processed now. The reality is harder to swallow. It's easier to remain in denial."

He knew that too.

"So, you're keeping your job?" he asked. He couldn't imagine Kenzie doing anything else. She was born to be an investigator.

"Yeah, we're lucky in that respect, I guess. Poor old Keith's been given the boot."

"Damn, that's tough." He didn't know Keith that well, but he liked the guy. He didn't mince his words. Reid appreciated a straight talker.

"I'll be managed by one of the online editors." She shook her head. "I haven't even met them yet. They're on a different floor than us."

"I'm sure it'll work out," he said, trying to be positive.

Kenzie sighed and took his hand. "I hope so. Now enough of my self-pity, let's go and have a drink. I'm sure you could use one too."

"Yeah, it's been quite a day."

"Wanna talk about it?" she asked, hopefully.

He grinned. "Why do I think you're hoping I say yes?"

"Del Gatto is my swan song," she told him, with serious eyes. "I want to make this story my crowning glory before I leave the paper."

He could tell she meant it. "Well, I might have something that can help you," he said carefully.

"Yeah?"

"We've got evidence that *Jewel's* captain, Hector Esparza, shot and killed Vince van Staden, the first mate and hired muscle on the crew."

Kenzie's eyes narrowed. "How does that help me?"

"Because one of the theories we're working on is that Hector is killing off the crew for Del Gatto."

She stared at him. "I thought you were convinced Del Gatto wasn't involved? What brought about this change of heart?"

"Del Gatto hired Hector and, from what we can gather, Hector is something of a pro. There's only one reason why Del Gatto would hire a professional killer to skipper his yacht."

"Because he was doing something illegal," Kenzie finished, her eyes gleaming.

Reid nodded. "The only problem is, Del Gatto is untouchable. The Feds couldn't even break him. We've got nothing on him."

"He won't do his own dirty work." Kenzie's eyes were like flint. "He keeps his hands clean. That way, he can never be implicated."

"It's beginning to piss me off," Reid growled.

"Hmm…" Kenzie drummed her fingers on the countertop.

Reid knew that look.

"What?" he asked.

"I think I might be able to help you get some dirt on Del Gatto."

"Really? How?"

She gave him a slow smile. "Pour me another glass of wine and I'll tell you."

CHAPTER 20

Vargas pulled up to the imposing black gates. Two burly security guards, both packing, came out of the guard's hut. "Can we help you?" the one said in a no-nonsense tone.

"I'm here to see Del Gatto." Vargas held up his ID. "Detective Vargas, Sweetwater PD."

The guards exchanged a glance. "What's this about?" the inquisitive one pressed.

"I'm here to give him an update on the investigation." Vargas didn't specify which investigation. Hopefully, the guards would think it was to do with the theft of Del Gatto's wife's necklace.

"Wait here." He returned to the hut presumably to get authorization, while the other guard remained outside, keeping a beady eye on him. Vargas wasn't intimidated. He kept his hands in full sight on the steering wheel and bopped along to the salsa number playing softly on his radio. No threat here.

He saw the guard in the hut nod.

Good, he was in.

"Go ahead," the second guard said, as the gates retreated silently. Vargas nodded and cruised up the side-lit drive to the mansion.

When he got there, Del Gatto's Head of Security, Samson Quinn, was waiting for him outside. "Detective." Quinn greeted him with a stiff nod. "It's a bit late for a house call?"

"I need to talk with your boss," Vargas said, getting out of the car. "There's been a development."

"Come inside." Vargas followed him into the vast marbled hallway, with the grand staircase curving upward in the background. The ceiling seemed to soar above him, while a splashy, abstract painting that he thought was a Jackson Pollock, caught his eye.

"Nice place," he said, as they walked through an elegant living room and out into a lush courtyard. Del Gatto was sitting in a chair, a glass of whisky or bourbon on the table beside him. He turned around as Vargas entered.

"Sorry for the interruption," Vargas said, extending a hand. He hadn't spoken to Del Gatto directly before and knew first appearances were everything.

The businessman shook it, studying him with curious eyes. "You're Garrett's man, aren't you? I've seen you at the station."

"That's right, sir."

Del Gatto gestured for him to sit. "What's this about?" It was a warm night, with only the softest breeze, and somewhere in the background classical music played.

He sat down opposite Del Gatto. "We have reason to believe the captain of your yacht, *Jewel of the Seas*, Hector Esparza is responsible for murdering two of the other crew members: Vince van Staden and Pedro Gonzales."

"That's ridiculous," Del Gatto snapped. Behind him, Quinn took a step forward.

"I'm afraid we have evidence," Vargas said, as calmly as he could. "We've issued a warrant for his arrest."

"You're kidding?" Del Gatto stared at him, and then at Quinn, who asked, "What evidence?"

"I'm afraid I can't discuss that, but I came here to ask you if you know where Hector might be hiding?"

"Of course not. How should I know?"

"Because you hired him," Vargas said. "You seemed to know him quite well, so we hoped you'd be able to help us with our search."

Del Gatto thought for a moment. "You've tried his apartment, obviously?"

Vargas nodded. "He appears to be on the run."

Del Gatto shook his head. He seemed genuinely upset. "I'd never have expected this of Hector."

"What about you?" Vargas turned to Quinn. "Any idea where he might go?"

Quinn shook his head.

"Does Hector have a military background, too?" Vargas asked. Quinn's expression darkened, while Del Gatto massaged his forehead. "I'm not sure. He certainly knew how to handle himself, but whether he had formal training or not, I couldn't tell you."

"Hector was born in Haiti," Quinn said quietly.

"He was?" Vargas turned back to the head of security. "I thought he was American."

"He is now, but he grew up in Haiti. He told me that's how he learned how to become a sailor, hanging around the docks as a boy."

"Were you close?"

"No, but we talked sometimes. He seemed like a decent guy."

"He never mentioned his past to me." Del Gatto glared at his head of security as if that was his fault. "His credentials checked out, he was an excellent seaman, and took really good care of the *Jewel*."

Until the hurricane, of course.

Vargas thanked them for their time and left the mansion. On the way back to the station, he thought about what Quinn had said. Hector was Haitian. How he'd obtained a U.S. social security number, Vargas didn't know, but that's how he'd integrated so seamlessly into the community.

Of course, he could have gone back to Haiti, Vargas mused, as he took the freeway back to Sweetwater. Or maybe he was hiding amongst the Haitian community in Miami. He could have friends there. It was a good place to start looking.

Vargas also wanted to do some digging into Hector's past. Now that he knew where Hector was born, it might be easier to trace him back there. Vargas had a sneaky feeling that Hector was going to have a lot of skeletons in his closet.

———

Kenzie watched Reid fill up her glass, the idea still percolating in her head. It *might* work, if they played their cards right.

"What did you have in mind?" Reid set the bottle down on the countertop.

"Remember I told you I'd had lunch at the Palmetto Pointe Country Club the other day?"

"Yeah, with Alex."

"Well, while I was in the ladies' restroom, I happened to run into Del Gatto's mistress, Christina Gomez."

"I remember you saying. Separate entrances, right?"

"That's right." She smiled. "Anyway, Christina was on the phone to a friend, or rather, she was sobbing into the phone to her friend."

"She was upset?"

"Yes, about Del Gatto. Apparently, he won't leave his wife for her."

Reid frowned. She could tell he was wondering where this was heading. "I can't say I'm surprised. Family is important to men like Del Gatto. He has an image to uphold. I doubt he'll ever leave his wife for some bimbo."

"She is a bimbo," Kenzie agreed, picturing the barely-there tennis skirt, fake boobs, and pouty lips. "But she is currently very angry with her lover and might be open to a little manipulation."

"Kenzie—" He had a warning tone to his voice.

She held up a finger. "Wait, hear me out."

At his nod, she continued, "What if she was so mad at Del Gatto, that she wanted to get back at him? An anonymous tip to a newspaper reporter on the murkier side of his business."

"Revenge?"

"A woman scorned and all that." Kenzie tilted her head to the side. "I think I can get her to spill the beans. What do you think?"

"It might work." Reid paused, thinking. "If she knows something."

"Of course she'll know something. Mistresses always know more about their lovers than the wives do. Plus, they've been together for four years, she's bound to know something about his illegal activities."

Reid pondered this. "Okay, but how are you going to make her go for it?"

Kenzie leaned over and patted his hand. "Don't worry about that, I've got a plan."

THE PARKING LOT outside the Palmetto Pointe Country Club was filled with high-end vehicles that glittered in the mid-morning sun. Kenzie parked her relatively new Chevrolet Volt next to a sleek Lamborghini Aventador boasting a vibrant, azure paint job. Its aggressive lines hinting at the power lurking beneath its hood. Not far away, a Bentley Continental GT exuded elegance, its classic design and creamy white finish the epitome of luxury.

Alex had left Kenzie's name at the gate, so she'd had no problem driving in, although her car raised a few condescending eyebrows. Walking toward the reception area, Kenzie passed a Ferrari 488 Spider in fiery red, an embodiment of speed and Italian craftsmanship. Getting out of it was a handsome golf pro, his golf bag sticking out of the passenger seat.

Kenzie marveled how each of the vehicles, symbols of wealth and prestige, seemed perfectly at home in the exclusive atmosphere of the Palmetto Pointe Country Club, unlike hers. Still, nobody inside the club would know.

Earlier that morning, Alex had attended a weekly tennis match and cornered Christina in the club house afterwards. She'd played her part to perfection and, when she'd called Kenzie later on to report back, she'd been triumphant. "I asked her if she was going to Salvatore and Bethany's Commitment Ceremony," Alex had said with a laugh. "The poor woman fell for it. She was dumbfounded. Didn't know what to say. I told her they were renewing their vows after twenty years of marriage and wasn't it nice to see two people so in love."

Kenzie hoped that would be enough to make Del Gatto's mistress even more resentful. With a bit of luck, she'd been fuming about it all day, working herself up into a tizzy.

Kenzie walked into the packed clubhouse bar. Tonight was the tennis league prize giving, and Christina was up for an award. She looked around, just to make sure Del Gatto wasn't lurking at any of the tables, but the coast was clear. It seemed he wasn't here supporting his mistresses' prowess on the tennis court.

Kenzie spotted Christina at the bar, working her way through a vodka tonic. Kenzie wondered how many of those she'd had this afternoon. By the way she was swaying on that bar stool, quite a few.

The man with her had his hand on her leg, and she was leaning forward, giving him an unobstructed view of her cleavage. Kenzie sidled up to the bar and took the seat next to Christina and ordered a huge glass of wine.

When Christina wasn't looking, she took out her phone and put it to her ear. "Of course I'm sure," she said, loudly. "I caught them together. Can you believe it? After everything I've done for him, I catch him screwing the nanny. What a cliché."

In her peripheral vision, she saw Christina straighten up a little.

"No, I can't speak to him about it," she hissed. "You know what he's like when he loses his temper." She sniffed and reached for her glass. "I wish there was some way I could get back at him, you know. Teach him a lesson."

Christina was definitely listening now.

"Okay, I'll let you know. Thanks for listening, hun." With another convincing sniff, she hung up.

Christina had turned around and was studying her openly. Kenzie looked up. "Men," she huffed, taking a large sip of her drink and showing off an enormous diamond ring and flashy gold wedding band in the process. They'd been purchased by the newspaper years ago for her undercover work. Excellent fakes, but only a pro would know the difference. "I hate him." Christina nodded and made to turn back to her admirer.

"Are you married?" Kenzie asked.

Christina hesitated. "No, but I'm in a relationship, so I know what bastards men can be."

"Right?" Kenzie leaned forward, studying her. "I'm Kenzie."

"Christina."

Kenzie nodded. "My husband and I have been married for nine years. Nine! And today I caught him screwing our nanny. I mean what was he thinking?" Her eyes filled with tears. "We've got two kids."

"You should leave him." Christina said. "There's no coming back from that."

"Is that what you'd do?" she asked, her eyes wide. "I mean, if your guy cheated."

"It's what I'm going to do," Christina replied, after a beat.

Kenzie gasped. "He cheated on you, too? What a scumbag."

"Yeah, we've been together four years, but it still hurts." Kenzie noticed she didn't mention her man was married, and she was the other woman.

"Of course it does. You're so brave. I wish I had the guts."

"We don't have kids, though," Christina said, not without a touch of longing. "So, it's easier to walk away."

Kenzie scowled. "I'm so angry, I want the bastard to suffer. You ever feel like that? So angry you could scream."

"All the time," Christina confided. "But I'm done with the bastard. He doesn't know it yet, but tomorrow I'm going to dump his ass."

Kenzie nodded. "It's so nice to meet someone who understands what I'm going through." She leaned in closer, lowering her voice to a conspiratorial whisper. "You know, I've been thinking of ways to make him pay, to really show him he can't just treat people like dirt and get away with it."

Christina's eyes sparkled with a mix of anger and intrigue. "Oh yeah? Like what?"

Kenzie paused, gauging Christina's reaction carefully. "Well, as it turns out, I'm a journalist and I have access to a platform that can expose men like my husband. Men who think they can do whatever they want without consequences."

Christina's interest was clearly piqued. "You mean, like, write an article about him?"

"Exactly," Kenzie replied. Then she sighed. "Except my husband's nobody."

Christina bit her lip, her mind racing. The thought of getting back at the man who had wronged her was obviously tempting. "My partner isn't a nobody," she said slowly.

Kenzie raised an eyebrow. "Oh? Who is he, then?"

"Have you heard of Salvatore Del Gatto?"

Kenzie frowned. "The billionaire?"

"Yeah, him. He'd hate it if he was splashed all over the front of the papers." Her cheeks colored. "Could you make that happen?"

"I'd need something to write about. Something that he won't want anyone knowing. Something that will make people see him for who he really is."

She thought for a moment. "He's been involved in some shady deals. I don't know all the details, but I can try to find out."

Kenzie nodded. "You have power here, Christina. You can make him pay for how he's treated you."

Christina looked down at her drink, then back up at Kenzie, a determined glint in her eyes. "Okay. I'll do it. He thinks he can just keep me around while he goes back to his wife. I'll show him. Everyone is going to know what a weasel he is."

Kenzie smiled, trying to hide her exhilaration. "You won't regret it, Christina. You find something we can use and I promise, we'll take him down together."

CHAPTER 21

"Hey, I thought we should get together and touch base," Reid said, even though he hated being the one to reach out. "You know, compare notes."

"Sure," came the smooth reply. "You wanna meet up now?"

"Why not?"

REID TOOK the thirty-minute drive to the FBI offices in Miramar to think about the various aspects of this case. Usually, there was some sort of incremental progress during an investigation, like every new clue they found slotted into the overall puzzle making the picture clearer, but this was nothing like that. There were so many differing threads, he didn't know which were real and which were dead ends.

Hector was still on the run and the evidence suggested he'd killed both Vince and Pedro, but then what was Del Gatto's role in the whole thing? It was his yacht that had washed up with the diamonds and Hector had skippered for him, so logically, one would assume they were in on it together. Could he believe Del Gatto had nothing to do with it? Was it possible Hector had orchestrated the smuggling operation without his boss's knowledge?

He gazed out of the window at the meticulously manicured gardens leading up the imposing glass and concrete fortress that was the new FBI headquarters. It was very impressive. Hopefully, the two FBI agents could shed some light on Del Gatto's role in the whole thing. He'd heard nothing since they'd come to his station and demanded to take over the case.

Agent Brush Cut greeted him in the entrance, a vast plaza where natural light filtered through high windows. Art installations and symbols of justice and integrity adorned the lobby, reminding the public of the bureau's mission and objectives. His department at Sweetwater was a hovel compared to this.

"Let's talk in private," the agent said, gesturing for Reid to follow him. There was a large folder under his arm and he still wore the same black suit he'd been in before.

They didn't clear security, instead going into a private office adjoining the lobby, presumably for discussions such as this with non-bureau law enforcement officers and individuals.

"Take a seat," Brush Cut said.

Reid chose one of four chairs around a circular table. There was nothing else in the room, no pictures on the walls, no vase of flowers, no rug. Purely functional.

"I'm glad you called," Brush Cut said. "I've been meaning to touch base."

Yeah right.

"That's why I'm here." He forced a grin. "How'd it go with Del Gatto?"

The agent pursed his lips. "Men like that are notoriously hard to interrogate. His lawyer stuck to him like glue and, to be honest, we didn't get very far. We wondered if you'd had more luck?"

Reid narrowly resisted a smirk. "I've spoken with Mr. Del Gatto several times since the diamonds washed up on the beach," he began. "And I'm not sure he had anything to do with the smuggling operation."

He watched the agent's face. Brush Cut blinked several times but didn't immediately reply. That was all the proof Reid needed. "What do you guys know that we don't?"

Brush Cut glanced down at the file but didn't reply.

"We found two of the crew members," Reid said. Maybe if he offered the agent something, he'd got some info in return. The agent's eyes lit up. "You did?"

"Yeah. Pedro Gonzales was a deckhand on *Jewel of the Seas*. We found him shot to death in his apartment earlier this week."

"He's dead?" Brush Cut blinked again.

"I'm afraid so, as is Vince van Staden, the first mate. We found him in a garage near Ronald Reagan Turnpike." He didn't say they'd found him when the hurricane hit, because then the agent would know he'd been withholding information. If it came out later, so be it. Right now, he needed leverage to see what was in that file about Del Gatto.

"What about the skipper, Hector Esparza?" the agent asked.

"You first." Reid nodded to the folder.

The agent sighed. "Okay, but this is classified information and part of an ongoing investigation."

"I get it."

Brush Cut opened the file and Reid saw a photograph of a man with silver hair, a large nose, and piercing black eyes. "This is Joe Molano," the agent said.

"The New York mobster?" Reid had heard about Joe Molano.

"One and the same." Brush Cut stared at the photograph. "I don't know if you know this, but Del Gatto started off as a runner for Joe Molano back in New York."

Reid's eyes widened. "I did not know that."

"Yeah, Molano was on the rise and Del Gatto was a smart kid. He had a head for business and a gift for strategic thinking. Molano saw promise in the boy and when Del Gatto finished school, he paid for him to attend Princeton."

"Seriously?" Reid couldn't believe what he was hearing. Del Gatto was connected to the mob. Suddenly, the investigation took on a whole new angle.

"Well, it was one of his shell companies, but same thing. We managed to trace the payments back to Molano, even though they hid their tracks really well."

"Do you think he's still working for the mob?" Reid asked, even though he knew the answer. Obviously, otherwise, there'd be no fat folder on the table in front of them.

"Let me tell you about Del Gatto," Brush Cut said. Reid sat back and listened.

"Del Gatto had formed his first company at the age of twenty-five, importing Italian food products from Europe. There was some talk of drug trafficking, but the DEA investigation into the company turned up nothing, so the investigation fell flat. Del Gatto had gone on to found several other companies, mostly in the import-export business."

Reid nodded, encouraging the agent to continue.

"By the time he was thirty, he'd made his first million. By forty, he'd moved to Miami and was buying and selling companies like they were baseball cards. Each time, he took an ailing company, turned it around and sold it for more than he'd bought it. The companies he couldn't turn around, he broke up and sold off in pieces for more than the whole."

"Smart," muttered Reid.

"Now in his late fifties, Del Gatto owns several hotels in addition to his many businesses. Ever since the DEA investigation thirty years earlier, he's kept his nose clean. He pays his taxes, he donates to charities and other worthwhile endeavors, mostly for the improvement of the city and its infrastructure."

"Congressman Leonard," Reid said, remembering what Kenzie had said about Del Gatto financing Leonard's projects with dirty money.

"He has several politicians in his corner, another reason why it's so hard to get close to the guy. The powers that be like what he does for them and they don't want us to mess with that."

That's why it would be hard for Kenzie to take them down, too. They'd already sued the paper once. Next time they might not be so nice.

"Okay, your turn," Brush Cut said, "Any news on the skipper?"

"We got his address, but he'd cleared out already," Reid said. "We've got a BOLO out on him and, if we hear anything, we'll let you know."

The agent nodded.

"You're not interested in Del Gatto or the diamonds, are you?" Reid said. "You're investigating his connections to the mob."

Brush Cut shrugged. "The two are connected, but yeah, we've been after Molano for years. Del Gatto could be our way in."

"And if he's not responsible for smuggling in the diamonds?"

"Then we're barking up the wrong tree, but I can't see it. I mean, his yacht washes up the same day as the diamonds and his skipper goes on the run. Please."

Reid had to admit, it did seem to be the logical conclusion. He thought about Kenzie, and her insistence Del Gatto was involved. It seemed her instinct had been right all along. Why was he not surprised? The only problem was, she may have bitten off a lot more than she could chew.

Bringing Del Gatto down would be hard enough, but the mob, that would be downright impossible.

CHAPTER 22

"It worked!" Kenzie told Reid. She'd called him on her lunch break, knowing he'd want to hear what happened last night. "I can't quite believe it myself, but she fell for it."

"Really? Did she give you anything we can use?" Kenzie liked the way he said *we*.

"Kind of. I mean, she talked about secret meetings at the mansion, people coming and going late at night."

"What kind of people?" Reid asked.

"Business types. New Yorkers, mostly. She said she used to live there, and she recognized the accent." Kenzie thought back to what Christina had told her. "They would talk all night and leave in the early hours. That's suspicious, right?"

Reid's tone changed. "Could she identify these men?"

"I don't think she knew who they were, but she described them as thuggish, and the guy in charge was called Joe. She heard Del Gatto greet him. He had snow white hair and talked in a deep, gravelly voice, like there was something wrong with his throat."

Reid went quiet.

"You know someone like that?" she prompted.

"Sounds like it could have been Joe Molano and his boys."

"Joe Molano, the New York crime boss?" Kenzie caught her breath.

"Yeah, he talks with a rasp because when he was younger, someone cut his throat. He's got the scar to show for it."

Kenzie had heard the stories. "Are you telling me Del Gatto is connected to the mob?" She could hardly keep the excitement out of her voice.

"Kenzie—"

"Holy crap, Reid! This is huge. How did I not know this?"

He sighed. "Because you don't have access to FBI files."

Not even Raoul could hack into the FBI database. "How did you find out?"

"They told me. Apparently Del Gatto's fancy Ivy League education was paid for by one of Molano's shell corporations."

Kenzie tried to control herself. "I can't believe this. How long have you known?"

"Since this morning."

"I hope you were going to tell me?"

He hesitated, only for a fraction of a second. "Of course."

"Reid—"

"We still don't know if he's involved in this."

Kenzie spluttered into the phone. "If Molano paid for Del Gatto's education, the mob owns him. That's not a debt you ever repay."

Reid was silent on the other end.

"Anything Del Gatto is involved in, the mob is too." She let out a slow, shaky breath. "The diamond smuggling could go way higher than Del Gatto's organization. He might just be the middleman, the Miami connection."

"Kenzie, the mob is the FBI's remit. We can't go after Joe Molano. We don't have the resources for that. My responsibility is to the victims who died here in Miami. To Vince and Pedro."

"That doesn't mean we can't expose them," she murmured.

"They're dangerous people, Kenzie," he warned, his voice full of concern. "Don't go there."

"Christina said she'd see what else she could find out," Kenzie said, and she heard Reid sigh. "In the meantime, I'll get Raoul on the case. Now we know what we're dealing with, he might be able to find some proof of Molano's involvement."

"Kenzie, listen to me, these guys are bad news. If they are involved, you could be putting yourself in danger by going after them."

"I'll be careful," she promised. "Let's see what Christina comes up with. She's determined to make Del Gatto pay." Kenzie had been surprised by the woman's hostility. Alex had done her job better than she could have hoped.

Raoul was beckoning her over.

"Oh, you know the diamonds you sent to the lab?" she asked, before she hung up. Seeing Raoul had triggered her memory. She was supposed to get the details from Reid and she'd almost forgotten.

"Yeah?"

"Do you know how many there were?" she added hastily. "I want to include the number of carats in my follow-up article to the one I wrote when they washed up on the beach."

Reid paused. "Give me a sec."

She heard him tapping on his computer and a moment later he said, "The lab put the weight of the bag at 639 carats."

Kenzie exhaled. "That must have been worth millions."

"Yep. Street value of nearly seven million dollars." That tallied with what the ledger said. Almost.

"What about the one in that guy's stomach," she added, as an afterthought. "Do you think he stole it from that shipment?"

"I believe that one was one and a half carats," Reid said. "The lab said it was from the same source, so my guess is it was part of the original shipment. You can't mention him in your article, though. That's still an active case."

"No, of course not. I was just curious," Kenzie said vaguely.

"IF YOU'RE DONE TALKING to your boyfriend," Raoul said, when she finally hung up the phone and went over to his desk. "I have something to show you."

"I was getting some information for us," Kenzie told him. "You were right. The 640.5 was the number of carats in the shipment. The lab confirmed it." If they included the one the dead seaman had swallowed.

"Excellent. It's starting to make sense now. I think we can safely assume this coded information is about the diamonds." He turned to the piece of paper on his desk and ticked that part of the entry.

Kenzie was hit by another pang of guilt. It was probably time she told Reid about the ledger. He'd told her about Del Gatto and the mob. She still couldn't believe that. Tonight, she thought, as she stared at the first line of code. Tonight, she'd tell him about the ledger.

"We still don't know what the first part means," Kenzie frowned. "KM-52."

"Actually, I think I might. I've been doing some digging, and diamond mines have different sectors, which are numbered. The KM could be the name of the mine and the 52 could be the specific sector."

Kenzie gasped. "Oh, my gosh. I completely forgot. I *know* the name of the mine, and it was something like that." She prodded the piece of paper. "What was it now? It sounded very African."

Raoul stared at her expectantly.

"Simba, Shaba, Kimba…" She petered off, thinking hard. Then she snapped her fingers. "That's it! Kimbala."

"KM." Raoul broke into a grin. "That's it. Well done, Kenzie."

"Kimbala, Sector fifty-two," she whispered.

Raoul turned to his computer. Kenzie watched as his fingers flew over the keypad. Seconds later, he brought up a large-scale diagram.

She squinted at it. "What's that?"

"It's the schematics for the Kimbala Mine." Kenzie's eyes widened as he leaned in and studied the key in the top right corner.

"Sector 52." He pointed to a section of the diagram on his screen. "There it is. That's where your diamonds are from."

Kenzie stared at the image. It was hard to imagine that the diamonds she'd found on the beach were from that dark little section of mine on another continent halfway across the world.

"That's crazy," she whispered, but Raoul's eyes were back on the ledger entry.

"And we can tick that one off, too." He picked up his pencil.

"We're making progress." Kenzie felt a surge of adrenaline. "This proves Del Gatto was involved in the smuggling operation. And if he was involved, it's probable the mob was too."

Raoul did a double take. "Did you just say mob?"

"The New York mob, yeah." She leaned in. "I just found out Del Gatto has a connection to Joe Molano."

Raoul gave a low whistle. "This investigation just took on a whole new dimension."

"I know."

"Perhaps we should take this to the police," he said, suddenly nervous.

"I will tonight. But don't forget, I obtained the photograph illegally. I broke into Del Gatto's study and took it. That means it's inadmissible in court."

"The police could search the house and retrieve the real ledger," Raoul suggested.

That was an option. If they could get a warrant.

Raoul shrugged. "It's your choice, Kenz. I'm just a researcher, what do I know?"

She squeezed his shoulder. "Thank you, Raoul. Let's keep going. If I can find out who these people are, then I really will have something to take to Reid. In the meantime, see what you can dig up on the Del Gatto-Joe Molano connection."

He nodded. "Leave it to me."

CHAPTER 23

The call came in as Reid was eating lunch at his desk. Pastrami on rye washed down with a soda. It was freaking humid. It seemed like the weather was making up for the hurricane by unleashing a mini heat-wave. As luck would have it, the AC was on the fritz. Everyone was struggling with the heat.

Monroe—his face purple from excitement or heatstroke, Reid couldn't decide which—came charging over like an out-of-control buffalo. He almost knocked Diaz flying, then rebounded off Vargas's desk in his haste to get to Reid.

"Whoa!" Reid reached out, as he wobbled to a halt. "What's the hurry?"

"Lieutenant, you're never going to believe this! There's been a burglary at the forensic lab." His chest was heaving.

Reid frowned, "The forensic lab? Why is that—?" Then he realized why Monroe was so excited. "Don't tell me, the diamonds?"

Monroe bobbed his head up and down. "You got it! They're gone."

"Holy shit," exclaimed Diaz, jumping out of her chair. "All of them?"

Monroe kept nodding.

Vargas stared at him, his mouth open.

"What the hell happened?" Reid asked, still reeling.

"Someone broke in overnight and stole them from out of the safe."

"I thought they were guarded." Reid ran a hand through his hair. It came away damp.

"They're only guarded when they're being analyzed or in transit, not when they're locked away in the safe overnight. The FBI were due to collect them this morning and, when they opened the safe, they were missing."

"Can you imagine their faces?" Diaz murmured, glancing from Vargas to Reid.

"What about security cameras?" Reid couldn't believe what he was hearing. How could seven million in uncut diamonds disappear from a forensic lab? Okay, granted, the labs were privately run, but it would have been vetted and cleared.

Monroe shrugged. "That's all I know. I just heard it come in on the wire. Miami PD's responding."

Reid got up. "I've got to call Pérez."

He took his phone outside and called the captain's direct line. Phew. It was hotter than Hades out here. Still, underneath the brutal heat was a slight breeze, which was better than sitting in the stuffy squad room.

"I take it you heard," was the first thing Pérez said when he answered the phone. "Idiots left the diamonds in a bloody safe overnight with nobody guarding them."

"You're kidding me. How'd the burglar get inside the building?"

"It appears that the thief used a stolen key card to get access. They waited until everyone had left, then cracked the safe and stole the diamonds."

"What about surveillance cameras?"

"The cameras in that area were temporarily disabled. We think the thief used an electronic jamming device."

"Okay, but what about the other sections? The corridors, the exit?"

"They're still going through the footage, but it appears the thief escaped via a first-floor window while the cameras were jammed."

"Taking seven million in diamonds with them," Reid finished. "Holy crap, Captain. That's a major heist."

"I know." He sighed. "We've got to keep this from the press. Can you imagine the media shit storm? I can see the headlines now. POLICE LAB LOSES SEVEN MIL IN DIAMOND HEIST." He gave a humorless snort. "Hell, we'd be laughing stocks."

"Technically, it's not a police lab," Reid muttered.

"Doesn't matter. They have the Miami PD contract. It's practically the same thing."

Reid exhaled. "Now what? Where do we go from here?"

"I don't know about you, but I'm going to get very drunk tonight," Pérez said. "After I've done some damage control."

Reid felt for the guy, he really did.

"Who knew the diamonds were there?" he asked, his mind spinning into gear.

"Enough people," Pérez growled. "You, me, a couple of other detectives, the lab assistant, appraisers, Kenzie, obviously, and then there's Del Gatto's lot. It could have been any one of them."

True, seven million dollars was a hell of a temptation.

"Do you think they acted alone or had help?" Reid asked. "Whose key card was stolen?"

"A lab tech called Maurice Perkin. He reported it missing this morning, but of course by then it's too late."

"Do you think he was the accomplice?"

"We're questioning him, but it doesn't look like it. I'll keep you posted."

"Okay, thanks Captain."

Pérez hung up without saying goodbye.

When he got back inside, Reid relayed what he'd learned to the rest of the team, all of whom were anxious for the latest update.

"It had to be someone familiar with the case," Diaz stated. "I mean, they'd have to know where the diamonds were being kept and when the Feds were going to pick them up."

"They'd also have to know there were no guards overnight and what kind of safe it was in order to crack it," Vargas chimed in.

Both valid points.

"The lab tech was targeted for his card because he had the right access," Reid said, scratching his chin. Problem is he only noticed it was missing this morning, which means it must have been stolen the evening before. He used it to exit the building, so the thief must have been watching him, waiting for an opportunity to grab it.

"Easy to lift a key card if you know what you're doing," Diaz said. "They should ask him if he remembers being jostled or bumped in the parking lot after work, or maybe on the bus or metro."

"I'm sure Miami PD has it under control," Reid said. He was glad he didn't have the case. What a nightmare. How do you explain that to the powers that be? They were going to come down hard on Pérez for that one.

They were just getting back to work after the shocking revelation when Diaz's phone rang. She listened, then after a curt nod, told the caller they'd be right there.

Reid glanced up expectantly.

"Remember that BOLO we put out on Hector Esparza? Well, there's been a sighting in Little Haiti. An off-duty officer said he's just seen him go into a bar."

Reid stared up at Diaz. "He's there? Now?"

"Yeah. You coming?" She inspected her Glock and, satisfied it was in good, working order, slipped it into her holster.

"Wouldn't miss it. Let's go get him."

They blue-lighted it to the expressway, wove through the bustling streets of downtown Miami and headed north, bypassing the Design District before reaching the vibrant heart of Little Haiti.

Reid cut the siren and lights long before they discreetly maneuvered the SUV into a narrow alley, parking a block away from a little-known bar tucked away in this quiet corner of Little Haiti. They hadn't bothered to dress the part this time. There was no disguising what they were there to do.

"I'll wait out back," Reid said, grimly. "You go in the front and see if Hector is there. When he spots you, he'll run straight out the back and into my arms."

Diaz nodded, her chin set at a determined angle, and walked toward the entrance, barely noticeable except for a faded sign.

Reid positioned himself under an overgrown flamboyant tree, wishing there was a breeze. Perspiration ran down his face, the oppressive humidity clinging to him like a second skin. He could hear the soft murmur of Creole music softly playing in the background.

Heart thumping with pent-up adrenaline, he tried to visualize the unfolding scene. Diaz would be stepping into the dimly lit bar, her presence slowly becoming known. She'd pause, scanning the room's shadowy corners for Hector. If the elusive sailor was there, he'd leap up, weaving his way past the mismatched tables and chairs to the back exit, and—On cue, Hector emerged from the bar's side door into the mellow light filtering through the alleyway's overhanging foliage. Momentarily disoriented by the shift from the bar's dim interior to the dappled sunlight of Little Haiti, he blinked rapidly. Then, spotting Reid, he launched into motion.

"Police, freeze!" Reid aimed his gun at the suspect, hoping he'd put his hands up and come willingly, knowing when he was cornered. Except Hector had other ideas. He snarled and lowered his shoulder. Before Reid could react, two hundred pounds of hardened sailor crashed into his torso. Reid's gun flew from his grasp as both men slammed violently into the ground. The air rushed from his lungs on impact.

Gasping, Reid struggled to get a grip on his sweaty adversary. Hector drove an elbow into his ribs, causing him to yelp in pain, then slithered free from his grasp. Reid scrambled awkwardly to his feet just as Hector pulled a wicked 6-inch blade from his boot.

"I'm taking you in," Reid growled through gritted teeth. He lunged forward, but Hector feinted, letting Reid stumble past before raking the knife savagely across his side.

Reid clutched at the wound as dark crimson bloomed, soaking through the fabric.

Shit.

He'd been cut.

Growling, Reid threw a wild haymaker, but Hector ducked easily. Off-balance, Reid left himself open to a vicious elbow that cracked against his jaw. Stars burst across his field of vision as he crashed backward over an upturned crate.

Hector picked up the gun and aimed it at Reid, but before he could pull the trigger, Diaz came hurtling out of the bar.

"Drop the weapon!" she screamed, pointing her Glock at him.

Hector turned and fired. It was so fast, Reid thought he'd got her, but Diaz dived for cover, the bullet flying harmlessly over her head. There was a soft thud as it lodged into the flat boarded wall behind her.

That split second reprieve was all Hector needed. He darted through the quiet side street, where a few curious locals glanced up from their daily routines and vanished into the labyrinth of alleys threading through the back streets of Little Haiti.

Reid tore after him. This was Hector's neighborhood, and his knowledge of the terrain gave him the advantage. Reid tried to keep up as Hector leaped over trash cans and pallets and zigzagged down alleyways with sure-footed familiarity. Reid lumbered after him, ducking under crisscrossing laundry lines and smacking damp sheets out of the way.

Soon, his shirt was drenched in sweat—or was it blood? He couldn't be sure.

Hector disappeared around a corner and Reid desperately flung himself after the fleeing suspect, slamming hard into a brick wall. He tottered and reached out a hand to stabilize himself. If only the world would stop spinning.

"Freakin' hell, Reid," came Diaz's angry voice. "What the hell do you think you're doing?"

"He's getting away." Reid clutched his side and sank to the ground.

"Stay put!"

Diaz sprinted past, picking up where Reid had left off. As she disappeared after the fleeing suspect, he propped himself up against the wall, breathing heavily. Slowly, his vision cleared, and things came back into focus.

A local vendor, balancing a tray of fresh mangoes on her head and a small, brightly colored bird perched on her shoulder, paused and looked at him with concern. "Sir, are you alright? Do you need me to call for help?"

Reid glanced down to see his shirt was soaked with blood. Lifting it up, he inspected the gaping wound. It was raw and bloody, but only about an inch long. It didn't seem that serious, and he didn't think the knife had punctured any vital organs.

"I'm okay."

"No offense, but you don't look okay. You're bleeding."

"I know. It's just a scratch."

She blew air out of her cheeks and moved on.

Reid pressed his hand over the wound to staunch the bleeding, then struggled to his feet. Simmering with frustration and self-recrimination, he stumbled back to the SUV. He should have come with backup. He'd underestimated Hector. He'd thought he and Diaz could handle it. He'd been wrong.

Opening the door, he slumped into the passenger seat, still holding his side. The bleeding was slowing down a little now, or maybe his shirt had just absorbed most of it. Apart from feeling a little woozy, he was fine.

Twenty minutes later, Diaz arrived, panting and sweat-soaked. She was alone. "I lost him." She collapsed against the truck. "I told you to stay put. You look terrible."

He grunted. "Bastard knifed me. I may need a few stitches."

"Let me see." She lifted his shirt and grimaced. "Er, yeah. I'd say so. Let's get you to the hospital."

Reid let her buckle him in. "I underestimated him," he gritted, as Diaz started the truck. "I'm sorry."

"We both did."

As she took off, siren once again blaring, he leaned his head back against the headrest. "Hector won this round, but next time we'll be ready for him."

"You bet we will." She shot him a worried glance as she navigated the traffic to the nearest hospital. "This is far from over."

CHAPTER 24

Kenzie was finishing up at work when she got a call from Diaz. Her heart immediately skipped a beat. Even though she liked her, they weren't friends. There was only one reason the Sweetwater detective would be calling her. Reid.

"Hello?" She couldn't keep her voice from wobbling.

"Hey Kenzie. I'm at the hospital with Reid. He's okay, but he's been stabbed."

Kenzie felt the ground tilt. She grasped the desk, her mind going blank. "Oh, my God. Is it serious?"

"He's lost some blood, but nothing too serious. They're stitching him up now. I just thought you should know."

"Thank you. I'll come right over. Which hospital?"

"Jackson Memorial."

"I'll be right there."

Kenzie dropped everything and drove straight there. When she arrived, she found a disgruntled Reid lying on an examination table in the Emergency Room, arguing with a doctor.

"It was a nasty laceration, Lieutenant," the doctor was saying. "An inch deeper, and it could have punctured your liver or kidney."

"But it didn't," Reid retorted. "I'm fine. I need to get back to work."

"You've lost quite a lot of blood. You should rest up until you recover."

"I can't. I've got to get back to work."

The doctor sighed. "At least let the nurse put on a sterile dressing."

Reid lay back with a grunt.

"I see you're behaving yourself," Kenzie teased, leaning over and kissing him on the cheek.

He grimaced, albeit good-naturedly. "Doc here won't let me leave."

"The nurse will be in soon to dress your wound." The doctor smiled at Kenzie as he left the ward.

"What happened?" Kenzie asked, perching next to him on the bed. While he looked paler than usual, he seemed to be okay. The awful fear she'd felt driving over here was beginning to lift.

"Got knifed by a suspect."

Kenzie arched an eyebrow. "That much is obvious. Which suspect?"

"The skipper of the *Jewel*, Hector Esparza. I'm sorry, Kenz, but he's definitely involved in this. I wouldn't be surprised if he's the mastermind behind the whole operation."

"He tried to kill you?"

"Yeah, he aimed my gun at me and was about to pull the trigger when Diaz arrived. Thank God she did or I'd be—" He grimaced.

"Don't even say it." Kenzie gripped his hand. She hadn't had a chance to thank Diaz, as the detective had left the hospital before she'd arrived. Kenzie supposed she had to report what had happened and coordinate a search for Hector, who would now be wanted in connection with assault with a deadly weapon, maybe even attempted murder.

"Did you say your gun?"

"Yeah." He shook his head. "I dropped it when he barreled into me like a crazed bull. The guy must weigh two hundred pounds, at least."

Kenzie cringed. Reid would get reprimanded for that. It was one of the basic rules of policing never to let a perpetrator gain control over your weapon. It could put the officer and others in immediate danger. Her academy days might be a long time ago, but she remembered that much.

"Try not to worry about it," she said. "It happens."

"Not to me. I should know better." She could see the muscles flex in his jaw. He was furious at himself for letting the suspect get away.

"Why don't I take you home?" Maybe sitting out on the deck and talking it over would relax him. "I can make us something to eat at your place."

He squeezed her hand. "I'm sorry I'm being such a grouch. That sounds great."

A nurse came in with a cart and began to dress the wound. Kenzie was about to sit down when her phone rang. Shooting him an apologetic smile, she went outside to answer it.

"Hello?"

A garbled voice. "Kenzie? Kenzie is that you?"

"Christina? Yes, it's Kenzie. Is everything okay?" Her senses started tingling.

There was a sharp intake of breath on the other end and Christina's voice came through rushed and laced with panic. "Kenzie, listen, I found out something—something terrible. It's about Samson Quinn, Salvatore's head of security. I heard them talking, and I think he—"

The call crackled and a muffled noise in the background interrupted her. Kenzie strained to hear more, but the line went dead, leaving only an eerie silence.

What had just happened?

A chill ran down her spine as she redialed, only to be greeted by Christina's voicemail.

Shit.

Kenzie's mind raced, piecing together the fragments of the conversation. What had Quinn done? She knew the ex-soldier was dangerous, but Christina's warning followed by the dropped call added a new level of threat.

She had to do something, but what? She couldn't race over to Del Gatto's place to check up on her. Del Gatto would never allow her in.

Panicked, she rushed back into the ward. "Reid, I've just had a call from Christina. I think she's in danger."

"Christina?" He tried to sit up, but the nurse tutted, and he fell back again.

"Del Gatto's mistress," Kenzie hissed, under her breath.

"What makes you think that?" He nodded to her phone. "What did she say?"

"She's found out something about Quinn, Del Gatto's head of security. She was about to tell me what it was when she got cut off." Kenzie bit her lip. "Reid, we need to get over there ASAP."

"He's not going anywhere," the nurse said matter-of-factly. "Your wound is bleeding again, sir. If you don't lie still, it will keep doing that."

Reid growled, but the nurse ignored him and carried on wiping the wound. "I'll send someone around," he said, twisting to reach his phone.

"Sir, please," the nurse complained.

"Damnit." Reid fell helplessly back onto the bed.

"Don't worry. I'll do it." Kenzie dashed for the door. "I'm sorry Reid, I know something is terribly wrong. I'll call you later."

"Kenzie wait—" He tried to get up, but a firm hand pushed him down again. Before he could say anything more, Kenzie was out the door.

KENZIE WAITED NERVOUSLY at the junction of the road leading to Del Gatto's mansion. Here, at the end of a long line of palm trees, she was out of sight of the guards at the gate. She'd called Miami PD while she'd been driving, figuring they were closest. Dispatch had said they'd send a patrol officer to the property as soon as possible.

"Tell them to hurry," Kenzie had begged as she drove like a maniac towards Palm Island.

Ten minutes later, a squad car drove past her on its way toward the mansion. She watched as it stopped at the sinister, carbon-steel security gates. A guard came out of a side hut and approached the vehicle. Kenzie held her breath while they spoke. Their exchange was short, but noticeably tense and, when the gates hissed open, she uttered a silent, "Yes".

"Get a move on," she willed the squad car as it cruised up the winding driveway. Nobody had left the complex since she'd arrived, but in the heart-stopping twenty minutes it had taken for her to get here, anything could have happened.

The patrol officer, after what seemed like an eternity, finally returned. She flagged him down and the officer pulled over and rolled down his window. "Yes, ma'am?"

"Kenzie Gilmore. I'm the one who called you," she said, breathlessly. "I'm a friend of Miss Gomez. Was she inside the house?"

He frowned, asked to see some form of ID, then once she'd shown him her driver's license said, "No, ma'am. I spoke to the owner, Mr. Del Gatto, who assured me she wasn't there."

Kenzie felt like crying. She was sure Christina had been at the mansion when she'd made the call. Kenzie replayed what she could remember of the few short seconds of the phone call in her mind. The last bit was the most telling.

*I heard them talking, and I think he—*She must have been at the mansion to overhear them talking. Where else could they be?

"Did you see any signs of a struggle?" she asked.

"Nothing like that, no. Everything appeared to be in order."

Kenzie rolled her hands into fists. "Are you sure?" she pressed, aware of how desperate she sounded. "She called me less than an hour ago and said she was in trouble."

"Did she call from this house, ma'am?"

"Yes, I—I think so."

The officer nodded sympathetically. "I understand your concern, but everyone there seemed calm. They allowed us full access—no objections. If she was there, she isn't now."

A deep, uneasy feeling settled on her. What more could she do? "Thank you, officer."

"You should check with her friends. She may have gone to one of them if she was upset."

She wasn't upset, she was scared.

Still, there was no point arguing. The officer had done all he could.

Kenzie gnawed on her lower lip. There was a possibility Christina had gone home. If it hadn't been for the dropped call...

As the squad car disappeared down the street, Kenzie stood alone under the palm trees, the ocean breeze tousling her hair, trying to subdue her rising panic.

Think.

The obvious next place to check was Christina's house, except she didn't know where the woman lived. Taking out her cell phone, she called Alex.

"Kenzie, hi. How are you? You must have telepathy. I was just thinking about you."

"Alex, I need a favor," Kenzie blurted out, unable to hold back the anxiety in her voice.

"Is something wrong?"

"I—I don't know. I think something's happened to Christina."

"Christina? You mean Del Gatto's—"

"Yes, that Christina." Kenzie cut her short. "Do you have her home address? It's urgent."

There was a pause. "No. I don't think so."

"Could you find out?"

"Maybe. I could ask this guy I know from the club. I think he's friends with her."

"Please, and hurry. Call me back on my cell. I'll be waiting by my phone."

"Oh, yes. Sure."

Kenzie hung up.

Five gut-wrenching minutes later, Alex called back.

"Did you get it?" Kenzie asked, adrenaline making her hands shake.

Alex rattled off an address in Coconut Grove. "Kenzie, what's all this about? Is something wrong?"

"I think so. I think Christina may have been caught eavesdropping. She was on the phone to me, saying something about Quinn, when she got cut off. Alex, she's in trouble."

"Did she mention Quinn by name?" Alex asked.

"Yeah, she said she'd found out something about him, and was about to say what, when she got cut off. I think he caught her talking to me. If I'm right...Oh, God, Alex. I'm the one who asked her to spy on them. If she's in trouble, it's my fault."

"Kenzie, calm down." Alex's voice was filled with concern. "Where are you?"

"On my way to Coconut Grove."

"I'll meet you there."

CHAPTER 25

Kenzie pulled up to the charming two-story townhouse, her sense of unease growing. Though nestled on a pretty, tree-lined street. It stood quietly by itself, the blinds drawn as if harboring some awful secret. The ivy-clad façade with its cozy front porch seemed weirdly out of place.

As Kenzie hurried up the walk, the setting sun sank behind a low-lying cloudbank and the manicured garden was cast in shadows. She shivered and rang the buzzer. It echoed hollowly inside the house.

Nobody came.

Heart pounding, she ran around the back of the property, clambering over a small gate to reach the back door. As soon as she saw it, her heart sank. It was ajar.

It might be nothing, she told herself, even if she didn't believe it. Christina had just forgotten to shut it when she'd got home, that's all. She ignored the warning bells clanging in her head.

Kenzie pushed open the door and listened. The house was deathly quiet. The only sound she heard was the beating of her frantic heart. Inspecting the handle, she saw the lock was still in place, which meant it must have been forced open. Sure enough, there were markings in the wood of the door frame.

She ventured into the kitchen and gasped. "Oh, God."

Christina lay on the floor, her eyes shut like she was sleeping. A sticky red trail of blood had oozed from both delicate wrists, gathering in a small crimson pool that echoed the shape of her arm.

"Christina!" Kenzie ran forward, dropping to her knees heedless of the blood seeping into the fabric of her pants. This close, she could smell the thick metallic scent of it. Kenzie grasped Christina's shoulders, shook her gently. "Christina, can you hear me?"

Del Gatto's mistress didn't move. She'd slit her wrists. The knife lay on the floor beside her right hand, as if it had slipped out. Dread rising inside, Kenzie felt for a pulse.

"Come on," she prayed, pressing her fingers against the side of Christina's neck. Her skin was deceptively warm. "Come on."

There was nothing. Not the slightest flutter.

No. No. No.

She couldn't be dead.

Kenzie began chest compressions. She pumped her hands hard against Christina's chest, once, twice, again, and again. She kept going, shoulders burning, refusing to stop. But finally, she slumped back, breathing hard, and admitted what she had known from the first moment.

Christina was dead.

Kenzie let out a shuddering gasp. It was only yesterday she'd spoken to her at the country club, persuaded her to see what she could find out. Now she had slit her wrists.

Because of her.

Kenzie hung her head and sobbed.

THE FRONT DOOR buzzer reverberated through the house. Groggily, Kenzie looked up. She had no idea how long she'd been crying on the floor beside Christina's body.

"Kenzie! Kenzie, are you in there?"

Alex.

In a daze, she got up and staggered through the house to the front door. Bizarrely, she noticed that the decor was surprisingly tasteful, but very different to the Del Gatto mansion. Christina had a more modern style than Bethany. With a start, Kenzie realized Christina would never walk this way again, never admire the black and white photographs on the wall in the hallway, never smile at a friend as she opened the door.

A physical pain flashed through her, making her double up.

Alex was pounding on the door now, making a racket. Soon the neighbors would hear.

Kenzie opened it. "It's my fault..." she choked out.

"What is?" Alex took in Kenzie's reddened eyes and ashen face. "What the hell is going on, Kenzie?"

"Christina's dead."

"Oh, my God. Seriously?" Alex's eyes widened, horrified. "How?"

"She's in the kitchen." Kenzie turned and walked like a zombie back down the hall to where Christina lay.

Alex followed, but stopped when she saw the body. Her hands flew to her mouth. "What happened?"

"Looks like she cut her wrists."

"Why? Why would she do that?" Alex stared at Christina, her mouth open.

"I'm not sure she did," Kenzie said quietly.

Alex's gaze flickered back to her. "I don't—What are you saying?"

"Samson Quinn. He was the one she was telling me about when we got disconnected."

"Quinn?" Alex gasped. "You think he did this?"

Kenzie shrugged. She didn't know what to think. The desperate phone call, the forced door, the knife lying on the floor covered in Christina's blood. There were just too many unanswered questions.

"Have you called the police?" Alex asked.

"Not yet."

Alex pulled out her phone and dialed 911. Kenzie heard her report the suicide and give the operator this address, but it sounded muted, like she was underwater or in a dream. *Suspected suicide*, she wanted to add, but couldn't find the words.

"They're on their way," Alex said as she hung up.

Kenzie stared dully at the body. In the background, she heard Alex ask, "Is there any sign of a break in?"

"The back door's been wrenched open."

Alex inspected the lock, then gave a grim nod.

Kenzie blinked, unable to move. It was like she'd been frozen to the spot, unable to drag herself away from Christina.

"Maybe we should wait in the living room." Alex led Kenzie out of the kitchen. "There's blood all over your pants."

Kenzie glanced down. Christina's blood. "She didn't commit suicide," she whispered. "I know it."

"It sure looks like it to me," Alex said quietly. "Apart from the door, of course."

"What if he did this?" Kenzie turned to Alex, feeling sick. "What if he did this because of what she'd discovered?"

"Then the police will get to the bottom of it," Alex said, reassuringly.

Kenzie swallowed over the rising bile. Would they? Would they even look past the suicide? She closed her eyes, but all she could see was Christina's face, so she opened them again.

"It'll be okay," Alex murmured, rubbing her back. "It'll be okay."

Except Kenzie knew it wouldn't.

THE REST of the evening passed in a blur. Two detectives, who she didn't know, arrived and asked her a barrage of questions. Kenzie answered as best she could.

She'd come to visit the victim and, when she couldn't get in, went around to the back door and found it ajar. Going in, she saw the blood, then Christina lying on the kitchen floor. What made her go around the back? She'd received a distressed phone call from the victim and rushed over here shortly after that.

Alex then gave her version of events. After that, they were led to a squad car. The detective in charge explained that they needed to come down to the station to give their fingerprints and a DNA sample. These were standard procedures in such cases to rule out any involvement of the people who found the body. Their fingerprints would be compared against those found at the scene, and their DNA would be checked against any biological material collected.

"I didn't go near the body," Alex protested, but the detective was firm.

"It's procedure, ma'am."

The screech of tires made them all look up. Relief washed over Kenzie as Reid's Ford pickup halted behind the squad car. She'd never been so glad to see him in her life.

"Reid!" she called as he got out. She noticed him wince as he made his way to where Kenzie was perched in the back of the squad car. He really shouldn't be out of the hospital. "What are you doing here?"

"I came as soon as I heard. Are you okay? Is it true?"

"Excuse me, sir," the detective began, rising to intercept him. Reid, with a careful motion that avoided any jarring of his right side, presented his badge.

"Oh, my apologies, sir. I didn't realize."

To be fair, Reid was wearing a white T-shirt with a Jackson Memorial logo, which he'd probably picked up at the hospital gift shop and, with his bruised face, ruffled hair, and blood-spattered pants, looked more like a ruffian than a cop.

"That's okay officer. I'll take responsibility for these two." Reid's reply was gentle, his focus shifting to Kenzie as he carefully helped her out of the car. Alex thanked him with a nod and walked away. "What happened? How did she die?"

Kenzie took a shaky breath and clung onto his hand. "The back door was forced, and we found a knife lying on the floor. It looks like she slit her own wrists."

"Suicide?"

Kenzie led him away from the squad car. "She sounded terrified, Reid. That call I got at the hospital, that was barely an hour before...before I found her."

Reid frowned. "What exactly did she say?"

"She'd stumbled upon something terrible involving Del Gatto and Quinn," Kenzie managed, her voice breaking as hot tears stung her eyes.

"Did she specify?" A flicker of discomfort crossed his face as he adjusted his posture to ease the discomfort in his side.

"Just that. Then I heard noises, as if the phone was snatched from her hand." She blinked furiously. "This is my fault, Reid. I asked her to spy on Del Gatto. She's dead because of me."

Reid wrapped his arms around her, holding her against his good side. His arms were strong and comforting. Unable to hide her emotions, she buried her head in his shoulder and gave way to the tears once more.

CHAPTER 26

Reid was shocked at the state in which he'd found Kenzie. She was usually so controlled, so together. This sobbing, guilt-wracked version of the woman he loved was both heartbreaking and unsettling. The worst part was he didn't know what to do to make it better.

She had asked Christina to spy on Del Gatto. Not only that, she'd manipulated her into doing it. Now the woman was dead. He didn't blame her for feeling guilty.

Sighing, he left Miami PD in charge of the crime scene and took Kenzie home. An officer would drive her vehicle back later and drop off the keys.

"I can stay if you like?" he offered as she collapsed onto the couch. He'd have liked to talk to her about what had happened, eased her pain a little, but she wasn't in the mood. He wanted to tell her about the diamond heist too, but Pérez had said no press, and that included Kenzie.

"Thanks, but I think I need to be alone for a while."

Reid frowned, worried. He knew how he'd felt after his colleague had been killed, back when he'd worked for the Miami PD. Wracked with guilt, he'd blamed himself, when it hadn't been his fault at all. He hadn't been the one to pull the trigger, and it was the same here. Kenzie hadn't been the one to force Christina to take her own life. She hadn't killed her, even if her actions had led to the murder taking place. It would take Kenzie a while to realize that and to learn to forgive herself. "Okay, but I'm here for you if you need to talk."

Kenzie forced a smile. "Thanks, Reid. I just want to sleep." She collapsed onto the couch.

Reid understood the desire to let sleep take over, so you didn't have to think about what had happened. It was the brain's way of dealing with the trauma. Shutting down so it had time to process and heal.

He pulled out the rolled-up blanket she kept beside the couch and placed it over her, groaning as he stretched out his side. Talking about rest, he should go get some himself. "I'll call you later to make sure you're okay. If you want me to come back, you just have to ask."

"Thank you, Reid." Her eyelids fluttered, then closed.

Reid watched her, his heart twisting in his chest. It wasn't easy, what she had to deal with but, knowing Kenzie, she'd get through it. It might take a while, but she'd recover and get back on her feet.

"Bye, Kenz." He left her there on the couch, and locked the door on his way out.

WHEN KENZIE OPENED her eyes the next morning, she didn't know where she was.

Oh, yeah. The couch.

Then the full reality of what had happened last night hit her. The frantic phone call...the race to Del Gatto's...Christina's house...Her body on the kitchen floor...

The blood...

Christina was dead.

Kenzie squeezed her eyes shut and willed the memory to go away, but it didn't. Wouldn't. It was something she was going to remember for the rest of her life.

Slowly, she sat up and stretched her neck. It ached from sleeping on the couch all night. Her eyes felt gritty too, like she'd been in a dust storm. Stumbling into the bathroom, she looked at herself in the mirror.

Wow. Haunted eyes, blotchy skin, hair that resembled a bird's nest. She didn't think she'd ever looked this bad. Then she scoffed. It didn't matter, she felt even worse.

Peeling off her clothes, she got into the shower. As she stood there, staring at the water swirling down the drain, she wished the awful events from yesterday could drain out of her life—but nothing was that simple.

After a strong cup of coffee, she called Keith at the office and explained what had happened. "I'll work from home today," she said, without much enthusiasm.

"Write about it, Kenzie," he told her. "It always helps if you write about it."

Keith had known her a long time. He'd given her her first real job at a newspaper as an entertainment reporter back when she was wide-eyed and idealistic. He'd seen her grow, change, and morph into the hard-nosed investigative journalist she was today, but not without some hard knocks along the way.

She couldn't believe that part of her life was coming to an end.

"Maybe."

It was too soon to put pen to paper. She felt too raw. Her head was still trying to make sense of what had happened. Had it been Quinn? Had he taken Christina home, killed her, and disappeared out the back door moments before Kenzie had arrived at the front of the house?

The body had still been warm. Christina couldn't have died more than half an hour before she'd got there. Had Quinn been at Del Gatto's place when the patrol officer went round? She recalled him saying he spoke to Mr. Del Gatto, but there was no mention of anyone else.

Gnawing on her lower lip, she tried to remember what the young Miami PD officer's name was. Peter? Peterson?

Taking out her phone, she called an old friend at Miami PD. She'd met Ortega at the police academy. He was a senior detective now and ran his own unit. They hadn't spoken in a while, but she was sure he'd still take her call.

"Kenzie Gilmore. My goodness, it's been a while."

"Hey Ortega. How are you doing?"

"I'm good. What about you? Long time, no see."

"Yeah, sorry about that. I've been busy."

"I know. I've seen you in the papers, making a name for yourself."

"I'm trying." She scoffed without humor.

"Let me guess, you realized you were wrong all those years ago and you really do want to go out with me." He chuckled.

"You're not that lucky."

"Damn. Okay, what is it? What do you need?" Still the same Ortega.

"Actually, just a name. A young patrol officer paid a visit to Salvatore Del Gatto's mansion yesterday, and I can't remember who he was. Could you find out for me?"

"A patrol officer? I don't know many of them personally, but sure, I could find out. Why do you want to speak with him?"

"It's a long story, but I need to know who else was at the house when he stopped by. It's important or I wouldn't be asking."

"Yeah, I know. Let me see what I can find out, and I'll call you back."

"Thanks, Ortega. I owe you."

"No worries. Buy me dinner sometime."

"You got it."

LATER THAT AFTERNOON, Kenzie had another visitor, this time it was Alex.

"I thought you might want some company." She held up a bottle of wine.

Kenzie didn't want company, but she didn't have the heart to turn Alex away. "Come on in."

Alex stepped into the living room and looked around. "Nice place you got here. Love the views of the bay."

"Thanks." She'd bought it with the money her dad had left her. It was her sanctuary, her place away from the newsroom and the deadlines and the stories she worked on. While she loved that stuff, it was always good to come home to her little piece of paradise.

Alex set the wine down on the dining room table. It was chilled, Kenzie could see the water droplets on the side. "I'll get us some glasses." She disappeared into the kitchen. When she came back, Alex had opened the bottle.

"Now I know you're probably beating yourself up about Christina, but what happened yesterday is not your fault."

Kenzie froze. Alex had a way of getting straight to the point. \

"Actually, Alex, it's entirely my fault." She set the glasses on the table. "It was *my* idea to get her to help us, *my* idea to ask her to spy on Del Gatto, and it ended up getting her killed."

"You couldn't have known." Alex reasoned.

"I *should* have known," Kenzie sighed. "That's the point. Del Gatto is a bastard, I knew that. I've been tracking him for years, watching from the sidelines. I knew he was up to no good. I was so desperate to catch him that I got his girlfriend killed in the process."

Alex filled up the glasses and handed one to Kenzie. "You didn't slit her wrists."

"No, but I may as well have." Kenzie accepted the wine and downed half a glass.

Alex touched her arm. "I'm sorry, Kenzie. I really am. I feel partly responsible, too. I mean, I planted the seed that made her so mad. If it wasn't for me, she wouldn't have been so eager to help dig up dirt on Salvatore."

Kenzie hung her head. "Even that was my idea."

"You know what you need?" Alex reasoned.

"No." There was nothing that would make her feel better.

"To catch the bastard who did this."

Except maybe that.

"Then, you need to write about it in the paper and give Christina the justice she deserves."

For the first time since it had happened, Kenzie felt a flicker of life in her veins.

"How? Del Gatto is untouchable. I can't get near his mansion. Quinn was the one who killed her, but Del Gatto gave the order, I'm sure of it."

"Then prove it." Alex fixed her gaze on Kenzie. "Take them both down."

Kenzie thought about the coded ledger and the initials of the contacts. If she could find those people, she might be able to work backwards and get proof of Del Gatto's involvement. Right now, it was the only lead she had.

"Okay," she told Alex, pulling herself together.

"Okay what?" Alex tilted her head.

"Okay, I'm going to take them both down."

CHAPTER 27

"I thought she slit her wrists," Reid said, frowning.

"So did I, but the forensic blood spatter analyst said the patterns were inconsistent with suicide. It looked like she was moving around when she did it."

"As in a struggle?" Reid asked.

"Exactly."

A frazzled Captain Pérez had driven out to Sweetwater to talk to him about the case. Reid had taken him to the local burger joint for lunch. Apparently, Del Gatto was refusing to be questioned by anyone other than his new best friend, Lieutenant Garrett, and Pérez didn't have the energy to argue. "If he wants you, he can damn well have you. This should probably be your case anyway, Garrett. This whole mess might be connected to the diamonds."

"Any news on the lab theft?" Reid asked.

Pérez shook his head. "They're conducting their own internal investigation, but our guys have gone in too. No prints. No DNA. Zilch. A total pro job."

Just like the Bling Bandit.

A cold chill shot through him. Was what he was thinking even possible? No way. It was a crazy idea. How would the high society cat burglar have found out about the uncut diamonds? They couldn't. Only those people connected to the case would know about it. Unless they had access to such information.

"Are you looking into everyone who had knowledge of the case?" Reid asked.

"Of course. We're working our way through the list. It's a long one. Longer than you'd think."

Reid nodded. It was Miami PD's responsibility, even though he'd brought Pérez the diamonds to begin with. Thankfully, Sweetwater PD didn't have to get involved. They had enough on their plate with a double homicide suspect, Hector, on the loose; Del Gatto and Quin suspected in Christina Gomez's murder; and Kenzie beating herself up about it.

"What did the coroner say?" Reid asked.

"The incisions were jagged, which is consistent with a self-inflicted wound."

Reid nodded. Usually, there were signs of distress or hesitation in a suicide, such as multiple superficial cuts, also known as hesitation marks, before the fatal ones. They didn't make smooth, controlled cuts. "But—?"

Pérez sighed. "But the angle of the incision was questionable. It appears she was right-handed and the cut on her right wrist was left to right, not right to left, which makes it very awkward, especially if she wasn't in a rational state of mind."

"So, it's unlikely she cut her own wrists," Reid summed up.

Pérez ran a hand through what was left of his hair. "Which means we've got another homicide linked to Del Gatto." He'd thinned out over the last few years. Frown lines cut deep grooves around his mouth and his shoulders hunched under an invisible weight. The promotion to captain had come at a cost.

Reid vowed he'd never get to that point. The lieutenant was as good as it was going to get for him. Anything higher and he'd have to start jumping through bureaucratic hoops and wouldn't be able to be actively involved in investigations. Hell, he shouldn't be now, but luckily his was a small department, and they needed the manpower. Besides, at Sweetwater he was the boss, he could do what he liked.

"You think he did it?" Reid asked, as the waiter came back with their burgers.

"Shit, I don't know. Not directly, no."

"What about his Head of Security, Samson Quinn?"

Pérez smeared ketchup all over his fries. "Maybe. Or the bastard hired someone. Who knows? After your girlfriend's call yesterday and what Officer Milano said after he'd been to the mansion, it's possible, yeah."

"Officer Milano?" Reid frowned. He didn't recognize the name.

"The rookie who went to check up on the mistress after Kenzie got the distress call," Pérez explained, slipping a fry into his mouth. "It came through to dispatch and Milano was closest, so they sent him round to do a drive by."

"I see." Reid picked up his burger but didn't take a bite. Kenzie's instincts had been right. She'd said they had to get over there ASAP, but he'd been in the hospital unable to leave.

Maybe if he had—He shook his head. No point in going down that road. There was enough to worry about without focusing on the things outside of his control.

"What did the officer say?"

"When he got there, a maid opened the door and showed him in. Del Gatto reassured him everything was normal. Miss Gomez wasn't there, and he hadn't seen her since the previous day. There were no signs of a struggle, so he left." Pérez shrugged. "What more could he have done? He didn't have a warrant to search the place."

Reid gave a somber nod. He knew the limitations of the job well.

"Why is that suspicious?" Reid asked.

"Because the victim's phone puts her at the mansion at five o'clock on Friday night. Time of death was between six and eight, but since Kenzie got to her house in Coconut Grove at about twenty past seven, we can narrow that down even more."

Reid frowned. "She was at Del Gatto's place two hours before she died?"

"Her phone was. Your Kenzie called her buddy, Sergeant Ortega, yesterday and asked for Officer Milano's number. She wanted to know if Samson Quinn had been at the house when he'd spoken to Del Gatto."

"What time did Officer Milano get to the mansion?" Reid wanted to know. He was surprised Kenzie had called Ortega after all this time. He'd worked with him at Miami PD and didn't like the guy, but he knew Kenzie had history with him.

"A little before seven."

"So Christina was dying when Officer Milano was at the Del Gatto house?"

"So it seems."

Reid was silent for a moment, thinking. Kenzie had been right to question whether Quinn had been at the Del Gatto mansion that evening.

"Did Officer Milano see Quinn at the house?"

Pérez shook his head. "No. He did not."

REID CHOSE QUINN FIRST. Del Gatto's Head of Security had waived his right to an attorney and came in on his own accord. That made things a lot easier. Reid thanked him for his cooperation and reiterated that he was not under arrest and that he was free to leave at any time. Then, he sat down opposite him at the steel table in the tiny interrogation room. Next door, he could hear a printer spitting out copies and there was a lingering smell of coffee in the air. The AC was still broken, which made it uncomfortable, but it wasn't hot enough to be unbearable. It wasn't ideal, but it would have to do.

Quinn didn't seem to mind the heat, the cramped space, or office noise. He sat comfortably in the chair, long legs out in front of him, arms crossed over his chest, waiting patiently for Reid to begin.

Reid went through the required protocol for the recording, then told him why he was here. "Mr. Quinn, we're questioning you in relation to the death of Miss Christina Gomez." The interview was being broadcast via a live feed to the police servers. Anyone with the appropriate clearance could watch.

"Mr. Quinn," Reid began, when all that was done. "When did you last see Christina Gomez?"

Del Gatto's head of security thought for a moment. "That would be Thursday morning at oh-eight-hundred hours."

Reid arched an eyebrow. "That's pretty specific."

"That's when she left the mansion."

"Does she always leave that early?"

"Yes, usually. Mrs. Del Gatto gets up at eight o'clock, so I make sure Miss Gomez leaves at that time."

"I see." It must be hard work juggling a wife and a mistress. Del Gatto obviously had Quinn making sure their paths never crossed. "That's part of your job, is it? To make sure the two women never meet?"

A shrug.

Reid moved on. "Did you see Miss Gomez out?"

A tight nod. "I let her out the side entrance, yes."

"Does Mrs. Del Gatto know about her husband's mistress?" Reid asked.

For the first time, Quinn hesitated.

"Does she?" he prompted.

"I don't know." He clenched his jaw. "She might."

Reid studied him across the desk. Concern flickered in his eyes, before the mask of control came down again.

"What do you think about Bethany Del Gatto?"

Quinn's forehead furrowed. "What do I think?"

"Yeah, do you like her?" Reid kept his tone casual, hoping to catch Quinn off guard.

"Everybody likes Mrs. Del Gatto. She's a warm, caring woman who does a lot for charity," he replied. "I have the greatest respect for her."

"Do you think she's capable of killing someone?"

His eyes darted to Reid's. "No, sir. I do not."

Reid parked that theory for now, although Quinn's response was interesting, and moved on. "What about the evening Miss Gomez called Kenzie Gilmore, asking for help?"

"I don't know about that," he replied smoothly.

Reid watched him closely. "That's strange, because she mentioned you by name. Said she'd found out something about you and was about to tell Kenzie what it was when she got disconnected."

Quinn kept his voice even. "Did she?"

Reid had to appreciate his coolness. Most men withered under his interrogation glare, but not Quinn. The man was as collected as if he were chatting to a friend at a sidewalk cafe. "Do you know anything about that?"

"Like I said, I haven't seen her since Thursday morning."

"What do you think she found out about you?"

"I don't know."

"Do you have secrets, Mr. Quinn?"

No reply. His eyes remained fixed on the wall behind Reid's head.

"Are you involved in any illegal activities?"

"No, I am not."

"What about diamond smuggling?"

"No, sir."

Reid didn't expect him to admit it, but it was worth gauging his reaction. Unfortunately, there wasn't one. Quinn must have ice running through his veins.

Reid masked a sigh. This was going nowhere. Still, he had to continue. It was important to get the questions down on record, so he could prove Quinn had lied if he was ever found guilty. "Did you over-hear Miss Gomez speaking to Kenzie Gilmore on the phone?"

"No."

"Did you escort Miss Gomez off the premises last night, take her back to her house, and kill her by slashing her wrists to make it look like suicide?"

"No." His voice remained lie-detector steady the entire time he was being questioned. This guy was used to high stress situations, or he'd been trained how to handle them. The military would do that to a certain extent, the special forces even more so. He made a mental note to dig deeper into the head of security's background.

"Are you sure? Because you weren't at the mansion when Officer Milano was there looking for Christina Gomez. Neither was she."

"What time was this?" He didn't miss a trick, either.

"Five thirty P.M. on Friday."

He broke into the tiniest of smiles. "I went for a run. I jog every evening if my schedule allows."

"Jogging?"

"Yes."

Reid narrowed his gaze. "Where'd you jog?"

"The boardwalk."

Great. Him and about a thousand other people. "Can anyone vouch for you?"

"The guards at the gate saw me leave."

They would follow up on that. Of course, anyone could be bought or persuaded to lie if it was in their own best interests. Still, there might be something on those fancy cameras Del Gatto had at the security gate. Strangely enough, he didn't have any in the grounds or the house, but he did at the gate. Maybe this was so his mistress could come and go undetected.

"Where does Miss Gomez park her car when she comes to visit?" Reid asked, a thought striking him.

"Huh?" The change in angle threw Quinn.

"Doesn't Mrs. Del Gatto notice her husband's mistress's car parked on the property?"

"No. Miss Gomez parks outside the estate. She uses the side gate to enter and exit the property." Reid guessed there were no surveillance cameras covering this side gate either, which meant Quinn could have left via the front gate, driven around to the side, parked his car, gone inside to collect Christina before taking her back to her house and killing her. No one would be the wiser. No one except Del Gatto, of course.

The only problem was there was no way to prove it.

DEL GATTO WAS LESS CONTROLLED, but he had his lawyer present, which counteracted that. They sat side by side in the interrogation room, the same tiny space where Reid had questioned Quinn only an hour earlier. Visibly upset by his mistress's death, he kept saying, "I don't understand why she'd take her own life."

"She didn't," Reid said, sliding into the chair opposite. It was even hotter now, and all three men were perspiring. Sometimes a broken AC came in handy, Reid thought slyly.

"What do you mean she didn't?" His dark eyes fixed on Reid.

"That's why you're here," Reid explained, glancing from Del Gatto to his lawyer. "We're questioning you in relation to Christina Gomez's murder." The coroner had finished the autopsy, and the results were in. There was no way Christina could have made the slashes on her right wrist. Not at that angle.

"Oh my God." Del Gatto ran a hand through his hair. Was it trembling? It was hard to tell. Maybe a little. Reid repeated that he wasn't under arrest and could leave at any time, but Del Gatto just waved his hand in the air. "Let's get this over with."

Reid nodded. "Do you know of anyone who would want to harm Miss Gomez?"

Del Gatto flinched. "Of course not."

Reid hesitated. "What about your wife?" It was an obvious question. Even though he didn't think Bethany Del Gatto capable of killing anyone, he had to cover all the bases. That look in Quinn's eye had worried him.

"Bethany? Are you crazy?" His lawyer put a warning hand on his forearm.

"I'm sorry, I have to ask."

Del Gatto looked appalled. "No, of course not. Bethany wouldn't hurt a soul."

"We are going to have to speak to her."

The lawyer nodded, but Del Gatto's voice dropped to a hiss. "You can't. She doesn't know about Christina."

"I'm afraid we have to, if only to rule her out."

He hung his head. "You're going to destroy her."

"I'm sorry, but she's a suspect in this case. One of our patrol officers is bringing her in as we speak."

Del Gatto paled. "Bethany has nothing to do with this, she's an angel."

Reid was confused. The way Del Gatto was speaking, anyone would think he loved his wife, and yet he was screwing around behind her back. He didn't get it.

"We'll be the judge of that."

"You're wasting your time, Lieutenant," Del Gatto growled. "Are we done here?"

Reid gave a smirk. "Not even remotely."

The billionaire sighed and leaned back in his chair.

Reid consulted the folder he had open in front of him. "When last did you see Christina Gomez?"

"Last week sometime. Thursday, I think. She left early in the morning, like she always does."

Reid glanced up. "Before your wife wakes up?"

Del Gatto shifted in his chair. "That's right."

"And you haven't seen her since then?"

The lawyer cut in. "He already told you he didn't."

Reid ignored him. "What about on Friday evening?"

"Lieutenant," the lawyer barked.

Del Gatto shook his head. "Are you suggesting I had something to do with her death?"

"I'm just trying to piece together her last movements. You see, she made a phone call that evening—from your house." The lawyer looked surprised.

Del Gatto frowned. "She couldn't have. She wasn't at my house."

"We have her cell phone data. It puts her location at your house at five o'clock."

Del Gatto thought for a moment, seemingly puzzled, then his brow lifted. "I think I can explain that."

"You can?" Reid sat back. He couldn't wait to hear this.

"Yeah. The housemaid found a cell phone in the kitchen yesterday morning. Could that be Christina's?"

"A phone? Your maid found a phone, and you didn't think to tell me?"

"I didn't know it was hers. It could have been anyone's. I have a lot of staff, plus we're having work done on the pool. People are traipsing in and out of the house all day long."

"Do you still have it?"

"It's in the house somewhere, yeah."

Reid nodded. If they could get the phone, they could check it for fingerprints. It wouldn't be hard evidence, but it would be something to go on.

"Why would Christina leave her phone at your house?" Reid rubbed his forehead. The phone had either been switched off after that or the battery had died. Either way, they hadn't been able to get a signal.

"I don't know. Maybe she dropped it."

Reid's eyes narrowed. "Or maybe she was making a hurried call to Kenzie Gilmore when somebody stopped her?"

"Kenzie Gilmore?" Del Gatto lost all his charm as his lips curled back in a snarl. "I wouldn't believe anything that bitch tells you. She's been gunning for me ever since Congressman Leonard and I sued her newspaper for libel a couple of years back."

Reid didn't appreciate his language, but he didn't show it. Fifteen years of being a cop had taught him how to conduct himself in interviews, and any rise out of him would be unprofessional. Besides, he knew the story. It had been before he'd met Kenzie, but the lawsuit had almost ended her career.

"As I said, we have her call records," he said coldly.

Again, his lawyer shot him a warning glance. Del Gatto shifted in his seat. "I think I'd like to go now."

"That's not a bad idea." The lawyer said, standing up.

"One last question," Reid said, before Del Gatto could get up. "Was Samson Quinn at your house on Friday evening when Officer Milano stopped by?"

"Officer Who?"

"The Miami PD officer who came by your house to check if there'd been a disturbance."

"Oh, him. No, Quinn wasn't there and, before you ask, I have no idea where he was. He doesn't work around the clock, you know."

Reid sighed.

So far, he had zilch. Maybe he'd have more luck with Mrs. Del Gatto.

CHAPTER 28

"Should you be here?" Keith asked as Kenzie as marched into the office with a face ready to do battle. "You can take a few extra days if you need them."

"I need to work," she muttered, going straight to her desk and dropping her backpack on the chair. "I know Del Gatto's responsible for this, and I'm going to find a way to prove it."

Keith's tone was gentle. "I know Christina Gomez was a source, but she agreed to spy on her boyfriend," he reminded her. "You didn't force her to do it."

"I lied and manipulated her," Kenzie retorted. "It's pretty much the same thing."

"Are the police sure it wasn't suicide?"

"A hundred percent. Her wrists were slashed to make it look like it, but the killer messed up. He cut her right wrist the wrong way. She'd never have managed that herself."

Keith patted her on the shoulder. "I'm sorry, Kenzie." he hesitated. "I lost a source once."

She glanced up, momentarily distracted by his words. "You did?"

"Yeah, in Iraq. I was posted there as a war correspondent, this is in the early days when I was still making a name for myself. I recruited a local woman. Soraya was her name. I befriended her, talked her into taking a risk, and the same thing happened."

"She got caught?" Kenzie whispered.

He gave a sad nod. "They found her body on a dusty street on the outskirts of Baghdad. She'd been stoned to death."

"I'm sorry," she murmured.

"It took me ages to get over it." His eyes stared through her into the past. "I blamed myself, of course, but in the end, it was just a shitty situation. She was mixed up with some bad people. Sure, I asked her to gather information for me, but I didn't kill her." He shook his head. "It's messed up, but that's just the way it goes sometimes. You can't control everything your source does."

Kenzie shook her head. She didn't want to hear that. Not now. Not when it was still so raw. Her anger—at herself and Del Gatto—helped drive her on. It gave her a reason to get out of bed in the morning. She wasn't going to just accept this and move on.

"Del Gatto and that creepy sidekick of his killed her, Keith. I know it."

Keith nodded. She knew he didn't expect her to give up. Not now.

"One final scoop for the paper?"

She gave a tearful nod. "Might as well go out in a blaze of glory."

KENZIE STUDIED THE INITIALS, or what she thought were initials, in the ledger entry: FM-100K and EJ-MF. A couple of ideas had sprung to mind, but she wanted to talk them through with Raoul to see if they made any sense.

As soon as he got in, she intercepted him. "So, I've been thinking, what sort of people do you need in a diamond smuggling operation?"

"Good morning, Kenzie," he muttered, scooting past her to get to his desk.

She followed, right on his tail. "You need a fence, right? Someone to sell the diamonds to a dealer."

"You need authentication certificates," Raoul interjected. "The diamonds would have to be laundered before they could be passed off as legitimate or ethically sourced. Any reputable or high-end retailer would demand proof of that."

"Who would take care of that?" She skirted around him as he took his laptop out of his bag and set it down on the desk.

"You'd need an appraiser, or a gemologist. I think that's the industry term. Someone who can assess the diamonds for cut, color, clarity, and carat—the four Cs. Then there are the watermarks, holograms, and even microprinting on some certificates, which requires advanced printing technology and expertise."

"You have been looking into this," Kenzie murmured.

"I've been looking into a lot of things," he said with a wry grin.

Kenzie wanted to ask what else he'd been working on but was too focused on the ledger to break her train of thought. "How much would a gemologist charge to forge the certificates?"

"Well, it would have to be worth their while. No genuine appraiser would risk their reputation by creating forged documents for an illegal shipment of blood diamonds otherwise."

"Say a hundred grand?" Kenzie raised her eyebrow at him.

He gave a thoughtful nod. "I'd say a hundred grand for 640.5 carats fits the bill."

"Okay, so FM could be our forger." She held the piece of paper up in front of him.

"It is possible," he agreed, sitting down. "Kenzie, do you mind if I get a cup of coffee before we go on?"

"Yes." She pointed to the second line. "EJ could be the fence in Miami. See, EJ in MF."

He sighed but didn't have to look at the entry. "EJ could be the fence, yes."

"But why isn't there an amount next to their name?" Kenzie asked.

"A fence, acting as an intermediary, may facilitate the sale of the diamonds for the smuggler, earning a commission in the process. This commission varies and is only paid upon the successful negotiation of a deal."

Kenzie narrowed her gaze. "So, I'm looking for an appraiser with the initials FM and a jewel fence with the initials EJ."

Raoul powered up his laptop. "Yes, now if you don't mind, I've got work to do."

Kenzie wandered back to her desk, deep in thought.

THE GEMOLOGICAL INSTITUTE OF AMERICA gave the names of registered appraisers. There were hundreds listed, but she couldn't find anyone with the initials FM. Never mind. There were other ways to broaden her search.

She delved into social media profiles, professional networking sites, and online forums where appraisers and gemologists interacted. It was a painstaking process, sifting through profiles, looking for any signs that might link them to the smuggling operation. No one jumped out at her, but she found several experts whose initials were FM.

Next, she researched local jewelry trade shows and gem cutting workshops. Scanning their websites for staff listings, she looked for names that might fit the FM alias. Again, there were a few, but no one with any unusual activity or connections that might be linked to a wider organization.

She also considered the possibility that FM might not be an individual's initials but part of a business name. She expanded her search to include business registries and trade directories, looking for any combination of words or names that could correspond to FM. Those names also went on her list.

By the time she'd finished, the office was empty. Even Keith had gone home and he was usually the last to leave.

Kenzie yawned. Every time she blinked she saw a sea of names and faces. How was she going to figure out which, if any, was involved in the smuggling operation?

She needed help. Who could she call who knew about the illicit deal making that went on in this city? One man sprung to mind.

Carlisle.

Kenzie gritted her teeth. She really didn't want to call Carlisle. Ever since New York, she'd steered clear of the enigmatic fixer. That little incident had pushed the limits of their professional relationship, but Carlisle had come through for her in the end.

Now, she needed his help again.

Would he even answer her call? He kept a notoriously low profile and, on paper, he didn't exist at all. He was a ghost. He wouldn't be able to do what he did otherwise.

Carlisle brokered multimillion dollar deals between businessmen, heads of state, gun runners, and other unsavory characters. He knew everybody's secrets, and therefore, he had to keep his identity secret, because the information he was privy to could quite easily get him killed.

Had she pushed it too far last time?

She sighed as she took out her phone. There was only one way to find out.

CHAPTER 29

Bethany Del Gatto was an elegant, soft-spoken woman in her late forties, although she had the slim physique of a much younger woman. Her bobbed hair was very blonde, almost platinum, but her pale coloring and the lack of regrowth made Reid suspect it was natural. She wore very little make-up other than a coral blush, mascara, and a pink gloss on her lips, but with her high cheekbones and clear blue eyes, she didn't need any more than that.

"Hello, Lieutenant," she said, as she slid into the seat opposite him in the interview room.

"Good evening, Mrs. Del Gatto. Thank you for coming in. I apologize for the late hour. We've been extremely busy."

"Bethany, please, and your officer didn't leave me with much of a choice." She gave a small smile. "I believe you want to question me about my husband's mistress?"

Reid blinked, surprised. It was then he noticed her eyes were almost the same color as the sapphires she wore in her ears. He couldn't help thinking they looked rather sad.

"You're shocked." She laughed softly. "Yes, I knew about Christina. A wife always knows when her husband is cheating."

Reid stared at her, momentarily thrown.

"I was sorry to hear she'd been murdered, though. I hope you don't think my husband or I had anything to do with it?"

It wasn't often Reid was left speechless. He took a moment to gather his thoughts. She'd thrown him with her directness. He was even more bamboozled by the fact she didn't seem that upset. Perhaps the separate rooms were her idea, not her husband's. Maybe the mistress was an act of desperation, rather than desire, on Del Gatto's part.

He cleared his throat. "That's what I'm trying to figure out. When last did you see Miss Gomez?"

Bethany's brow furrowed slightly. "Last week sometime. I think it was Thursday morning. I saw her leave the house around eight o'clock."

"Did you speak to her?"

"No, we've never spoken. My husband takes great pains to make sure we never meet. Luckily, the house is big enough that we never had to." She gave a sad smile. Not for the first time, Reid wondered why on earth Del Gatto was having an affair.

"So you didn't see her when she came back to the house the following evening?" he asked.

Her eyes widened. "I didn't know she had."

"Her cell phone puts her at your house at five o'clock on Friday afternoon."

"Really? Well, I wouldn't know, I was out all afternoon." Bethany gave a little shrug. "I do a beach yoga class most evenings, if I can."

"Beach yoga? Which beach would that be?"

"Miami Beach. It's every afternoon during the week. The only session I miss is a Monday, because that's when I go and visit my sister."

"Your sister?"

"She's at Weston Hospital. Cystic fibrosis. It's palliative care. There's nothing they can do."

"I'm sorry," Reid said, and meant it. That must be tough. It explained the sadness behind her eyes.

"I don't know if you know, but I'm a patron of a cystic fibrosis charity," she added, her blue eyes clouding a little. "We raise money for research and development. At the moment, we're funding a new range of antibiotics that might give Ellie and people like her a fighting chance." She shook her head. "But I don't think it'll be ready in time. Not for Ellie, anyway. There've been a lot of setbacks."

"I'm sorry," he said again. It was clear she was dedicated to her sister and finding a cure for her condition. He couldn't see her hurting anyone, let alone killing her husband's mistress. Still, he needed to get her alibi.

"Can anyone vouch for you at beach yoga?"

"Plenty of people. I can give you the instructor's number, if you like?"

"That would be helpful, thank you."

She nodded and took out her phone. He passed her a notepad, and she wrote the number down. "That's her cell. Her name is Zoe."

Vargas called Zoe who confirmed Bethany's alibi and Reid apologized for wasting her time and got an officer to give her a lift home.

"Boss, you're never going to believe this," Diaz said as Reid walked past her desk on his way out. He stopped, turned, and went back to her desk. He wasn't sure how much more he could handle today. His brain was spinning, and he just wanted to call Kenzie before it got too late to see how she was doing.

"I'm not?"

"Hector Esparza is actually Jean-Baptiste Michel. He was born in a small fishing village called Anse-d'Hainault in 1989, which makes him thirty-four years old. Not forty-seven."

"How do you know this?" He gazed over her head at the screen.

"I sent that photograph of Del Gatto's to the Haitian authorities. It seems Jean-Baptiste has quite the backstory."

"I'm listening."

"He has a juvenile record for drug dealing and gang violence," she began, pointing to the record that she'd opened on the screen. "Instead of serving time, he was given the option of joining the police force."

Reid cringed. Haiti had a long and tumultuous history of political instability and the security forces were not always regarded in a good light.

"Yeah," Diaz said without turning around. "He was an officer in the Police Nationale d'Haïti when the earthquake hit. That's the Haitian National Police to you and me."

Reid had read about the 2010 earthquake and its aftermath. While it wasn't a political event, it did lead to massive loss of life and widespread destruction. The wake of the earthquake saw a significant amount of political turmoil, including problems with the relief efforts, corruption, and the outbreak of cholera. "It must have been a tough time to be in the police force."

"That's all I've got from that source," she said. "However, the police and other security forces were blamed for several human rights violations in the aftermath of the earthquake, and he would have been actively involved in the earthquake response, including search and rescue operations. He would have witnessed a lot of violence."

"Or been part of it," Reid muttered grimly.

IT WAS LATE when Reid finally left the station, but not too late to call Kenzie. "How are you doing?" he asked when she picked up. "I've been worried about you."

"I'm okay." He could hear by her voice that she wasn't.

"If you want to talk about it," he began.

"Thanks, Reid, I appreciate the offer, but I don't think talking about it is going to do me any good. I need to move on."

"If you're sure."

"I'm sure." There was a pause. "Reid?"

"Yeah?"

"There is something I need to talk to you about, though, when you have time."

"Sure. I'd come over now, but it's late and I need a shower. I don't want to come near you in this state."

She made a soft snuffling sound. At least he'd made her smile.

"Okay, but can we talk tomorrow? It's important."

"Of course. Why don't you swing by the station in the morning and we can go get a coffee or something?"

"I'll do that."

"Night, Kenzie."

"Good night, Reid."

***

IT WAS two in the morning when Kenzie got a call back. The way it worked with Carlisle was she would call a burner phone number and leave a message. He would call her back if he was in the country and able to meet. The number changed all the time, and she never knew if she had the most recent one. That's how he operated.

"Good evening, Kenzie," came the clipped voice down the line. "I hope I didn't wake you."

"Of course not," she lied, sitting up in bed and turning on the light. "Thanks for calling me back. Can we meet?"

"Yes, let's. I've been meaning to call you."

"You have?" Now that was a surprise. Carlisle only ever called her when he needed some help with 'propaganda', as he put it. A well-placed article singing someone's praises or a damming line causing stock to plummet. It wasn't ethical, but compared to what he did for her...it was nothing.

"I read your recent article about the diamonds washing up on the shore. Very dramatic."

"It was. I was there, I found them." The follow-up to her initial article about the yachts destroyed in the hurricane had caused quite a stir.

"I know." There was a pause. "How does tomorrow morning suit you?"

"Fine. Where do—?"

"I'll see you then." The connection was lost.

Kenzie sighed. Carlisle never arranged a definite time or place. He'd find her, she knew that. She wouldn't have to do a thing.

CHAPTER 30

Vargas settled into a corner at a pop-up burrito spot in Little Haiti. The breakfast burritos were legendary, and he hadn't had one in far too long. Once upon a time, he'd been a regular around here, back when he'd dated a girl who lived in this neighborhood and he'd gotten to know it pretty well.

His contact, a woman whose teenage son he'd saved from a drug bust, had called only that morning to say she thought she knew where Hector was hiding out. While he ate, he waited for her to show up.

It was nearly time for him to leave when he spotted her crossing the road. Hard to miss in that vibrant, floral-patterned dress that fluttered about her as she walked. Her head was wrapped in a matching scarf, its ends trailing behind her. So much for incognito, but that was Madame Dubois, as she was called. He couldn't imagine her being anything other than her usual flamboyant self.

Luckily, he'd dressed the part. She couldn't be seen meeting a detective, so he wore a worn baseball cap, torn jeans, and a shirt with a splashy print design. Just another out of work migrant living in Little Haiti.

"William," she said in her broad Creole accent. "It's so good to see you. How is yuh Madda doin'?"

She pulled up a chair and sat down next to him. He couldn't help grinning at the elaborate display of affection. "She's fine, Auntie. She sends her love."

"Excellent." She drew out the word.

"Can I get you something?" He gestured to the food on display.

She shook her head and instead slid a tatty piece of paper across the table toward him. "Your boy is at this address—in the basement flat."

"Thank you, Auntie." He put the paper in his pocket. "Are you sure I can't get you anything? A burrito to go?"

"Oh, no." She got to her feet. "I must be off. Give your Mada my best."

"I will."

He watched as she walked away in the direction of the food market, her sandals clicking softly against the pavement.

THE OPPRESSIVE MORNING air was thick with the tension as Reid, Vargas, Diaz, assisted by the Miami PD tactical squad, gathered outside the nondescript basement flat. Reid had decided to act immediately, to give Hector as little chance as possible of getting away. The neighborhood was eerily quiet, as if it was holding its breath in anticipation of the drama about to unfold.

Reid surveyed his team, a silent nod was enough to convey his command. Each member, protected by ballistics vests, checked their gear one last time. Weapons at the ready, they ran across the street toward the property.

Reid, Vargas, and Diaz moved to the front, forming the initial breach team. The rest of the squad fanned out, securing a perimeter to ensure Hector had no escape route. Reid gave the signal to approach and, like shadows, they descended the stairs to the flat's entrance.

The breacher, a robust figure carrying the hydraulic buster, positioned himself by the door. On Reid's nod, the tool was activated, its forceful precision breaking through the lock without the chaos of a traditional ram. The door swung open, revealing the dark interior of the flat.

"Police! Hands where we can see them!" Reid's command was sharp, a clear warning to Hector. The team had been briefed on the importance of taking him alive. If they had any hope of finding out who was behind this, it would be through the *Jewel's* skipper. If he was acting alone, then they needed confirmation of that, too.

The team entered swiftly, splitting into two groups to clear each room. The interior was cramped, cluttered with fast food wrappers, makeshift bedding, a table littered with maps and various documents, all evidence of a fugitive's life.

As they approached the back of the flat, a noise—a slight rustle—halted their advance. Reid paused, signaling his team to prepare. With a coordinated movement, they breached the final room.

There, amidst a clutter of clothes and electronic equipment, was Hector. He was alone, caught in the act of packing, his escape plans laid bare around him. The surprise on his face was evident, the realization of his capture dawning as he saw the tactical squad fill the room.

Reid stepped forward, his voice calm but authoritative. "Hector Esparza, you are under arrest."

Hector immediately sprang into action. He twisted around and dove into what looked like a closet behind him, kicking the door shut. As he'd turned around, Reid had spotted a concealed weapon tucked in the back of his jeans. Reid heard a click as the door lock sprung into place.

Unwilling to wait, Reid aimed his service weapon at the lock and fired. The team advanced, with Reid kicking the flapping door wide open. What he'd thought was a closet was, in fact a bathroom, and worse, there was a narrow window above the toilet—and it was open.

Hector had somehow managed to climb through.

"He's outside!" Reid yelled into his radio to the tactical team that had formed a perimeter around the house. "Head's up, he's armed."

The rest of them were already charging for the door. As Reid stepped out into the sunshine, he heard a barrage of shots coming from the back of the house.

Sprinting in their direction, he saw one of the tactical team holding a gun and Hector lying on the ground.

His heart sank. He *needed* him alive.

Reid raced toward the groaning figure of Hector. He was rolling around, holding his stomach. A gut shot.

Shit.

"I aimed for his leg," the police shooter said. "He ducked, and I got him in the stomach."

"Is it bad?" Vargas asked, running up.

"Call for an ambulance," Reid barked, putting his hand over the hole in Hector's abdomen. Blood was running out onto the pavement, and the skipper's face was contorted with pain.

"Stay with me, Hector," Reid said, pushing down. His hands were slippery with blood. "Stay with me."

Hector stopped moving and closed his eyes. His arm fell back and Reid glimpsed the anchor tattoo on his tanned forearm. The guy clearly had a deep-set love for the sea, regardless of his background.

"We're losing him," Reid yelled, not sure what anyone there could do about it. Damn, they needed to keep him alive. Hector was the key to everything. The diamond smuggling, the double homicides, everything.

"Hector, look at me," Reid demanded, his voice edged with ice.

Hector's eyelids fluttered, like he wanted to open them, but couldn't. Where the hell was the ambulance?

"Come on!" Reid shouted. He could feel Hector's heartbeat fading, slower and slower, as the blood leaked out of him. "You are not going to die."

Finally, sirens could be heard coming up the street. The ambulance stopped right beside the body and the paramedics jumped out.

"Gunshot wound to the abdomen," Diaz told them as they rushed to give medical assistance. Reid stood back as one paramedic cleared the victim's airway while the other continued to apply pressure to the abdomen wound to stem the bleeding.

Please let him make it, Reid prayed.

An oxygen mask was put over Hector's mouth, so he got enough oxygen. It seemed to help his labored breathing. Next, an IV line was set up administering a steady flow of fluids to combat shock. Reid was impressed with the speed and efficiency with which they worked. If this didn't save him, nothing would.

"Is he going to live?" Reid asked, but he didn't get a reply. The two paramedics were focused on their patient, ensuring the bleeding had stopped and his vitals were stable.

In his peripheral vision, he saw Vargas talking to the tactical squad, who were packing up and getting back in their vehicles. The officer who'd shot Hector would have to turn in his gun and undergo an internal review for an officer-involved shooting. If Hector died, it would be more intense, but as far as he was concerned, the shooting was justified.

Hector had pulled a gun on him and even though he had not discharged it, the threat had been there. He'd been through several such reviews himself and they weren't fun, but nevertheless, they were an unfortunate part of the job.

"Let's get him ready for transport," the one paramedic said, and the other fetched the stretcher. Reid kept a close eye on Hector's vitals. They seemed stable.

Together, they lifted Hector onto the stretcher and secured him before they loaded him into the ambulance.

"How's it looking?" Diaz said, coming over.

Reid exhaled. "I hope he's going to make it."

CHAPTER 31

It didn't take Carlisle long to find her. Kenzie had gotten used to his methods over the years since he'd been one of her sources. The sleek, black Mercedes gliding up the street, the door opening, a strong hand grabbing her and pulling her in. It was all very secretive and under the radar.

This time was no different. She drove to work, parked in the underground parking lot in her designated spot, and had just locked her car when a sleek, black, SUV with heavily tinted windows glided to a halt behind her. The driver's window slid down and a man in a Hawaiian shirt said, "Get in."

Kenzie glanced around, but there was nobody in the parking garage. She was late, later than usual, so most people were already there. She pulled open the side door and the massive four by four swallowed her up.

"Hello, Kenzie." She turned and smiled at Carlisle. He hadn't changed from the last time she'd seen him in New York. Immaculately dressed, silver haired, cold blue eyes. "I take it you're well."

"Yes, thank you. You?"

He smiled. "Very. How do you feel about the newspaper restructuring?"

"You know about that? I didn't think it was public knowledge yet."

"Everything is public knowledge if you know where to look."

Of course. That was his business, the flow of information—the power of which couldn't be underestimated. After that debacle in New

York where Reid had been kidnapped and she'd had to ask Carlisle to help her get him back, Warner Sullivan, the President's son had been arrested for murder, bribery and corruption, and consequently, the President himself had announced he wasn't running for a second term in office. The political landscape had changed in a meticulously brokered nanosecond, all due to the flow of information.

"I'm devastated," she admitted, unable to keep the bitterness from her voice. "I'm being absorbed by the digital division. They've got a subscription service, it's going to take our readership online."

"Interesting," he mused. "I'm sure you'll do very well there."

She frowned. "I might not be of much use to you there. Digital doesn't have the gravitas that print does."

"You could always move. I'm sure many newspapers would be grateful to have you."

The thought had entered her mind, but she hadn't had the time to dwell on it. Not with everything that was going on.

"Maybe."

"Anyway, what can I do for you today?" The knowing look in his eyes told her he already had an inkling.

"The diamonds," she began. His lips curled back in a smile.

"Ah, yes. The seven million dollars in uncut blood diamonds. I heard they were recently liberated from the police laboratory."

"What?" she balked.

"Oh, didn't you know? I am surprised. You're slipping, my dear."

"They were stolen from the lab?" Reid hadn't said anything to her about it, but then, she'd barely seen him since...since Christina had been murdered. He'd called numerous times, she just hadn't felt up to it.

"Yes, Sunday night, if my sources are correct."

"I haven't read anything about that." She frowned.

"Press blackout, I believe." He chuckled. "And rightly so. It's embarrassing. Besides, the public would lose what little faith they have left in the police force."

Kenzie shook her head. "Do they know who stole them?"

"Not that I'm aware."

Then no, they didn't.

Kenzie gathered her thoughts. "Carlisle, I'm looking for the person involved in forging authenticity certificates for the diamonds, as well as a fence. I thought maybe you'd know, since you know about every underhanded deal that goes on in this city."

His eyes crinkled. "Careful, Kenzie, or I might take offense."

She waited.

"Why do you want to know?" he asked.

"Because I know Del Gatto is behind the diamond smuggling, with or without his mob connections. I know he ordered his henchman, Samson Quinn, to kill Christina Gomez and make it look like a suicide, and I want the world to know how corrupt he is."

A moment of silence passed where Carlisle studied her. "Del Gatto," he said eventually. "Didn't he sue the *Herald* for libel?"

"Yeah, him and Congressman Leonard. They're thick as thieves, those two."

"Stalwarts of Miami big business and local politics," he muttered. "It's going to be hard to bring them down."

"She was my source," Kenzie whispered. "It's my fault she's dead."

Carlisle nodded. A deep silence engulfed them. Kenzie knew he was debating whether or not to help her, so she didn't say anything.

"I think we can negotiate," he said quietly.

She glanced up, blinking. Carlisle didn't do emotion. Only cold, hard deals. "You do?"

"I'll see what I can find out for you and I daresay I'll be able to give you your forger and possibly your fence as well. The diamond industry in Miami is small, you just have to know the right people to ask." Which he did, of course. "But I'm going to need something in return, and you're not going to like it."

"What's that?" Kenzie narrowed her gaze.

"I need you to hold off on Del Gatto."

She frowned. "Why? He's the reason I'm doing this. He's why I'm here."

"I have a deal pending," he began, then paused. "I need to keep him in play for a little while longer. Once the deal is done, you can have at him."

"How long?" she whispered.

"A couple of months."

Kenzie bit her lip. What good was the forger or the fence if she couldn't take down the big dog?

"You'd bring down an international diamond smuggling operation," he pointed out, "and Christina's killer."

"But Quinn's not the man who gave the order."

"Not yet. But Del Gatto's not going anywhere."

Kenzie thought about this. It wasn't ideal, but something was better than nothing, and if she could gather the evidence she needed to link Del Gatto to the smuggling and the killing, she could sit on it for a while.

"The newspaper won't be around in a few months," she said, an edge to her voice.

He shrugged. "The *Herald* isn't the only way to publish information."

It was true. She could freelance, she could go and work for another newspaper, she could even put it on a podcast. The world was changing, and she had to change with it or she'd be left behind.

"Okay, you've got a deal," she said.

"Excellent." The back door whispered open. "Go well, Kenzie. I'll be in touch."

RAOUL INTERCEPTED her the moment she walked into the office. "Kenzie, holy smokes! Where have you been? I've been waiting for you."

"I was delayed." She flicked her hot hair off her neck. The meeting with Carlisle had irked her, but she had no choice but to live with it. The deal was done, and she had to honor it.

Raoul grabbed her arm and led her to his desk. "I've found something so bizarre I don't know what to make of it."

"Heavens, what is it?" Kenzie went with him, intrigued by his behavior. It wasn't often she saw Raoul so ruffled. "What have you found?"

"Sit down. You have to see this."

Grabbing a chair, she swiveled around to face him.

"Steel yourself, Kenzie, Alex is not who you think she is."

"Alex?" Kenzie stared at him. "What do you mean?"

"Remember you asked me to look into her background?" Raoul took a deep breath. "Well, this is Alexandra Delacroix." He pulled up a photograph of a teenage girl of about sixteen with dark hair and sad, sloping eyes.

"That's Alex?"

He nodded. "It wasn't easy finding this, I had to ask an old school-teacher in Orange County. She dug it out of the archives."

"Wow." Kenzie stared at the photograph. "That doesn't look anything like Alex."

"I know." He adjusted his glasses. "That's what I thought. So I looked at the college records. No photographs, but in 2010, there was an incident at UCLA where a girl committed suicide in one of the dorms."

"That was Alex's friend," Kenzie said suddenly. "She told me about that."

"This is the girl who died." Raoul pulled up a photograph taken by the coroner. A close up of a girl with pallid skin, tinged with gray, lying on a steel table. Kenzie immediately looked away. "Seriously, Raoul? That's a postmortem shot."

"I know. Look at it, Kenz, and tell me what you see."

Slowly, Kenzie turned back to study the photograph. Dark hair, narrow face, the same slanting eyes, albeit closed. Her hand flew to her mouth. "It's the same girl as in the other photo."

"Correct, which leads me to assume, the girl who committed suicide was in fact Alexandra Delacroix, and not—" He leaned in to read the name on another document. "Eleanor Johnson, as was printed on her death certificate."

Kenzie stared blankly at him. "I—I don't understand. Alex and this girl shared a dorm. That's Eleanor, not Alex."

"I was confused too," Raoul said, pulling up yet another document. "So I looked at the coroner's report. Guess who ID'd the body."

Kenzie went cold. "Alexandra Delacroix?"

CHAPTER 32

Kenzie gripped the table, her eyes still on Raoul's screen. "Let me get this straight. Alexandra died, but her roommate told the coroner it was Eleanor Johnson, then she assumed Alex's identity—or am I way off base here?"

"I think you might be right."

"How could she get away with that?" Kenzie whispered.

"It's not as hard as you think. School was over, most of the kids had already left campus. Nobody would have questioned Eleanor when she went to the morgue to ID the body. They just assumed she was telling the truth. I mean, people don't usually lie about something like that."

"No, they don't," Kenzie murmured. She turned back to the photograph of a young Alex. So sad. A troubled child, a suicidal teenager. Eleanor, a nobody who saw an opportunity to be someone.

"It's crazy, isn't it?" Raoul said.

Kenzie nodded. The more she thought about it, the more sense it made. "Eleanor moved to Miami, where no one knew who she really was. Both Alex's parents were dead, and she probably had Alex's driver's license and social security number, since she shared a dorm room with her."

"It's audacious," Raoul said, a tinge of admiration in his voice.

"Eleanor even looked the part, with those classic high cheekbones, full lips, and green eyes." Kenzie shook her head. "People will see what they want to see. Even I thought she looked like Vivien Swanson, Alex's famous movie-star grandmother."

Now he'd delivered his bombshell, Raoul sat back and studied her. "What are you going to do?"

"I don't know. I need a moment to process." She got up, feeling a little unsteady. "Think I need to take a walk."

What did it mean? Alex had lied to her, to everyone. Here she was, living in a fabulous skyrise bought with Calvin Delacroix's money, frequenting the most exclusive country club in Miami, and mixing with the rich and famous. She'd inherited Alex's father's estate, her mother's estate as well as the famous Vivienne Swanson's estate—all because her poor roommate, a sad, troubled girl, had committed suicide.

Raoul was right, it was audacious, but she'd gotten away with it. Nobody had even questioned the young college student with the Hollywood pedigree. It made sense that Eleanor Johnson, a nobody, had died, and Alex Delacroix, the glamor girl, had identified the body.

Wow. What a scam. Kenzie blew a hair out of her face. It was hot outside, but the sun seemed to burn through the fog in her mind and help her think clearer. That night in the mansion, what had Alex really been up to? She couldn't have stolen Bethany's necklace, she didn't have the equipment, unless she'd left it somewhere on the grounds. That was possible. Maybe she'd even gone back to collect it the next day.

She'd picked the lock on the study door, saving Kenzie, and even though Kenzie hadn't seen it at the time, she now thought Alex must have known about the side door. Maybe she'd cased the joint beforehand. After all, she was friends with the Del Gatto's. They moved in the same circles. That wasn't the first time she'd been to their house.

As Kenzie walked, the fog lifted even more.

Alex was a scam artist. She'd fooled everyone into thinking she was someone else—so why couldn't she be the Bling Bandit, too?

Kenzie shivered, despite the heat.

How much was Calvin Delacroix really worth? Before his death, she'd heard rumors he owed a lot of money. Alex may have needed to supplement her lifestyle and stealing jewels from the people she knew would help her do that. She had access to their homes, she knew their routines, she knew what pieces they owned. It was a perfect cover.

Kenzie stopped walking as a thought hit her. "Oh, my God," she whispered to no one in particular. Alex had even known that the diamonds had been taken to the lab for analysis. She'd told her herself. She'd willingly given up that information when Alex had asked.

Kenzie exhaled. Alex had played her, right from the start.

She thought about how she'd found Alex, washed up on the beach. There's no way she could have faked that, too. The near drowning had been real. The question that bothered her the most, though, was why had Alex been there in the first place?

Was the excuse she'd given nonsense? Kenzie was willing to bet Alex hadn't been washed off the rocks at a party. She'd been after the diamonds and been washed off *Jewel of the Seas* as it was smashed against the harbor wall. Somehow, Alex had known there were diamonds on board that yacht.

But how?

Had she overheard Del Gatto and Quinn talking, just like Christina had? Alex was clever, she'd outsmarted everyone. Except the hurricane had messed up her plans. She'd nearly died trying to get those diamonds off the boat, so when she'd found out they were at the lab, she'd jumped at the chance to grab them.

That must be it. Kenzie sat down on a bench, her heart pounding. It was a flamboyant, far-fetched theory, but it made sense. Suddenly, she knew what she had to do. She had to speak to Reid. Now.

Jumping up, she raced back to the office. Unfortunately, such was her haste that she didn't see the cyclist coming straight for her. The last thing Kenzie remembered before falling to the ground was a hard object hitting her in the back of the head.

Then nothing.

CHAPTER 33

"Can I see the gun?" Reid asked the Miami PD tactical team leader before they left the scene.

Hector's gun had already been bagged, but he pulled it out to show Reid. "Colt M1911. Great stopping power. Very effective in close combat situations. Don't see many like that on the street."

He wasn't telling Reid anything he didn't already know. Reid, who was wearing gloves, took the weapon and studied it. Same make. Same model. This could well be the gun that killed Pedro. He inspected the magazine.

"Six in the magazine and one in the hole," the squad leader said. ".45 ACP cartridge."

One shot fired.

One casing found outside Pedro's apartment.

"Did he take a shot at your officer?" Reid asked.

"No, Lieutenant. He did not. This weapon hasn't been fired recently."

Reid nodded. Hector'd had the opportunity to fire but hadn't taken it. Was that because he hadn't had time to get off the shot or he hadn't wanted to shoot a fellow cop?

Then again, he hadn't hesitated when Diaz had come out of the bar the other day. He pursed his lips, thinking. That shot had gone high, a fairly rookie mistake for someone of Hector's skillset, which begged the question: What if it hadn't been a mistake? Maybe he'd intentionally aimed high so as not to kill Diaz.

Reid grunted. Maybe he was reading too much into this.

"Okay, thanks." He handed the Colt back to the squad leader. "Can we get copied in on the ballistics report? I want to know if that gun's been fired and when?"

"Sure, thing, Lieutenant."

They shook hands and the squad leader rebagged the weapon and returned to his vehicle. As they drove away, Vargas came up to him. "Is it the same gun?"

"Sure looks like it."

"That confirms Hector's our shooter."

"He appears to be, yeah."

Vargas nodded. "Probably killed Vince van Staden, too."

Reid hesitated. "Probably."

Vargas gave him a funny look. "Everything okay, boss?"

"I'm not sure." He shook his head. "Something doesn't add up, but I can't put my finger on it."

"Oh?"

"Why didn't Hector take the shot? If he'd fired, he could have stopped that officer in his tracks and gotten away."

"Poor reflexes?" Vargas said.

"He was the skipper of a million-dollar boat, and I fought with him. I don't think he has slow reflexes."

Vargas frowned. "You think he held back on purpose?"

"I don't know. Let's see what ballistics comes back with. If this is the same gun that killed Pedro and with the boots with Vince's blood on them, we've got enough to charge him. He'll go away for a long time."

BACK AT THE STATION, Reid was settling down to write his report on the morning's activities when a call came in from Dispatch. Apparently, a body had been discovered in the rubble of a collapsed building that went down during the hurricane, and Miami PD had diverted the call to his department.

"Why'd they do that?" he asked Monroe.

"Because the ID on the victim says his name is Carl Ramos. When they entered his name, they found an open casefile with your name on it."

"Carl Ramos. That's the navigator on *Jewel of the Seas*," Diaz said, looking up. "Another crew member."

"He's dead too?" Vargas swung his chair around to face Reid. "That's three of them down."

"And Hector's in hospital in a coma," Reid said, grabbing his keys. "Let's go take a look. Is the CSI team there?"

"Yeah, they've been there for some time."

"We'd better get a move on, then. Tell them we're on our way."

REID STEPPED out of his car onto the gravel beside the dilapidated building and looked at the splintered mess of wood and glass. The roof, torn away and in pieces, lay precariously to one side. Miraculously, the front wall was still standing, but in place of the door was a gaping hole, and the windows were hollow voids, the glass shattered, allowing the elements to wreak havoc on the inside.

"Matteo did a number on this place," Vargas muttered as they pulled on their forensic gloves and crunched up to where several workmen, their faces pinched, stood behind a bright yellow tape flapping in the breeze. They were watching a white-clad crime scene officer and a pathologist work the scene. One was taking photographs while the other was on his hands and knees next to the body.

Reid ducked under the flap and stepped over debris strewn about by the storm before greeting the two crime scene investigators. "Lieutenant Garrett, Sweetwater PD." They glanced up, nodded, and the one on his knees stood up and shook Reid's hand.

"Hello, Lieutenant." Reid recognized him. They'd met before at some other crime scene, another time, somewhere else in the city.

Vargas went over to talk to the workmen and get their statements. A heavy, uprooted tree lay beside the structure, its broken branches intermingling with the fragments of the building frame. It looked like that could've been the reason for the collapse.

"IS THAT CARL RAMOS?" Reid nodded to the body, covered in rubble. The man lay in the fetal position, his hands over his head as if sheltering from flying debris of the collapse of the roof. Covered in layers of dust, it was hard to see what he looked like, or how long he'd been lying there.

"That's what his ID says." The pathologist nodded to a fold—up wallet on the ground next to the body.

"May I?" The pathologist nodded, and Reid opened the wallet. Inside was a Mexican driver's license and a crew card for the *Jewel*, like the one Vargas had found at Vince's house.

"Yep, that's our guy." Reid handed the wallet back. "Any idea how he died?"

The pathologist pointed to the victim's shoulder. "Well, right off the bat, I can tell you he's been shot. That's a gunshot wound, right there. What I can't tell you is whether it killed him." He glanced around the derelict structure. "He's covered in bumps and bruises. They were all obtained antemortem. I'd say he was still alive when this place came down on top of him, but I'll know more after the autopsy."

Reid grimaced. "So he's been here since the storm?"

"Judging by the state of decomp and the condition of the body, I'd say so, yeah."

"What was he doing here?" Reid murmured as Vargas came over to join him. This was a largely underdeveloped parcel of land adjacent to Matheson Hammock Park, south of downtown Miami. The park itself was coastal, facing Biscayne Bay, which put it directly in the path of the storm. The dense mangrove forests that surrounded the park meant it was pretty secluded, despite being in the Miami metropolitan area.

"This was an old boathouse at one point," Vargas said, relaying what the workmen had told him. "It was used by fishermen in the bay area, but it had fallen into ruin and been abandoned a long time ago."

"What are they doing here, then?" Reid nodded to the workmen.

"Clean up mission. The city is trying to remove unsafe structures as a result of the storm." Reid nodded. They moved away from the body to let the pathologist and crime scene investigator finish up.

He looked at Vargas. "Okay, so Carl Ramos has an altercation with the shooter. He runs into the park, hoping to hide, but gets shot. The storm is about to make landfall, so like Vince, he looks for a place to shelter. He comes in here, but the damn building collapses on top of him, trapping him and leaving him to bleed out. How does that sound?"

"Sounds plausible, but why were they here to begin with?"

"There's a marina on the other side of the park," Reid said. "Maybe they were there."

"It's not where the *Jewel* was moored," Vargas pointed out.

"I know, but there aren't any vehicles abandoned around here and he didn't live around here, so that's the only possibility." He went back to the pathologist and asked to see the wallet again. Taking out the crew card, he took a photograph with his phone camera. Thanking him, Reid returned to Vargas. "Okay, let's go see if anyone at the marina recognizes him. Maybe they can tell us who he was with."

"It's a long shot," Vargas muttered, falling into step beside him.

"Yeah, but it's the only shot we've got."

CHAPTER 34

The Matheson Hammock Marina shimmered like a sapphire under the bright Florida sun. Serenely idyllic, it was lined with an array of boats ranging from sleek sailboats to luxurious yachts, each bobbing gently in their slips, waiting to set sail on the open sea or explore the winding mangrove channels nearby.

"You speak to the dockmaster," Reid said, "while I try to find the manager."

Vargas nodded and headed off in the direction of the harbor master's building, a sturdy structure on stilts that extended over the water. It stretched at least three floors up, giving it an expansive view of the marina and all the vessels in it.

Reid entered the main building, set adjacent to the entrance to the marina. It took him five minutes to find the administrative offices and speak to someone who could direct him to the appropriate person.

"Mr. Higham is in the office at the end of the hall," a woman said, nodding in the direction he'd come.

Reid showed her the photograph on his phone of Carl Ramos's crew card. "Do you recognize this man?"

She looked at it and shook her head. "No, I don't think so. Is he a member?"

"I doubt it." Reid followed her directions down the hallway to Mr. Higham's office. He knocked and heard a high-pitched voice call, "Come in."

Reid pushed open the door. "Mr. Higham?"

"Yes, can I help you?" A diminutive man with soft, effeminate features looked up from his desk. His appearance matched his voice.

"Lieutenant Garrett from Sweetwater PD." He held up his badge. "I'm looking for this man. I was wondering if you'd seen him around here. He's probably not a member, more of a social visitor." He approached the desk and held out his phone.

Higham stared at it for a while, then blinked. "I don't think so. I'd know him if he had a boat moored here, but if he's a social member or just frequents the clubhouse, I wouldn't know him." He thought for a moment. "You could ask Stephanie who runs the bar in the clubhouse. She's more likely to recognize him if he's been here."

Reid nodded. "Thank you. Where would I find Stephanie?"

He checked his watch. "She should be on duty now. The clubhouse is the next building over. You can't miss it, really."

Reid strode next door to the clubhouse. Higham was right, it had a large outdoor deck area overlooking the marina, umbrellas flapped softly in the light breeze and he could smell the briny scent of salt coming off the water.

As he walked in, he saw a blonde woman in her early thirties standing at the cash machine behind the bar. "Stephanie?"

She looked up. "Yeah? Can I help you?"

"Mr. Higham said I'd find you here. Lieutenant Garrett from Sweetwater PD. I'm looking for this man, do you know him?" He held the phone up. She took a long, hard look at it, then nodded. "That's Carl. Carl Ramos. He comes in here from time to time. Crews on the *Jewel*, I think, or he did." It seemed everyone had heard of the tragic fate of the *Jewel*.

Reid took a sharp breath. He hadn't really expected anyone to recognize Carl. His phone chose that moment to buzz in his pocket, but he ignored it. "When was the last time you saw him?"

She frowned. "Why? Has something happened?"

"If you could just answer the question, please, ma'am."

She thought for a moment. "It was a while back. I think it was the night before the storm hit."

"Are you sure?"

"Yeah, I remember now. He came in soaking wet and stayed till he dried out. The weather was already turning bad. We closed early on account of it. That's the last time I saw Carl. He hasn't been in since."

Because he'd been lying under a ton of rubble in the old fisherman's shack.

"Was he with anyone?" Reid asked.

"Well, he knows a couple of people around here," she said. "I saw him arguing with a big guy before he left, though. Looked like a body-builder, you know the type?"

Hector.

Reid pulled out his phone. "This the guy?"

She shook her head. "No, that's not him. That's Hector, he captained the *Jewel*. Carl and Hector are good buddies. Haven't seen either of them for a while."

Reid scratched his head. "Could you describe the man you saw Carl arguing with the night before the storm?"

She half-closed her eyes, trying to recall. "Five eleven, heavy set, big muscles, good looking in a hard kinda way, you know?"

"Hair?" Reid asked.

"Blondish. Had a scar above his right eye."

Reid's expression turned grim. "Thank you, Stephanie."

He thought he knew who Carl Ramos had met at the bar, and who he'd run from.

Back in the bright sunlight, Reid beckoned to Vargas, who had just appeared from behind a row of boats with his phone in his hand.

"Let's go. I think I know who killed Carl Ramos, and possibly the others."

Vargas dropped his arm.

"What?" Reid could see by his face that something had happened.

"It's Kenzie," Vargas said. "She's been hit by a cyclist. They've taken her to Jackson Memorial Hospital."

CHAPTER 35

A cyclist? Reid couldn't get his head around that.

Where? How?

Vargas didn't know any more and, neither did Dispatch, only that she was unconscious when the paramedics found her, so he put his foot down and blued and twoed it across town to the hospital.

"Kenzie Gilmore?" he called to the ER staff as he ran in. Vargas had dropped him at the entrance and was going back to the station to organize a warrant for Samson Quinn's arrest.

Suddenly, none of that mattered now. All he could think about was what condition Kenzie was in and whether she was going to be okay.

"She's still with the doctor," the nurse said. "Take a seat."

Reid didn't stop. "Which room?"

"Sir, you can't go in—"

He flashed his badge. "Which room!"

"1E, down the hall."

Blood pumping in his ears, Reid strode down the hall and plucked back the curtain that guarded the entrance to assessment cubical 1E.

Kenzie lay on the assessment table, an IV in her arm. He couldn't see her face because the doctor was leaning over her inspecting a wound on the side of her head.

"Kenzie?" he said. The doctor looked up. "Who are you? No one is allowed in here."

"Lieutenant Garrett from Sweetwater PD," he said. "I'm also her partner." Saying the words out loud made them seem even more real. "Is she going to be okay?"

The doctor's gaze flitted over the badge, then he turned back to his patient. "She's had a nasty knock on the head and a concussion, but I think she's going to be okay."

Reid felt so weak with relief, he had to sit down.

"Reid, is that you?" Kenzie's voice, a soft whisper.

"Yeah, it's me. I'm here." The doctor didn't say anything as Reid plonked himself in the chair beside Kenzie. She had her eyes closed, and was so pale, she was almost the same color as the beige wall behind her.

"We need to take her to X-ray to make sure she doesn't have a skull fracture or intracranial hemorrhages," he said grimly. "That baseball bat left quite a bump."

Kenzie groaned softly.

"Baseball bat?" Reid sat up. "I thought she was hit by a cyclist."

"She was attacked," the doctor said, turning to face Reid. "Whoever was on that bicycle took a swing at her and connected with her head. This wasn't an accident."

An icy chill slithered down his back.

Kenzie attacked?

"How'd you know it was a baseball bat?" he asked, frowning. Samson Quinn's name sprung to mind, as did Del Gatto's. Christina Gomez had been on the phone to Kenzie when the call had dropped. Two hours later, she was dead.

Were they coming after Kenzie now? Had she found out something damning about Del Gatto? Had she stirred up the hornet's nest?

"I've seen enough baseball bat assaults to know what they look like," he said flatly.

Kenzie stretched out her hand. He took it. "It's okay," he murmured. "I'm here now. It's going to be okay."

"Let's get her up to x-ray," the doctor said as a nurse came in. "Lieutenant, you can wait in the radiology waiting room, if you wish."

"I do wish," he said, standing up so they could wheel her out. As he followed her down the corridor to the radiology department, he was hit by a surge of fury so strong, it made every muscle in his body tremble. Whoever had done this to Kenzie was going to pay. He'd make sure of it.

V ARGAS AND D IAZ, accompanied by Hamilton and a young female officer called Martinez, drove up the gates of Del Gatto's property. Vargas handed the warrants to the guards and demanded to be let through. No pretending to be nice now.

The gates opened and the two police vehicles growled through, clawing their way up the path to the mansion. Samson Quinn, accompanied by Del Gatto, met them outside.

"What is this about?" Del Gatto bellowed.

"We have an arrest warrant for Samson Quinn." Vargas nodded to the two officers who approached Quinn and put him in cuffs. "And a search warrant for these premises."

"What are you arresting him for?" Del Gatto demanded as Vargas handed him the paperwork.

"For the murder of Carl Ramos," Vargas snapped. Reid had just been on the phone and told him about the attack on Kenzie. Even though the arrest warrant wasn't for the assault on her, Reid had asked him to keep an eye out for a baseball bat or a bicycle.

"Carl Ramos? Who's that?"

"The first mate on your former yacht," Vargas told him. "We found his body today in Matheson Hammock Park. He'd been shot."

"Jes—" Del Gatto raked a hand through his hair and turned to Quinn. "What the hell is going on?"

"I don't know, sir," Quinn said quietly as they loaded him into the squad car. As cool as ever, he wasn't resisting arrest. That wasn't his style. Vargas was beginning to think he was a bona fide psychopath.

"Don't say anything until my lawyer gets there," Del Gatto snapped.

Quinn nodded, before the door slammed shut and Hamilton and Martinez drove off with the suspect. Reid had been clear, keep him in lock up until he could get there to interview him.

Now for the search warrant.

"Sir, we're going to come in and search the premises."

Del Gatto stood back as his wife, Bethany, appeared on the steps in a yoga outfit, a roll-up mat under her arm. "What on earth is going on, Salvo?"

"These men are searching the house," he said bitterly. "I don't know what they're looking for."

"If you could stand back, ma'am," Vargas said, as the uniformed police officers filed past her in the house. She mouthed like a guppy but didn't try to stop them.

They spread out, but it was a big house and would take some time. They'd been briefed on what to look for. A weapon, a Colt M1911, any .45 caliber bullets, diamonds, a bicycle or a baseball bat. It was quite the shopping list.

Personally, Vargas felt the gun was a waste of time. The ballistics report from the Colt that Hector had hadn't come back yet, but when it did, Vargas was sure it would show that it was the gun that had killed Pedro and Carl Ramos. Still, Reid wanted to cover all the bases.

Vargas kept watch on Del Gatto as the officers searched. Bethany Del Gatto had got into her car and eased down the drive saying she didn't want to miss beach yoga. She obviously wasn't too concerned with what they'd find in the house.

Four hours later, Vargas was close to calling it a day. They hadn't found jack shit, and it was getting dark, and he was getting hungry. That's when he got a call from Reid, adding an item to the list of things they were searching for.

A ledger.

CHAPTER 36

Kenzie's head was throbbing, a relentless pain that seemed to dance behind her eyelids with every heartbeat. It was worse than any headache she'd ever had before, it was more like a herd of elephants trampling through her brain. The hospital room's sterile scent, a mix of antiseptics and muted despair, did little to soothe her discomfort. It was so bad, she could hardly think straight, and now Reid was shouting at her too. She closed her eyes momentarily, trying to block out the harsh fluorescent light.

"Are you okay?" he asked, his tone shifting from frustration to concern, his voice a soft echo in the cold room.

"Please don't shout," she whispered. They were in a hospital ward where she was being kept for observation, just until her x-rays came back. The beeping of nearby medical equipment was a constant reminder of her vulnerability. As soon as the doctor gave her the all-clear, she could go home to the comfort of her own bed, away from here.

"I'm trying not to." He lowered his voice, his frustration palpable. "But why didn't you tell me any of this before?"

"I was afraid you'd be upset with me." She gave a wry snort. "Turns out I was right." Inside, she was wrestling with a tangle of regrets. Of course, she should have told him sooner. It was foolish not to.

He shook his head, disbelief etched in the lines of his face. "Let me get this straight. When you were snooping around Del Gatto's study, you found this ledger that I've now asked Vargas to find?" In his eyes, a storm was brewing—a mix of incredulity and dawning realization. "In it were a bunch of coded entries that you and Raoul have related back to the diamond smuggling operation?"

She gave a feeble nod, the weight of the room pressing against her, or maybe that was guilt.

"In what way does it prove Del Gatto's involved?" Reid asked, his voice a steady current in the sea of her turmoil.

"It specifies dates of transport, number of carats, grading of the diamonds, and some other pieces of code that I'm still trying to figure out."

"Well, I'll be—" His gaze pierced through her like a searchlight in the darkness. "All this time we've been looking for information on Del Gatto and you've been sitting on it."

"I didn't know what it meant until the other day," she insisted, her words tainted with desperation. "Besides, I took the photograph illegally and without consent. It's never going to stand up in court. You can't use it."

"No, but I can use the original ledger."

She nodded, a fragile hope blossoming within her. That's why she'd told him now. It had been Raoul's suggestion all along. Her only concern was Carlisle. She'd promised him not to expose Del Gatto until he gave her the go-ahead. Still, that didn't mean she could control Reid and what they did. Who's to say Reid wouldn't have come across this information on his own accord? Carlisle would never know she'd told him. The police were conducting a search on the premises as they spoke. That was in play long before she'd mentioned the ledger.

"There's more," she added weakly.

His eyes widened. "More?"

"Yeah, lots more." She braced herself, feeling as though she were about to step off a cliff into the unknown.

"Is this why you were attacked?" The incredulity had given way to concern.

"No, I don't think the attack had anything to do with this." Alex had no idea Kenzie knew who she really was, not yet.

"Okay, shoot."

Kenzie took a slow, deep breath, the air cool and sterile in her lungs. "It's about Alex. Alex Delacroix."

"Your friend." Reid fixed his eyes on her. "What about her?"

"She's not really Alexandra Delacroix." The words hung in the air between them, heavy with implication.

"What?" Reid blinked several times as what she'd said sunk in. "Then who is she?"

The words tumbled out of her. "She's actually Eleanor Johnson. Eleanor was friendly with Alexandra Delacroix at college, they shared a dorm, but when Alexandra took her own life, Eleanor stole her identity."

It was very rare that Kenzie got to see Reid speechless, but this was one of those times. He shook his head, scratched his stubbly jaw, then said, "Run that by me again."

Kenzie told him the story, bit by bit, including the part where Eleanor had falsely ID'd Alexandra's body at the morgue. "That's screwed up," Reid muttered when she was done.

"Clever though," Kenzie said. "You see, nobody in Florida knew any different. They just assumed she was Alex Delacroix, because she said she was."

"Ballsy," Reid acknowledged. "She's been living a lie this whole time?"

"Yeah, since 2010."

"That's fourteen years," Reid murmured.

Kenzie nodded. "She inherited the Delacroix legacy, including the three estates, that of Alex's mother, father, and grandmother, the movie star."

Reid just shook his head, stunned by her revelation. "Does Alex know that you know?"

"Not yet, I'd just found out when I got attacked."

"You don't think—?" Reid started, his question hanging in the air.

Kenzie shook her head. "Alex doesn't know. Trust me, this was not her."

Reid pulled out his phone, a decisive gesture. "We're going to have to bring her in, you know that?"

Kenzie nodded, a sense of inevitability settling over her. "Before you do, there's something else you should know."

"I don't think I can handle any more surprises." He shot her a nervous smile.

She gave a soft chuckle. "It's just a suspicion. I don't have anything concrete."

"I'm listening."

"When I was locked in the study, Alex got me out."

"Yeah, you said."

"Reid, she picked the lock with a bobby pin."

His eyes narrowed ever so slightly, the shadows beneath them deepening. "So, she knows how to pick a lock? Why is that significant?"

"Well, it's not something everybody knows how to do," Kenzie said, biting her lip. "Besides, she said she just happened to be walking past, but I don't buy that."

"You don't?" He frowned, unsure of where this was going. Maybe she wasn't being clear enough. The concussion had fuddled her brain.

"I think she may have stolen Bethany's necklace." She lowered her voice. "Reid, I think Alex might be the Bling Bandit."

CHAPTER 37

Reid left Kenzie to grab a coffee and call Vargas. His head was still swimming with everything she'd told him. At least he'd managed to pass on the instruction to look for the ledger to Vargas before they'd ended the search. He had no idea if they'd found it yet.

Her revelation about Alex was astounding. All that stuff about her being Eleanor Johnson and assuming Alexandra Delacroix's identity. That would take some substantiating, but now they knew where to look. Kenzie had said she'd speak to Raoul and get him to pass on who he'd spoken to and his sources for getting the information.

He'd get the team on it first thing. Once they had enough evidence, they'd bring her in. A search warrant wouldn't go amiss either. If she was the Bling Bandit, which he still wasn't sure about, then she might have the stolen emeralds at her house or in a safety deposit box.

Could she have broken into the lab and stolen the diamonds, too?

He massaged his temples. It was all too much. First Hector's shooting and now this.

Hector. Wasn't he in Jackson Memorial, too?

Frowning, Reid went down to reception and asked the woman behind the desk. She had two phones to her ears and was scribbling something on a notepad, but she nodded and held up a finger. Wait.

He did, and eventually, she hung up one of the phones, put the other on hold and set down her pen. "Hector Esparza, did you say?"

"Yeah, that's him."

She looked it up on the computer. "Room 402, that's on the fourth floor."

He thanked her and went to find an elevator. The fourth floor was laid out in a similar fashion to Kenzie's, but he had to show his ID before he could get past the nurse's station. He was pleased about that. It meant people couldn't just wander in without a reason.

"How's he doing?" Reid asked the on-duty nurse.

"He was in a bad way when he came in," she told him. "He'd lost a lot of blood and subsequently went into cardiac arrest, but we managed to stabilize him. He's now in an induced coma to allow him to get over the trauma."

Reid nodded. "Any idea how long he'll be in a coma?"

"Depends." She shrugged. "It's the doctor's call."

"Okay, thanks. Will you let me know when he wakes up?" He gave her his card. She glanced at it, nodded, and flashed a tired smile.

He thanked her again and went back downstairs to call Vargas.

"WE COULDN'T FIND THE LEDGER," were the first words out of Vargas's mouth. "It wasn't there. We found the hole behind the painting, but it only contained a few documents and some cash."

Reid clenched his jaw. "Bastard must have moved it before you arrived."

"Makes sense, especially if he had something to hide."

"Any sign of a baseball bat or a bicycle?"

"There was a baseball bat in a cabinet, but it was signed by Derek Jeter and hadn't been used. We brought it with us anyway. No bicycle anywhere on the property, unless you count the indoor bike in the home gym."

Reid sighed. "What about Quinn? He come quietly?"

"Yep, just like you said he would. I've put him in the holding cell until you get back. Del Gatto called his lawyer, though. He'll be here soon."

"I'll be back soon." He stifled a yawn.

"How's Kenzie?" Vargas asked.

"She's okay. Her scans will be back soon, then, hopefully, they'll let her go home. She's groggy and concussed, but she's talking. I think she'll be fine."

"That's great news."

"Hey Vargas, she told me some stuff about her friend, Alex Delacroix.

Could you call Kenzie's research assistant at the *Herald*, Raoul—I can't remember his last name—and get him to come in first thing tomorrow and give a statement?"

"Sure. What's this about?"

"Kenzie thinks Alex might be the Bling Bandit."

"Crap, really?"

Reid couldn't help a weary grin at his colleagues' incredulity. "Maybe. Can you check if she's on that list of friends and family of the victims that you put together?"

"She was, boss."

His eyebrows shot up. "She was? You're sure?"

"One hundred percent. I checked the list myself only this morning. Alex Delacroix and Bethany Del Gatto are the only two that know all the other victims and we know it can't be Mrs. Del Gatto, since it was her emeralds that were stolen."

The night of the party, Reid thought. Alex happened to be wandering past the study in which Kenzie was locked.

Finally, it was all adding up.

———

KENZIE CLOSED her eyes and let the waves of nausea wash over her. This was normal, she was assured, but if it got worse or she started vomiting, then that was cause for concern. She was lucky she had a very hard head.

The doctor had told her to try and stay awake, so she went through everything she'd discovered so far in her head, hoping it would stave off the grogginess that kept threatening to engulf her.

She was losing the battle when she heard the door to the ward open. There were three other patients in this ward, all awaiting results of some form or another. Waiting to see whether they could go home or whether they'd be admitted for further treatment. Kenzie was praying her scans were clear.

A voice she didn't recognize said, "Kenzie Gilmore?"

Opening them, she looked into the face of a man she didn't recognize. He was casually dressed in jeans and a T-shirt, his hair a nondescript brown and he wore dark glasses. Her pulse ratcheted up several notches. Was this the guy who'd hit her with the baseball bat? Had he come back to finish the job?

She reached for the orange button to sound the alarm when he leaned forward and handed her something. The cry died in her throat. "What's this?" she croaked.

"A message from Carlisle. He says to get better soon."

Carlisle.

Her eyes shuttered closed. Thank God. This wasn't an assassin coming to murder her in her hospital bed. When she opened them again, the man was gone, and she was left holding a small, folded piece of paper.

She hadn't even had time to read it when the doctor came in. "Good news," he beamed. "Your scans don't show any sign of bleeding. There is some indication of contrecoup swelling, however it's minor and should resolve in a few days."

"Oh, that's great. Does that mean I can go home?"

"We'd like to keep you overnight, just to be safe. You've had a severe head trauma. I feel sending you home now would be remiss."

Her heart sank, but another wave of nausea hit her, so she nodded and lay back and closed her eyes.

"I'll tell the nurse to admit you and you'll be taken to another ward. I've let your partner know, he's waiting outside."

"Can you send him in?" she asked, trying to hold back the tears.

"Of course. I'll be around to check on you later."

"I think you should stay here tonight," Reid said to Kenzie's surprise. "It's the best place for you."

"Might I remind you how adamant you were to leave after your stab wound," she said.

He had the grace to look embarrassed. "That was different. It was a flesh wound, not a head wound. Head wounds are serious. Someone bashed you with a freaking baseball bat, Kenz. That's no joke."

"Okay, I'll stay." She hadn't really contemplated leaving. It still hurt to lift her head off the pillow. She didn't mention the visit she'd had or Carlisle's note that was cradled in the palm of her hand. Surreptitiously, she slid it under the blankets. Reid didn't notice.

"How'd it go at Del Gatto's place?" she asked, as Reid sat down beside her and took her hand.

"Not as well as I'd hoped. They didn't find the ledger."

"Oh, no." She tried to sit up, winced, and lay back down again.

"Don't move," he told her.

"But we need that to prove his involvement."

"That's why he got rid of it," Reid said wearily. "He must have known we were coming."

"How?"

"Guilty people are always paranoid. Anyway, we've got Quinn in custody. Vargas has put him in the holding cell."

"Are you going to interrogate him?" Kenzie asked.

"Vargas or Diaz can do it. They're both more than capable."

Kenzie studied his face and saw the lines of tension etched into his brow, the tense jaw, and the stiff shoulders. He was amped up and dying to let rip at Quinn. "You don't have to stay," she said quietly.

"Of course I'm going to stay."

"Reid, I'm fine. The doctor's given me the all-clear. He's just keeping me in as a precaution. Go and interrogate Quinn. That's more important."

"Nothing's more important than you, Kenz." he squeezed her hand.

Kenzie felt a lump form in her throat. "I know," she whispered. "I feel the same way about you. When Diaz called and said you'd been stabbed, I—" She petered off, unable to continue.

He smiled. "Well, you don't need to worry. I was fine too."

She nodded, then wished she hadn't. Wasn't it time for another painkiller?

"Hey, I was thinking," Reid began, his voice husky. She reopened her eyes. "When you get out of here, I think you should come and stay with me for a while."

"At your place?"

She could have sworn he was blushing. "Yeah, at my place. Just until you're better and we get these guys. Kenzie, someone tried to kill you today and we aren't sure who that was."

"It was Del Gatto, obviously. He probably sent Quinn after me."

"We don't know that," he repeated. "More importantly, if we can't find any evidence to hold Quinn, he's going to walk. Del Gatto's already got his lawyer on the way."

"Then you'd better go," Kenzie said, releasing his hand. "Go. You need to get this guy, Reid. For me. And for Christina."

CHAPTER 38

Del Gatto's lawyer was waiting at the police station when Reid got there. It was the same hawk-nosed man as before, this time in a slightly more wrinkled suit. He'd obviously come straight from the office after being hastily briefed by Del Gatto.

"I demand to see my client," he barked as Reid walked in.

"Sure." The lawyer was entitled to some time with Quinn before the questioning began. "You got ten minutes." That was all he was going to give him.

"What are the charges?" the lawyer asked, even though Del Gatto would have told him.

"The suspected murder of Carl Ramos."

The lawyer nodded, and Vargas took him to the interview room. Soon after, Quinn was also led, still in cuffs, into the room. Reid had told Vargas to keep them on, since he didn't trust the guy one bit.

After yet another cup of coffee, Reid felt the weariness subside and his brain kick into gear. Good, he needed the buzz to make him extra alert. Kenzie's words hung in his head.

You need to get this guy. For me. And for Christina.

For Carlos Ramos.

He walked in, nodded to both men, and sat down at the table. The atmosphere was thick with anticipation and the lawyer's aftershave.

"Thanks for your patience," he told Quinn, who merely nodded. The suspect didn't seem phased, which worried Reid. As much as he wanted to bust Quinn now, he knew his chances were slim. This would be more of a fishing expedition than anything else.

"Do you know Carl Ramos?" Reid began, establishing a threshold.

"Yes, he's one of Mr. Del Gatto's employees."

"What's his occupation?"

"He worked on *Jewel of the Seas* as a member of the crew."

Reid nodded. "Were you friends?"

"No, but we knew each other."

"When did you last see Mr. Ramos?"

Quinn didn't have to think about that one. He knew why he was being arrested, and he'd formulated all the answers already. "Two weeks ago at the clubhouse at the Matheson Hammock Marina. We met for a drink."

"I thought you said you weren't friends." The fluorescent lighting cast harsh shadows on Quinn's face, making him seem harder and more ruthless. Still, his demeanor was anything but.

"We weren't."

"Yet you met at a yacht club for a social drink?" Reid's eyes bore into Quinn's who remained as calm as Biscayne Bay on a summer's day.

"We were discussing the repairs to the yacht," he explained coolly.

Reid kept his gaze locked on Quinn. "Do you always meet at a boat club to discuss business?"

"Not always, but I was off duty and he keeps a boat down there, so we met there."

"A boat? What kind of boat?"

"Just an old fishing boat. Nothing special."

Reid nodded. "That was the night before the hurricane hit."

Quinn gave a nod of recognition. "Yeah, the bar shut early, and they tossed everyone out."

"What time did Carl leave?"

The suspect pretended to think about this. "Around seven. He said he had something to do, and he left quite suddenly as I recall."

"Did he seem agitated?" Reid asked.

"Yeah, actually. He went to the restroom and when he got back, he seemed angry."

"Angry with you?"

"Not with me. With Hector."

Reid frowned. "Hector?"

"Yeah, Hector was there too that night. That marina is one of his favorite hangouts. Carl stopped to talk to Hector, then came back and said he had to leave. I asked him if he needed a lift, but he declined."

"He leave on foot?"

Quinn nodded. "He just walked out. I barely got a chance to say goodbye."

"What about Hector?" Reid asked. "Did he also leave?"

"Yeah, he left straight afterwards."

CHAPTER 39

"You let him go?" Kenzie couldn't believe it.

"I can't keep the guy for no reason, Kenz. Trust me, I tried, but it looks like Hector might have killed Carl Ramos."

"You're taking Quinn's word for it? He's a liar and a killer. You shouldn't believe a word he says."

"He's not the only one who saw Hector in the bar," Reid explained. "We spoke to the bar manager who confirmed he was there that night. Quinn's story checks out."

She huffed, frustrated. "What about Alex?"

"Raoul is coming in first thing to give a statement and then we'll double-check everything he's told us, get statements from his sources, and make sure everything's watertight. Then we'll arrest her for identity theft."

"What about the jewel heists?"

"The only evidence we have is that she knew all the victims. That's not enough to charge her."

"Maybe I was wrong about that," Kenzie said, cautiously.

"Oh? What made you change your mind?"

"I was thinking about that night at the charity fundraiser. There's no way Alex could have broken into a safe without the proper equipment."

"It was a complicated safe," Reid agreed. "It would take some professional kit to crack it."

"All she had with her was a tiny purse."

Reid was silent for a moment. "The only other name on the list was Bethany Del Gatto, but it can't be her. She's nearly fifty and a victim herself."

Kenzie didn't respond.

"Kenz, are you okay?"

"Yes, I'm fine. My head's still a little bit foggy. I'm sure I'll be okay tomorrow."

"Can't wait to have you home."

"Same."

"So you're coming to mine?"

Kenzie hesitated. This was a big step. She'd never stayed at his for any length of time before. This would require her bringing clothes over, toiletries, putting them in his bathroom cabinet. It meant sharing the cooking and generally being in his space. "If you still think I should."

"I do." No hesitation there.

Kenzie smiled. "I'll let you know when I'm discharged."

"Great, I'll come to get you and drop you at mine. Have you let Keith know you're taking a few days off?"

"I wasn't planning to take a few days off," she said, surprised he'd think she'd do that.

"But your concussion?"

"If the doctor thinks I can go home, then I can work."

"I'm not sure that's a good idea, Kenz. You've had a bad head injury. You should rest."

She heard the concern in his voice and didn't have the heart to make him worry. "Okay, I'll speak to Keith. Maybe I can work from home. Your home, that is."

"That's a better idea."

"You do have WIFI?" she asked. The connections in the Glades weren't always the best.

"I have a WIFI hub," he said. "It allows me to work without relying on the local connection, which isn't that great."

"That's fine, then."

Kenzie didn't tell him she wasn't planning on staying at his place all day. Carlisle's information had changed everything. Now she knew who the forger and the fence were, she had to trace them back to Del Gatto. That was the link she had to find.

The only problem was she hadn't quite figured out how she was going to do that.

After saying goodbye to Reid, her eyes dropped to the crumpled piece of paper she still clenched in her hand. Penned in Carlisle's neat handwriting were two names. The names were:

FELIX Martins
Eleanor Johnson.

CHAPTER 40

Kenzie snuck down the corridor to the elevator. It was dark and not many people were around. Visiting hours were over and only the night nurses were on duty. She didn't see a single soul as she made her way up to the fourth floor.

Reid had told her Hector was in the hospital, too, after his gunshot wound to the abdomen, and she couldn't resist the opportunity to talk to him. The skipper held the answer to a lot of the questions that were flying around her head, rendering her unable to sleep.

The painkillers had dulled her headache, and the room didn't spin every time she sat up anymore. Walking was still difficult, and she kept one hand on the wall for balance just in case she had a wobble, but for the most part, she was fine.

The elevator came to a stop, and the doors slid open. Stepping out into the dimly lit central room, she saw one nurse at the nurses' station and another hovering near a machine in the far corner. Neither looked up at her as she stepped out.

Kenzie had purposely worn her hospital gown and was carrying a glass of water. If she were stopped, she'd say she thought she was on the second floor, not the fourth. She had a concussion and was easily confused.

A beeping came from one of the wards and the nurse checked her computer, got up, and went to check on the patient. The one in the far corner was still taking readings off a machine. Kenzie took the opportunity and snuck past the nurses' station to pad in her socks down the corridor to room 402.

There was a light glowing softly from inside. Reid had said Hector was in an induced coma, but when Kenzie had called reception and enquired after her dear friend in room 402, the duty nurse had said he'd just been brought round. Reid would probably get the call in the morning.

Kenzie pushed open the door and slipped inside. Hector was in a ward with two others, just like her, and like the patients in her room, were also fast asleep. Only Hector sat upright, staring at the wall, a frown on his rugged face.

"Hector?" she whispered, so as not to wake the others.

He swung his head round. "Who are you?"

"My name is Kenzie. I'm also a patient here."

He relaxed somewhat but didn't lose the frown. "What are you doing here?"

"Can we talk?" she asked, softly. "About your boss, Salvatore Del Gatto."

The frown deepened. "No, I think you should leave."

"He murdered a friend of mine," she said quickly. Hector didn't need to know Christina wasn't a friend.

His eyes fluttered as he processed this.

Kenzie corrected herself. "Or rather, he got that killer Samson Quinn to murder her. I know he did, but I need to find a way to prove it."

Hector shook his head. "I can't help you."

Kenzie padded over to the bed. "I think you can, Hector. You see, I know Del Gatto has been smuggling diamonds illegally from west Africa. I also know he used you and the crew to do it, and now he's killing you off, to cover his tracks."

"How do you know that?" Hector hissed.

"Because I was the one who found the diamonds. When the yacht hit the harbor wall and broke into pieces, the diamonds washed up on the beach. I found them and gave them to the police."

He stared at her, trying to work out if she was for real or if this was a trap. She saw it in his suspicious gaze. "I'm not trying to set you up," she said. "I'm not working with the police, I'm a reporter and I'm trying to expose Del Gatto for what he is, a corrupt, murdering scumbag."

There was a cold silence, where the beeping of the hospital monitors was the only sound.

"Will you help me?"

After what seemed like a long time, Hector nodded.

"How did it work?" Kenzie asked.

"We were told to meet the container ships at night in international waters. It was extremely dangerous. The *Jewel* is so much smaller than a giant container ship and they don't have great stopping power, so if you mistime it—" He made a slicing motion with his hand.

Kenzie got the picture.

"Once you got back to the marina, what happened to the diamonds?"

"We left them on board in the safe. Vince and I were the only two that knew the combination, along with the contact."

"The contact?"

"There was this woman, she would come and collect the diamonds once we'd left the yacht. I didn't ask what happened to them, I just know they were gone when we set off on our next voyage."

"Did you get paid extra for this?" she asked.

He nodded. "Del Gatto made it worth our while. I sent my money back to Haiti. I didn't want his blood money."

"Did you know they were conflict diamonds?" Kenzie asked.

"I knew. Vince knew too. He was hired security to protect the stones in case anything went wrong."

"Did you know he was found dead with a diamond in his stomach?" Kenzie studied the rugged seaman. Hector swallowed and nodded. "I knew, because I was there."

"You were?"

"I met him and we went to check out some equipment for the boat, but while we were there, Quinn took a shot at us. Luckily, it was howling a damn gale, the hurricane was making landfall, and a tree whipped him in the face. Anyway, the gun went wide, and Vince and I split up. I knew then he was going to try to kill us."

"Why?" Kenzie asked. "Why was Quinn trying to kill you both?"

"Because we'd had enough," Hector said. "Vince swallowed the diamond to show the authorities. He thought it was more likely they'd believe us if they could see one of the diamonds."

"Except he never got that far."

Hector nodded. "Quinn caught up to him in the street and hit him over the head with a piece of wood. I heard the crack and saw him go down. He was bleeding pretty badly. Quinn raised his gun to shoot Vince, but I tackled him from behind. The gun went flying, and I told Vince to run. He did, but I don't know where he went. After Quinn took off, I picked up his gun and went to find Vince, but the storm was so bad by then, I had to find shelter."

Kenzie listened carefully.

"What about Pedro Gonzalez? What happened to him?"

"I met Pedro and told him what had happened. He was scared, I mean, really scared. Then that cop showed up and Pedro and I fled. I think Pedro got busted, but I didn't hang around to see it."

"They got to Pedro," Kenzie told him. "After he was released, Del Gatto's lawyer took him home and there was a guy lying in wait. He was shot outside his apartment."

Hector clenched his hands into fists. "Bastards. Pedro was little more than a kid."

"I know. This is why we have to take these guys down, Hector. They're murderers."

He gazed at her with newfound respect, and she saw a flash of determination in his face. "Tell me what you need me to do."

"Do you recognize this woman?" Kenzie showed him a photograph Raoul had sent her of Alex.

He nodded. "Yeah, that's the woman who collects the diamonds."

Kenzie smiled. She had her proof. Unbeknown to Hector, her phone was recording every word.

CHAPTER 41

Reid was surprised to find Kenzie waiting for him downstairs in the hospital lobby. Looking spritely, she said, "Hector's awake."

He stared at her. "How do you know?"

"Because I had a little chat with him last night. It was very enlightening."

Reid frowned. "Kenzie, Hector's a dangerous man. What on earth did you think you were doing? He's a suspect in a multiple homicide."

She snorted. "Hector didn't murder anyone. He's been on the run from Samson Quinn this whole time."

Reid couldn't believe she'd be that gullible. "Of course, that's what he'd tell you. We have evidence—"

"Reid, before you continue, will you listen to something? Afterwards, Hector is waiting to talk to you. He wants to tell his side of the story."

Reid gave her a hard stare. "If Hector's awake, I should really go talk to him first."

"You need to listen to this." She pushed play on her phone and he heard Kenzie's voice come through the phone's speaker.

I think you can, Hector. You see, I know Del Gatto has been smuggling diamonds illegally from west Africa. I also know he used you and the crew to do it, and now he's killing you off, to cover his tracks.

Reid took the phone, turned down the volume, and put it to his ear. He listened to the whole thing, without speaking, and then handed it back to her.

"Does he know you took this?"

She shook her head. "No, I didn't want to tell him in case it spooked him. If he tells you the same story, he doesn't ever have to know. I just wanted it as back-up." Kenzie was a seasoned reporter, she knew the advantages of getting a source on tape.

He shook his head. "I can't believe you got him to open up to you."

"I caught him at a vulnerable moment," she said with a small smile. "He'd only just come out of his coma and was feeling quite emotional."

Reid couldn't picture Hector being emotional. The tape explained a lot, like how he'd got Vince's blood on his shoes, how he ended up with the Colt, and why he'd gone into hiding. It didn't explain, however, how Pedro had been shot with a similar .45 or how Carl Ramos had died after leaving the marina.

"He's actually a good guy, Reid." Kenzie was saying. "He deserves to tell his story without judgment."

"I'll keep an open mind," he promised. He remembered how Hector had aimed high at the beach bar when Diaz had come out guns blazing and how he'd hesitated to shoot the tactical officer in Little Haiti and took a bullet to the gut as a result. Maybe everything he'd told Kenzie was true.

"Do you mind waiting while I go and have a word with him?" he said. "It might take a while."

Kenzie smiled. "Be my guest. I'll get a cab home and start packing. You can pick me up there when you're done."

Reid was torn. He wanted to take Kenzie home and make sure she was okay, but Hector was waiting for him and the skipper held the key to this entire investigation. "I'm going to get Vargas to meet you at your place, just to make sure it's safe."

"That's really not necessary. I'm only going to pack and wait for you. I'll keep the door locked."

Reid frowned. He'd put a tail on Quinn, so he didn't think she'd be in any more danger. "You sure you're okay?" Her eyes were clear, and she seemed to be in good spirits. Not groggy and out of it like yesterday. He'd been really worried about her then.

"I'm great, just eager to go home."

"I'll let you know when I'm on my way." He kissed her and took off in the direction of the elevator.

THE FIRST THING Kenzie did when she got home was have a long, hot shower. Her head was still painful where she'd been hit with the baseball, but she managed to wash her hair without too much cursing.

Afterwards, she made a coffee and sat down to plot her next move. Alex was the fence, but she had the forger's name too. She called Raoul, who answered almost immediately. "Kenzie, I heard what happened. You okay?"

"Yes, I'm fine. Got a bit of a sore head, but I'll survive."

"I heard you got hit with a baseball bat."

"So I'm told. I didn't see it coming."

"I'm glad you're okay." She heard the concern in his voice. "Listen, I can't really talk now, I'm on my way to your boyfriend's office to give a statement."

"Yeah, about that," Kenzie said. "Can you hold off for a few hours?"

"I suppose so, although Detective Vargas did specify to come first thing."

"I know, but I've got something pressing that I need you to do. Can you come to my place? I'm not supposed to be at work."

He hesitated, then said, "Sure, I'll turn around. See you soon."

Twenty minutes later, Raoul pulled up in front of her condo. Kenzie opened the door to let him in. "What's so urgent that you had to make me postpone my police appointment?"

Kenzie put a hand on his shoulder. "I got us the names. FM and EJ, I know who they are."

"Seriously?" His glasses slid down his nose. "How?"

"I asked a source and you'll never guess who EJ is."

Raoul stared at her for a full minute, before whispering. "Tell me it's not Eleanor Johnson?"

"The very same."

"Well, damn." He took a deep breath. "Your fake friend Alex is the fence."

Kenzie nodded. She is a con woman, after all. Is it surprising she's mixed up in this?"

"I guess not." Raoul scratched his head. "But how does that work?"

"She's known Del Gatto for years. I think they're in it together. He smuggles the diamonds in using his yacht and the crew to do it. She collects the diamonds at this end, gives them to the appraiser who forges the certificates, then she sells them on."

"With the authenticated certificates, they're effectively laundered," Raoul summed up.

"That's right. I have the forger's name too, but no idea how to find him."

Raoul sat down at her dining table and took out his laptop. "Give it to me."

Ten minutes later, she had an address.

FELIX MARTINS LIVED in a high-end apartment block in South Beach. According to the management website, it had underground parking, a concierge, a gym, and a private swimming pool.

"He's a freelance appraiser and makes a damn good living from it, judging from his investment portfolio." Raoul tilted his head to the side as he scanned the list of stocks and shares.

Kenzie shook her head. "How do you find these things? You know what, it doesn't matter. I don't want to know."

"I'm sure he's not declaring all of this," Raoul said, sardonically.

"Well, it's not our job to tip off the tax man."

"What are you going to do, Kenzie?" Raoul asked. "You can't break into his apartment."

"I'm not going to break into his apartment, I'm going to break into his office. I need proof that he's working for Del Gatto."

"How do you know he doesn't work from home?"

"Way too risky," Kenzie said. "He'll have rented office space close to where he lives to forge the certificates. All I have to do is track him and I'll find it."

"How are you going to do that? You can't follow him around, Reid will get suspicious."

"I'm not going to follow him around, I'm going to track him with this." She held up a tiny micro tracking device.

"Where'd you get that?"

"Tools of the trade, dear boy."

Raoul rolled his eyes. "You say I'm bad. How are you going to plant it on him?"

"Easy, I'll just bump into him outside his apartment."

Raoul got up to leave. "I need to get going. Sweetwater PD are expecting me."

Kenzie nodded. "I'd better get packing. I'm going to stay at Reid's for a few days, just until this is over."

"I see things are getting serious." He grinned.

"It's a precaution," she told him.

"Yeah, sure." He winked at her and left the condo.

Kenzie stared at the tiny device in her hand. She'd used them before, on the job, when she'd needed to trace someone's movements. After she'd wiped it clean, there'd be no way for anyone to trace it back to her or the newspaper. The only problem was knowing when Felix Martins would be leaving or returning to his apartment. She didn't have the time to scout it and learn his routines. She'd have to take a chance and head down there first thing tomorrow morning. Maybe she could catch him going for his morning coffee or heading to the office. That would be even better.

She thought about Reid at Del Gatto's, looking for Quinn, and felt a pang of guilt. The last thing she wanted to do was go behind his back, but she needed this information to take down Del Gatto. She needed to know every nuance of the smuggling operation, and when the time was right, when Carlisle gave her the go-ahead, she was going to bust it right open.

For Christina. For herself.

CHAPTER 42

Reid pulled up outside Kenzie's condo and got out of the pickup. The talk with Hector had been immensely useful, and he had to agree with Kenzie that the former *Jewel* skipper was one of the good guys.

With his evidence, they'd be able to build a case against Samson Quinn. As soon as he was well enough, he'd be moved to a safe house, and then Reid would talk to his contacts at the DOD about witness protection.

Unfortunately, Del Gatto, in typical fashion, had managed to keep his hands clean of most of the dirty work. It was Quinn who'd been the point of contact with the crew, Quinn who'd given them their instructions, Quinn who'd hunted down Carl, Vince, and Hector to silence them. Apart from del Gatto's yacht being used as the vessel in which the smuggled goods were transported, there was no physical evidence leading to his involvement whatsoever. A testimony from the Head of Security would be vital in prosecuting Del Gatto.

He knocked on the door and smiled when Kenzie opened it in a cornflower blue dress, her blonde hair hanging loosely around her shoulders.

"You look great." He reached for her. "So much better."

"Thanks. I feel better." She stood up onto her tiptoes and kissed him.

"Ready?" He grinned, unable to help himself.

She smiled back. "Ready."

They were halfway home when Diaz called on the police radio. "Boss, we've got a situation."

He frowned. "What is it?"

"Del Gatto's just called and reported that his wife's been kidnapped."

"Bethany?"

"Yeah, he says she was abducted by his Head of Security."

"What?" exclaimed Kenzie. Reid pulled over into a bus stop so he could think. "Say that again?"

"Samson Quinn, Del Gatto's head of security, has just abducted Bethany Del Gatto."

"But, why?" Reid couldn't understand it. What on earth did Quinn want with his boss's mild-mannered, genteel wife?

"I don't know, boss, but we'd better get over there ASAP."

Reid glanced across at Kenzie. He couldn't take her to Del Gatto's, the man hated her.

"Take me home," she said. "I'll be okay."

"Shoot, I'm sorry about this Kenz."

"It can't be helped. You've got police work to do. I'll drive over to yours later." As his face twisted with indecision, she squeezed his arm. "It'll be fine, don't worry."

He nodded, eager to get to Del Gatto's, and turned the car around.

Del Gatto was beside himself when Reid arrived. "What's Quinn playing at?" he raged, pacing up and down outside his house. "Does he want my money? Is he going to ransom her, is that what this is about?"

"Maybe." To be honest, Reid had no idea. Quinn was so calm, so collected, this was completely out of character for him.

"When did this happen?" Reid asked the demented billionaire. From the way he was carrying on, you'd think he was totally besotted with his wife, not that he'd been having an affair for years.

"An hour ago. I got home to find him holding poor Bethany at gunpoint. He was demanding she hand over the diamonds." He looked baffled. "Bethany doesn't know about the diamonds."

Reid wondered if that was a confession. "Are you admitting you were smuggling diamonds?"

He blinked, as if the thought hadn't occurred to him. "No, I'm talking about the diamonds you said washed up on the beach. The diamonds you accused me of smuggling. I'm assuming that's the diamonds he was talking about. What other diamonds are there?"

Good answer.

"She was terrified," he continued. "He dragged her to my car and ordered her to get in."

"Which car is this?" Reid asked. Del Gatto gave him the make and model and Reid immediately got Diaz to put out a BOLO on the vehicle and its occupants.

"Did he say anything else?"

Del Gatto shook his head. "Quinn is a man of few words at the best of times, but I don't understand this at all. Please, you've got to find her."

Reid assured him they'd do everything in their power to get her back.

KENZIE WAS astounded by what had happened. Samson Quinn had abducted Bethany Del Gatto. Why? What possible motive could he have for doing that?

In the back of her mind, she heard Reid's voice saying: *The only other name on the list was Bethany Del Gatto.*

Somewhere in the back of her mind, a light flicked on. Bethany might be nearly fifty, but she had the body of a much younger woman. All that yoga had made her strong and flexible.

Kenzie thought about Del Gatto's elegant, poised wife. A soft-spoken, charming hostess. A major donor for the Breathe Hope Foundation.

On the evening of the party, Bethany had insisted that the necklace was present when she'd dressed, but discovered it missing upon her return, even though the safe had remained untouched.

Bethany had known that the diamonds had gone to the lab for testing. She'd known because her husband would have told her or she'd overheard him talking to Quinn about it.

A thought struck her, but it was almost too audacious to consider seriously. Kenzie sat down on the couch and stared unseeing ahead of her. Was it possible that Bethany was the Bling Bandit?

Had Bethany broken into the police lab and stolen the diamonds, and that's what Quinn was after? Somehow, he'd found out about her little side hustle.

Feeling breathless, she pondered her idea. Was it based in reality or was it her foggy mind jumping to conclusions?

Raoul. She needed Raoul. He could help her clarify some things.

Her researcher was still at the police station, waiting to be seen. "Kenzie, this really isn't a good time," he hissed.

"Raoul, I think Bethany Del Gatto might have the diamonds. I think she could be the Bling Bandit."

"Are you sure you're not still concussed?" He tried to keep his voice low.

"Can you check something for me?"

"Not now, I can't."

"Well, when you're done then."

"Okay, what?"

"Can you look to see how much Bethany has donated to the charity in the last few years? The donor records should be available somewhere online."

He sighed. "That's easy. I can do it on my iPad. It shouldn't take long."

"Thanks," she told him. "You're a star."

A few minutes later, he confirmed. "She's donated an inordinately large sum to the charity over the last few years. Close on two million dollars, and there's more—a lot more—from an anonymous donor."

"Could you send me a screenshot of the dates of these donations?"

"Yeah, coming through now."

Her phone buzzed in her hand. "Thanks, Raoul."

Kenzie opened the image and stared at the dates. Next, she googled the Bling Bandit's more recent escapades. They weren't an exact match, but close enough to be suspicious. Kenzie exhaled long and slow. She could be on to something here.

Where did Bethany get two million dollars? Possibly more if the anonymous donations were hers too. She didn't work, her husband sure as hell wouldn't give her that amount of money to donate to a charity, and she had no other visible sources of income.

Kenzie thought back to what Alex had told her. Bethany's sister was dying, and she was desperate to find a cure. How easy would it be to gaze at the wealth displayed around the nipped and tucked necks and dangling from the ears of your rich, selfish friends and think of the good it could do if it were repurposed? It wouldn't be that hard to take note of the valuables, where they were kept and how much they were worth, then go back when the owners weren't home and steal them.

Nobody would suspect her, of course, but just in case they did, she arranged for her own emerald necklace to disappear. She even got her husband to report it to the police. Del Gatto probably had no idea Bethany had taken it herself.

Kenzie gasped as the realization hit home. Every good thief needed a fence. How else would Bethany sell the stolen items of jewelry? It just so happened, she knew a good one, too. Someone her husband used in his illicit diamond trade.

Kenzie sat back and thought about the night of the charity ball. There were certain things that didn't add up. She'd thought it strange that the inner door that led to the stairs that took you down to the side exit at Del Gatto's house had been left unlocked. It was an extra layer of security that hadn't been employed. With all those security guards hovering around, why was it left open? Because Bethany had left it open for Alex.

Had Alex stolen the emerald necklace that night, too? Had Bethany left the safe open, or given her the combination? That touch, those few whispered words at the party. Bethany was telling Alex the coast was clear.

Phew. This was huge. Alex had been working for Bethany, as well as Del Gatto. Kenzie needed to speak to her, and she knew just where to find her.

CHAPTER 43

Kenzie drove to the Palmetto Point Country Club and pulled over outside. Without her name being left with Security, she wouldn't be allowed in and for that, she needed Alex.

"Hey," Kenzie said as Alex answered. "I'm outside the country club. Can we talk?"

"Sure, is something wrong?"

"No, I just want to pick your brain about something." It wasn't a lie.

"Okay, give me a second and I'll get reception to call through to the gate."

"Thanks."

Sure enough, a few minutes later, Kenzie was cruising down the drive toward the parking lot. This time, she parked next to a glossy Miami blue Lamborghini Aventador. Its sharp, aerodynamic design making it look like something out of the future.

Alex met her at the entrance. "Hi, I've been meaning to call you. How have you been?"

Kenzie leaned in and whispered. "Alex, I know everything."

The socialite's eyelids fluttered briefly before she laughed and said, "Whatever do you mean, Kenzie?"

"I mean, I know that you're really Eleanor Johnson. I know about what you do for a living, and I know that you're part of this whole diamond smuggling operation that Del Gatto's been running."

The smile vanished from Alex's lips. "I think you'd better leave or I'm going to call security."

"Don't worry," Kenzie hissed. "I'm not interested in you. I want to expose Del Gatto and his illegitimate enterprises. I want the world to know he's a homicidal scumbag who had his crew murdered so they wouldn't talk and his mistress killed because she found out what he was up to."

Alex grabbed her arm and pulled her through the lobby and out into the garden. Kenzie was surprised at her strength. They walked in silence until they were far away from the terrace where well-exercised members were benignly sipping their pre-dinner cocktails.

"How did you find out?" Alex whispered. She looked shaken. Her usual cool exterior was flushed, the cracks beginning to show.

"That night at the ball, I found a ledger in Del Gatto's study. I took a photograph of one of the pages. It was coded, but it contained particulars of the latest shipment of diamonds. Your initials were there. EJ. I didn't know who you were, then."

"But you found out?"

"Actually, my researcher discovered the truth. He stumbled across an old photograph of Alexandra Delacroix, which happened to look just like that girl in your dorm who committed suicide." Kenzie fixed her gaze on her.

"Damn," she muttered softly. "I thought I'd destroyed all those old photos."

Kenzie shook her head. "No, there was one left. It was a clever plan, though. Did you think of it on the spot, or was it premeditated?"

"On the spot." She shook her head, her eyes a witchy green, remembering. "Alexandra was such a drag. Surprising, really, given her family's legacy. She couldn't cope with her mother's death, her father's neglect, her grandmother's estate. It was all too much. She chose journalism because she thought she'd go into marketing rather than acting, but the expectation was always there. College was a sanctuary for her. After we graduated, she decided to end it by hanging herself in the dorm room."

"It was you who found her, wasn't it?" Kenzie breathed.

Alex nodded. "I was shocked. Everybody had left campus, except for me. I had nowhere to go. My father was...well, let's just say I didn't have the best family life either."

"Your father was in prison," Kenzie whispered. She'd researched Eleanor Johnson while she'd been lying in that hospital bed with a concussion.

A wry smile. "You have done your homework. Kenzie Gilmore, the award-winning journalist. I should have known you'd find out my secret."

"Honestly, Alex, I'm not interested in who you are or what you do." That wasn't strictly true, but the police would fact check Raoul's research and arrest her for that. "I'm only interested in exposing Del Gatto."

Alex shook her head. "The game is up, though. Isn't it? Do the police know?"

Kenzie nodded. "But they're tied up at the Del Gatto mansion. I don't know if you heard, but Samson Quinn has abducted Bethany Del Gatto."

"What?" Alex's eyes grew huge. "Why?"

Kenzie smiled. "I think you know why."

Alex sank down onto a nearby bench. "You know about that, too?"

"I wasn't sure, but it fit. That night of the party, she left her safe open so you could take her necklace, didn't she?"

Alex stared at her but didn't reply. She didn't have to. Her silence gave her away.

"That's how you knew how to get out of the house. Bethany had told you the side door would be unlocked and you could escape that way." Kenzie took a seat beside Alex. "You know, I had a suspicion you weren't all you seemed to be when you picked that lock to the study."

Alex cringed. "I knew that was a risk, but I couldn't leave you there to get discovered."

"Why not? It would have given the guards a distraction. You could easily have snuck back downstairs and left the party, no one would have known you had a priceless emerald necklace in your purse."

Alex dropped her voice. "These are not nice people, Kenzie. Despite what you think of me, I'm not a killer. Quinn, well, Quinn is dangerous. He wouldn't hesitate to torture you to find out what you knew and then make you disappear."

Kenzie gulped. It was an involuntary reaction. "I had a run in with him yesterday," she said. "He hit me on the head with a baseball bat."

Alex gasped. "No! Are you okay?"

She turned her head and felt the bump. "I am now, but I spent last night in hospital with a concussion. Lucky his aim was off and I have a tough noggin."

Alex inhaled sharply. "Kenzie, I know you want to get Del Gatto, but trust me, you do not want to mess with these people."

"He's only human," she said. "Not some monster."

Alex shrugged. "He might not be, but—" She faded off.

"You're talking about his mob connections. Joe Molano and the New Yorkers?"

Alex didn't immediately reply. "Be very careful, Kenzie. You don't want them on your back."

This was true, but Kenzie had no intention of getting involved with the mob. Her interest was purely in Del Gatto. The FBI could handle the mafia.

"What exactly do you do for Del Gatto?" Kenzie asked.

Alex sighed. "I don't work for Del Gatto, I work for myself. Quinn calls me when a shipment comes in, I collect the diamonds and take them to a forger."

"Felix Martins?"

"Wow, Kenzie. I'm impressed. Is there anything you don't know? Am I just wasting my time telling you all this?"

"What do you do after you get the certificates?"

"I sell them to various dealers, some of whom are aware of the dirty origins of the goods, some who aren't. They get slotted into the mix and come out clean, ready to be sold at high-end jewelers all over the country."

"Neat," Kenzie commented. "How does the money flow back to Del Gatto?"

"It doesn't."

Kenzie frowned.

"Quinn takes care of everything. It's done through a Panamanian shell company that they'll never trace. Del Gatto's name isn't even on the paperwork. Nothing leads back to him."

Kenzie gritted her teeth.

"So you see, Kenzie. It's all for nothing."

Alex got up. "I've got to go, before the police come for me. I'm sure you understand. It's been...enlightening talking to you. Be careful, Kenzie. This is a dangerous game you're playing."

And she sashayed across the lawn back to the clubhouse. Kenzie exhaled. She'd leave Alex to the cops, she had enough for her story. Everything Alex had said she'd recorded on her phone.

Kenzie reached into her pocket to switch it off, but her phone was gone.

CHAPTER 44

"Why was Quinn asking Bethany where the diamonds are?" Reid said to Diaz, squinting in the glaring afternoon sun. They were standing beside her squad car outside Del Gatto's sprawling mansion, the ground radiating waves of heat. Trying to decide what to do next, they could hear the faint wail of sirens in the distance as every police officer in Miami searched for Del Gatto's sleek black Jaguar. Quinn's photograph had been distributed to every police station in the state-the alert clear:

Armed and dangerous. Approach with extreme caution. Arrest on site.

Diaz shook her head, strands of dark hair falling across her face. "How would she know?"

Reid frowned, the bright sun forcing him to narrow his eyes into slits. He remembered what he'd told Kenzie at the hospital. "The only other name on the list was Bethany Del Gatto," he said slowly.

Diaz glanced at him. "What list?"

"The friends and family of the jewel theft victims." Reid wiped the perspiration off his forehead.

Diaz gasped, the sound sharp in the heavy air. "You're not saying she's the Bling Bandit?"

The possibilities churned in his mind. "I think she might be."

They stared at each other for a long moment, the buzz of a nearby fly the only sound. Then Diaz said, "Are they in it together?"

"I don't know. It's possible, I suppose." Reid thought for a moment. "Could be this isn't a kidnapping at all. Maybe they've run away together with the diamonds."

"Then why make it look like one?" Diaz was right. It would have been simpler to just disappear together. No mess, no fuss.

"I'll ask Del Gatto," Reid finally said.

The businessman was shaking his head before Reid even got to the end of the sentence. "Bethany, a cat burglar? Are you insane?" Del Gatto mopped his brow with a monogrammed handkerchief.

"She knew all the other victims," Reid said reasonably. "She could easily have found out when they'd be out and used that knowledge to burgle them."

Del Gatto was staring at him in disbelief, eyes wide. Reid was beginning to feel for the guy. He was an arrogant prick, but this had clearly shaken him to the core.

"Was Quinn close to your wife?" he asked gently.

Again, Del Gatto shook his head, mouth set in a grim line. "Not that I know of. They hardly ever spoke."

"So, they weren't lovers?" Diaz cut in.

"Hell, no." He looked genuinely horrified at the notion.

"Did you tell your wife that the diamonds were at the police lab?" Reid asked evenly, watching Del Gatto closely for any reaction.

Del Gatto shifted his weight from one Italian loafer to the other. "No, I don't think so. How would I know where they were? I didn't have anything to do with—"

"Because the FBI told you," Reid interjected, his tone steady. "You know they'd taken over the case and the diamonds were going to be analyzed at the police lab. It's common sense."

"I didn't know," Del Gatto murmured unconvincingly, but Reid could see he was lying, his left eye twitching almost imperceptibly. He was struggling with the concept that Bethany had broken into the police lab and stolen the diamonds right out from under his nose-his precious diamonds. "Why would she do that?" he whispered.

"I can give you seven million reasons why," Reid said meaningfully, glancing at Diaz.

"Any idea where she would have kept the diamonds?" Diaz asked Del Gatto. "Obviously not in the house, that would be too risky." Del Gatto had gone blank. He seemed at a loss for words.

"Mr. Del Gatto?" Reid prodded. "Is there anywhere she could have hidden the diamonds? Does she have a safe deposit box anywhere? Or an office?"

"There's the charity," he whispered. "That's the only other place she goes. The charity and to see her sister at the hospice."

Reid glanced at Diaz. "The hospice."

She shrugged. "Worth a shot, nobody would think to look there."

They left a couple of uniformed cops at the mansion, in case there was word from Quinn, jumped into Diaz's cruiser, and took off down the drive.

———

ALEX'S PORSCHE PANAMERA was accelerating out of the carpark when Kenzie got to her car. Damn her for stealing the phone. Kenzie hadn't even felt the con woman lift it out of her pocket. She was good, Kenzie had to give her that much.

Still, Alex wasn't the only one with a trick up her sleeve. Kenzie may not have been able to record the conversation, but she had planted the tracking device on Alex without her noticing. Seems they were both light fingered.

Opening her laptop and setting it on the seat next to her, Kenzie pulled up the software Raoul had installed. On a map, she saw the little green dot that was the tracker. "There you are," she whispered as she started the engine.

Kenzie followed at a distance, wondering where Alex was going. The Porsche headed west onto MacArthur Causeway and, at the intersection, took the turnoff to Miami's downtown area. Was she going home? Surely not. She must know the police would soon be looking for her. Perhaps she figured she had time to grab some belongings before she took off. Kenzie was sure she was going to make a run for it. Like she said, the game was up.

Before she got downtown, Alex turned onto the Dixie Highway toward Coral Gables, the engine of her sleek Porsche growling as it accelerated. Frowning, Kenzie followed, the air rushing by her open window. She kept several vehicles back, out of sight of the Porsche, using the pulsing green dot on her laptop screen to navigate instead of visually tracking the car ahead.

They passed Coconut Grove, where Christina lived, the sweet fragrance of pink bougainvillea lingering in the air as they continued south. Suddenly, as she approached Coral Gables, Alex turned right onto a broad palm tree-lined avenue. Kenzie hung back. The traffic was lighter, and she did not want to be spotted. The map said Le Jeune Road. What on earth was down here?

After a couple of miles, the Porsche turned off onto Old Cutler Road, which Kenzie realized went directly to the entrance of Matheson Hammock Park. Was this a trap? Did Alex know she was being tailed?

Kenzie couldn't see how. Alex likely thought she still had the upper hand, with Kenzie's phone in her possession. She had to know she needed to get out of town quickly before the police caught up to her.

Once inside the lush tropical park, Kenzie pulled over and waited to see what Alex would do next. The buzz of cicadas and screech of parrots filtered in through her open window. She watched the pulsing dot's slow creep forward on her screen. Finally, it came to a stop in the Matheson Hammock Marina.

A boat!

That's how Alex planned to make her escape - she had a boat waiting in the marina. Her little electric car sprung silently into action and she raced down the park's winding road toward the marina entrance. The parking lot was vast and semi-full, dappled shadows from swaying palms providing pockets of shade.

Kenzie tucked her little car into a spot behind a massive SUV with a boat trailer attached, hoping its bulk would hide her from view. The green tracker dot was still steadily pulsing on the screen.

CHAPTER 45

Reid and Diaz raced back across the causeway to the mainland, the cruiser's GPS guiding them through the city to the hospice where Bethany's sister, Ellen, was living. Half an hour later, they pulled into a neat, efficient parking lot with light sensors and clearly demarcated lines for ambulances and other emergency vehicles.

"Entrance is this way," Diaz said, hopping out of the driver's seat. Reid had called ahead and the administrative assistant on duty, a Mrs. Daphne Lawson, was waiting to greet them. "This is all very unusual," she told Reid. "We don't usually get the police here."

"I know, and I apologize for the intrusion," he said, keeping his voice calm and steady, even though inside he was itching to get to Ellen's room and have a look around. "Could we possibly speak with Ellen?"

"She's not having a good day today," Daphne said, the edges of her mouth tilting downwards. "But if you keep it brief, I'm sure she wouldn't mind."

They followed her along a narrow corridor with overly bright lighting, as if it were trying to compensate for the natural cheerlessness of the place. At a bottle-green door, Daphne paused. "I'll just see if she's awake."

Reid could scarcely hide his frustration.

"Okay," Daphne beckoned them in. They stepped into the merrily decorated hospice room. Bethany, or whoever came here, had tried to make it as uplifting as possible. There were framed photographs on a small dresser, ornate lamp shades casting a cozy glow around the room, and a soft knitted spread on the bed.

Sitting, propped up against some fluffy pillows, was a frail, gaunt version of Bethany. Her hair was completely silver, like her sister's, but her skin was sallow and she had dark shadows beneath her pale blue eyes. The number of tubes and pipes sticking out of her was alarming.

"Hello, Ellen," Reid said softly.

She managed a weak smile. "I hear you want to talk about my sister?"

"Yes, I hope you don't mind."

"No, how is Bethany? She comes to see me every week, you know."

"I've heard. That's nice."

Diaz thanked Daphne and led her from the room. Reid needed her gone so he could search the place.

"Your sister said she'd left something here for us," Reid prompted, making it up as he went along. "You don't know what that would be, do you?"

Her face crumpled into a frown. "No, she didn't tell me anything."

"You sure she didn't leave a package here last week and ask you to look after it for her?"

"Oh, that." Her eyes lit up momentarily.

Reid felt his heart jump. "Yes, that."

"She sent a friend to come and get that not half an hour ago."

Reid stared at her. "Someone else was here, in this room?"

"Yes, I was awfully surprised to see him, but Bethany's talked about him before, so I knew it was okay."

"Who was it?" Reid asked.

"That nice man who works for Salvo, what's his name again?"

Reid's tone hardened. "Samson Quinn?"

"That's the one."

Reid raced out of the room. Diaz was still in the hallway with Daphne. "Did Ellen have another visitor this morning?"

"No, why do you ask?"

"She said a man came to visit her not half an hour ago."

Diaz's head shot up. "He was here?"

"Who was here?" Daphne was looking like she might burst into tears. "Ellen didn't have any other visitors today."

Reid made for the exit. "They've just been here. Quinn must have snuck in when nobody was looking."

Diaz hurried after him. "Then they've got the diamonds. Quinn's got the diamonds. That means he won't need Bethany anymore."

Reid swallowed. She'd just said what he'd been thinking, what he was afraid might happen. Bethany was now a liability and he wouldn't hesitate to get rid of her.

REID RADIOED BACK to the station and got Vargas. He told him what had happened. "We're still looking for the Jag," Vargas said. "They can't have gone far."

Reid sat quietly fuming in the passenger seat as Diaz drove them back to Sweetwater. Where the hell would he go?

"He can't just shoot her in the car," Diaz said. "Could he?"

Reid said grimly, "Let's hope not."

They were almost there when Vargas's voice echoed through the radio. He was shouting and running at the same time. "Boss, Del Gatto's Jag has been spotted on the US-1 South heading toward Coral Gables. I'm heading there now."

Diaz pulled over. When the traffic had slowed, she put the siren on and did a U-turn in the middle of the road and headed back in the direction from which they'd come. "What's in Coral Gables?" she asked.

Reid thought for a moment. Nothing, as far as he knew. Only residential suburbs, parkland, mangrove swamps and...He gasped. "Matheson Hammock Marina."

"The marina?" Diaz frowned, her hands gripping the steering wheel. "You think he's going to escape via the marina?"

"Yes, of course."

She glanced over at him. "What?"

"Carl Ramos kept a boat there. He's going to use Carl's boat to get away."

Diaz gritted her teeth together. "With the diamonds."

Reid felt a surge of adrenaline. "Step on it," he said, "we may still be able to get there in time to save Bethany."

"You think she's still alive?"

"Yeah, I think he's going to kill her and dispose of her body overboard."

Diaz put her foot on the gas.

CHAPTER 46

Kenzie got out of her car, the heat hitting her like a wall as she crept through the parking lot toward the boat slips where vessels bobbed gently, rigging clanging. It was a stunning afternoon, the water a dazzling sapphire blue, the sun hanging at a lazy forty-five degrees in the jewel-bright sky.

Grabbing her secret burner phone from the glove compartment, she filmed Alex as she strode purposefully down the weathered planks of the jetty. Kenzie zoomed in on the phone's small screen as Alex approached a fishing boat moored at the end, the white fiberglass hull gleaming brightly. It was an older center console model, maybe an 18-footer, that rose and fell with the gentle swells as if eager to cast off.

Kenzie zoomed in as Alex boarded. To her surprise, Samson Quinn appeared from below, his dark-blond hair glinting red in the sun.

What was he doing here?

Shifting the phone to her other hand, she zoomed tighter and caught a glimpse of silver hair inside. Bethany!

Fumbling, Kenzie tried to call Reid but realized she didn't have his number on this phone. Cursing inwardly, she kept filming with a sweaty palm as Quinn embraced Alex, kissing her hard on the lips.

Holy crap...Alex and Quinn? In a weird way, it did make sense— Quinn orchestrating the smuggling, Alex fencing the goods. They must have hatched this plan to steal the diamonds from an unsuspecting Bethany, who'd liberated them from the police lab in order to donate the money to her charity. After all, they'd only end up in an evidence locker at the FBI headquarters and a fat lot of good they would do there. Kenzie agreed, the money could be better spent.

Glancing back at the entrance, she chewed her lip anxiously. Where was Reid? She had to stop them leaving or Bethany would undoubtedly be killed out on open water.

Trying to steady her filming hand as her pulse raced, Kenzie called 911. The tinny voice that answered patched her through and she urgently explained the situation to the officer. The line clicked off and almost immediately rang back with Monroe's familiar tones.

"Kenzie, is that you? Reid's on his way to the marina, hang tight."

She thanked him and hung up. He'd better damn well hurry. Quinn cast off lines into the water with a low splash. The tide was going out—once they left the marina, they'd rapidly pick up speed.

Damn it. She couldn't wait. She had to intervene now.

Breaking cover, she sprinted across the parking lot, catching a whiff of creosote and dead fish. A gunshot cracked loudly from the boat and she ducked, gasping as the bullet blew a cloud of sand from the pebbled ground behind her.

Shouting wildly, she waved both arms above her head at a man entering the dockhouse. "Stop that boat!" she screamed desperately. "They've got a hostage!"

"THERE THEY ARE!" Reid yelled, as Diaz drove straight through the marina parking lot towards the slips, tires crunching on gravel. She skidded to a halt just yards from the dock's edge, much to the consternation of the members who were enjoying sundowners on the wooden deck of the clubhouse, conversation turning to alarmed murmurs.

Holding his weapon, he leaped from the cruiser and ran towards the fishing boat, whose engine idled with a low grumble. Alex was at the helm, back rigid, while Quinn was on the deck, the ropes falling slack from his hands into the lazily lapping water as he untied the moorings.

"They're getting away!" Reid bellowed, feet pounding down the weathered planks of the jetty as gulls shrieked overhead, boat lines clanging against aluminum masts.

He registered dimly that Kenzie was yelling to him, her voice shrill over the cries of indignant seabirds. What on earth was she doing here?

No time to ponder that now as the boat's engine roared louder in his ears. Quinn spun, sunlight flashing on the metal barrel of his raised pistol. Reid threw himself to the planks just as the gun cracked loudly. Splinters flew as he tucked his head down, returning fire but missing amidst the chaos of screaming patrons fleeing the decks.

Another shot split the air and Quinn collapsed onto the deck with a roar of pain. Scrambling to his knees as cries echoed across the marina, Reid scanned the boat. Alex stood firmly on the gently rocking boat, clutching a small pistol. She'd shot Quinn in the leg—he writhed wildly, curses ringing out as crimson seeped into his jeans.

"Alex, stop!" Reid bellowed desperately over the idling engine's throaty rumble. She turned dismissively and pushed the throttle forward in a definitive roar. The boat reared up, white wake boiling, then shot forward across the glittering blue water. Kenzie was sprinting desperately down the pier too now, phone extended in front of her as she filmed the chaos.

Still confused by her sudden presence there, Reid knelt by Quinn, whose ragged moans were audible even over the engine's fading drone. He kicked Quinn's fallen gun away roughly across the weathered planks before yanking the bleeding man's hands behind his back and cuffing his wrists.

"Bitch shot me," Quinn choked out bitterly between groans of pain as Reid pulled him to unsteady feet. Blood darkened the weathered wood beneath them.

"Yeah, she did," Reid confirmed bluntly.

"Bethany's on deck!" Kenzie suddenly cried from alongside him. She gestured wildly out at the boat. It had stalled momentarily a hundred meters off as Alex dragged Quinn's stumbling hostage from the cabin by her slender arm. Her platinum blonde hair shone silver in the sunlight.

Reid's heart sank like a stone—no, she wouldn't dare shoot her too, not in open water. But he needn't have worried. A thin scream cut through the salt air, followed rapidly by a distant splash as Alex hurled the flailing woman over the side, before sprinting back toward the helm.

The boat roared to life once more, whitewater churning from the propeller as it leapt forward across the glittering blue bay. Shielding his eyes, Reid could just make out Alex turn and lift a slender hand in mocking farewell before the boat disappeared around the point.

CHAPTER 47

It was a local fisherman who pulled a terrified Bethany Del Gatto out of the water. "I thought they were going to kill me," she said, standing on the dock, teeth chattering.

Kenzie put an arm around her and led her up to the clubhouse. "Quinn probably would have, but Alex isn't a killer."

Reid shot her a sideways glance. Diaz had gone in the ambulance with Quinn and would take him into custody once his leg had been seen to. Luckily, the bullet had passed through without injuring any major arteries.

"Good thing she shot him in the leg," Reid said.

"Yes," Kenzie agreed. "Wasn't it?"

"Are the diamonds on board?" Reid asked.

Bethany nodded. "Quinn took them from the hospice. He tied me to the steering wheel, said if I cried for help, he'd kill Ellie."

Kenzie shook her head. "So, she used Quinn to kidnap you and get the diamonds, and now she's gotten away."

"She has my emerald necklace too," Bethany said miserably.

"Oh, yes, I was wondering what had happened to that." Kenzie gave a slow nod. "She was going to fence it for you?"

"Yes. She fenced all my...well, everything."

"How did you know she was a fence?" Kenzie asked. "Did you know your husband used her to fence the conflict diamonds?"

She shook her head. "Alex came to me. She'd realized what I was doing and said she'd like to help, that we could make a mutually lucrative deal. Until now, she's been great."

"She hasn't gotten away yet," Reid muttered under his breath, but she could hear the disillusionment in his voice. He knew as well as she did, they'd never find Alex. She would reinvent herself and disappear. She'd already done it once before.

"Am I under arrest?" Bethany asked.

Reid nodded. "I'm afraid so."

"You might want to get your husband to call his lawyer," Kenzie said, earning herself another glare from Reid.

"I wasn't keeping any of it," she sobbed. "I was trying to find a cure for Ellie."

Reid's eyebrows went up. Kenzie nodded. "I know you were. You were doing it for a good reason, but unfortunately, it's still against the law."

Bethany sniffed. "I suppose you're right." She turned to Reid. "Lieutenant, I'm ready to face the consequences of my actions."

Reid cleared his throat. "I'm glad to hear that, Mrs. Del Gatto, but I think you should take Kenzie's advice and consult with your attorney. That way, you'll get the best possible representation."

Kenzie smiled and linked her hand with his as they walked back to the clubhouse.

"How did you figure out Alex was the fence?" Reid asked as they swung gently in the hammock on his deck, the fibers creaking softly. It had been two days since Quinn and Bethany were arrested, and Alex had escaped with the diamonds. Two fruitless days of searching up and down the coast, through the murky glades and the myriad canals threading south Florida had turned up nothing. Carl Ramos's boat had simply vanished.

In front of them, the setting sun turned the glassy swamp surface into a dazzling palette of pinks, oranges, and glowing yellows. It was hard to believe predators lurked beneath that tranquil vista, waiting for twilight to emerge and feed.

"I deciphered the entry in the ledger," Kenzie said, the dying light playing over her features, "With Raoul's help, we discovered Alex was actually Eleanor Johnson—she had to be the fence."

"I can't believe you met with her, knowing what you did," Reid admonished, though not unkindly. "You should have called me."

"I wanted to," she admitted, sending him an apologetic grimace, her lips pressed thin. "But you were tied up with Del Gatto and Bethany's abduction. I knew it would take time before you even got to Alex. Given the circumstances, I suspected she was about to run and tried to get her on record first." Kenzie sighed. "But she saw it coming and snatched my phone."

"She was smart," Reid conceded into the growing darkness, a night heron cried sharp overhead. "I'll admit she never pinged my radar until you uncovered her lies about her identity."

"You were occupied," Kenzie demurred, giving his hand a gentle squeeze, her skin felt smooth against his calluses.

"Hector's agreed to testify," he told her with a sudden grin. "Thanks for getting to him first, by the way. Gave me leverage I needed."

"You caught him fair and square," Kenzie laughed. "I just beat you to it because of my hospital vacation."

"Well, I'm glad you made good use of the time off. You know, if you need a job after the newspaper goes digital, I bet Sweetwater PD would snap you up."

"Wouldn't pass the physical, remember?" She nodded to her knee. Crisscrossed with scars, it had been severely injured in a car wreck days before her graduation from the Academy.

"Does it still pain you?" he asked, brow furrowing.

"Only sometimes, when the weather shifts," she assured him breezily. "Luckily, I live in Florida, so it's not usually a problem." Her eyes twinkled at him as she winked.

"YOUR SCOOP MUST HAVE BROUGHT in a lot of revenue for the paper. Is the situation still so dire?"

"Unfortunately, the decision has been made," she said. "But it was a good scoop. I'm so glad the FBI managed to shut down the diamond smuggling operation and Quinn got what he deserved."

"You didn't get Del Gatto, though." It was a sore point. Reid knew Kenzie had been desperate to expose him, but as it turned out, there simply wasn't enough evidence to press any charges. The billionaire businessmen had remained unscathed by the whole dirty business.

"His time will come," she said quietly.

To be honest, he was surprised she was taking it so lightly. "I'm sure you'll get him one day."

"Oh, I will." He didn't doubt her.

"But seriously, what will you do for work now?" Reid pressed gently. "I know you've only got a couple weeks left at the paper before it folds." He knew she'd mentioned writing for the digital platform, but somehow couldn't envision her talents being best leveraged there.

Kenzie exhaled heavily. "That's actually what I've been wanting to discuss with you."

Ah. His belly swooped anxiously. "You have?"

"Mm-hmm. But you were finishing up the case, so I decided to wait. Still not sure if now's the right time, honestly..."

"Too late," he interjected. "Spill it."

"Okay, well...I was approached with a job offer. From another paper."

"Hey, that's great news!" he exclaimed, genuinely thrilled for her, though her expression gave him sudden pause. "Isn't it?"

"It's...it's with the New York Times," Kenzie said.

It took a long second to process the implications. New York Times. New York City. Eight states away instead of eight minutes.

When she laid her head on his shoulder, he felt the wetness of her tears instantly soak through his shirt. Swallowing hard past the apple-sized lump in his throat, he rasped, "You should take it."

Her head snapped up, eyes wide and searching. "Really?"

"It's the *Times*, Kenz," he made himself say steadily. "What reporter doesn't dream of working there?"

They talked for a while longer as the darkness slowly engulfed them. He held her close, ignoring the hollow ache blooming inside his chest.

"New York isn't that far," Reid finally offered weakly.

"Only two and a half hours by plane," Kenzie confirmed in a small voice.

He squeezed her gently. "We'll make this work."

She burrowed tighter to him. "I know we will."

THE STORY CONTINUES in Night Watch. Click the link below to Pre-order now!

Night Watch

<u>The Kenzie Gilmore Series</u>

Afterburn

Dead Heat

Heatwave

Burnout

Deep Heat

Fever Pitch

Storm Surge

Night Watch (Coming Soon!)

<u>Dalton Savage Mystery Series By L. T. Ryan & Biba Pearce</u>

Savage Grounds

Scorched Earth

Cold Sky

Frost Killer

Crimson Moon (Coming Soon!)

<u>Detective Rob Miller Mysteries</u>

The Thames Path Killer

The West London Murders

The Bisley Wood Murders

The Box Hill Killer

Follow the link for your free copy of *Hard Line: A Kenzie Gilmore Prequel*

ALSO BY WITHOUT WARRANT

More Thriller Series from Without Warrant Authors

Dana Gray Mysteries by C.J. Cross

Girl Left Behind

Girl on the Hill

Girl in the Grave

Girl Betrayed (Coming Soon!)

The Kenzie Gilmore Series by Biba Pearce

Afterburn

Dead Heat

Heatwave

Burnout

Deep Heat

Fever Pitch

Storm Surge

Night Watch (Coming Soon!)

Willow Grace FBI Thrillers

by Without Warrant and C. C. West

Shadow of Grace

Condition of Grace

Hunt for Grace

Time for Grace

Piece of Grace (Coming Soon!)

Gia Santella Crime Thriller Series

by Kristi Belcamino

Vendetta

Vigilante

Vengeance

Black Widow

Day of the Dead

Border Line

Night Fall

Stone Cold

Cold as Death

Cold Blooded

Dark Shadows

Dark Vengeance

Dark Justice

Deadly Justice

Deadly Lies

Vigilante Crime Series by Kristi Belcamino

Blood & Roses

Blood & Fire

Blood & Bone

Blood & Tears

Queen of Spades Thrillers by Kristi Belcamino

Queen of Spades

The One-Eyed Jack

The Suicide King

The Ace of Clubs

The Joker

The Wild Card

High Stakes

Poker Face

ABOUT THE AUTHOR

Biba Pearce is a British crime writer and author of the Kenzie Gilmore series and the DCI Rob Miller series.

Biba grew up in post-apartheid Southern Africa. As a child, she lived on the wild eastern coast and explored the sub-tropical forests and surfed in shark-infested waters.

Now a full-time writer, Biba lives in leafy Surrey and when she isn't writing, can be found walking through the countryside or kayaking on the river Thames.

Visit her at bibapearce.com and scan the QR code below to join her mailing list at to be notified about new releases, updates and special subscriber-only deals.

Printed in Great Britain
by Amazon

41664386R10145